Twisted Up In You

USA TODAY BESTSELLING AUTHOR

DAWN MARTENS

1st Edition Published January 2016
Cover designed by Glenna Maynard
Photo from Shutterstock
Formatted by M.L. Pahl of IndieVention Designs
Edited by Kendra Gaither and Crystal Sosa
Proofed by Angie Brennan

ISBN-13: 978-1519728760
ISBN-10: 151972876X

10 9 8 7 6 5 4 3 2 1

Acknowledgments

First, of course, I have to thank my G-baby – Glenna Maynard, of course! Duh, she's my everything, my best friend, and just simply amazing! G-baby, you do so much for me, and nothing I do will ever be enough to even out the friendship scale!

My Divas – you ladies rock! Each and every one of you is seriously amazing.

Cori, Pami, Melly, Nikki, Angie, Crystal B, and so many others – your chats, your friendships, and your love have been such blessings to me.

To my most favorite Emily in the universe – Mrs. Snow, I adore you.

Stacy and Ashley E – Gah, I love you both.

To my readers – thank you for putting up with my crazy. You all are amazing people.

Dedication

This one is for my girl, Cori, since duh, I named this character after you!

Twisted Up In You

Surviving a harsh upbringing, Corinne Treyton's new life comes courtesy of the Angels Warriors MC. No one will ever use her body again, unless she wants them to. Cori, a party girl, doesn't believe in relationships, but she'd be willing to try if only Blake, who happens to be her boss, could really see her for who she is. She hides her lifestyle from him, afraid he would think less of her.

Blake Lexington has crushed on Cori since the day she started working for him. He knows a bit about her past, living with the Angels Warriors, and he doesn't care. He refuses to make a move, thinking it will scare off his shy assistant. For years, he's thought she would never be attracted to someone like him.

Finally realizing that he needs to take action, her reaction surprises him. Cori believes he sees her as a slut and wants to use her. Secrets from the past will be revealed, causing everything to unravel.

Will real love bring them together, or is Cori too damaged to give true love a chance?

PROLOGUE
Cori

"Corinne Leanna Treyton, where the hell are you?" I hear my mom yell for me, her voice shrill. She's always yelling at me about something.

"I'm coming, Mom," I say, running out of my room to meet her in the living room. It's best not to keep her waiting.

"I need you to babysit tonight. I have a date," she tells me, giving me a dirty look. Her eyes are narrowed and her mouth tight.

I bite my tongue and nod.

She tilts her head to the side, appraising me. I wait for it, the onslaught of her telling me how ugly I am, how much of a burden I am to her. But I get nothing; she just sniffs and walks out the door. The room is stale with the scent of her cheap perfume.

Confused by her sudden departure, without any word as to when she will return, I peer out the window, watching her as she gets in a car I don't recognize. It isn't unusual for my mom to take off with different men, but it is usually one of three. *Where is she going? Whose car is that?* The tires squeal, and she is gone.

I move to the bedroom my sister, Melissa, is napping in and peer down at her over the crib. "Hi, Melly Belly. Wake up," I whisper down to her. I tickle her tummy, causing her to laugh. She has the biggest smile; her face always lights up when I come into her room to play with her.

Melissa is way too big to be in the crib. She's four now, but Mom doesn't want to go and buy her a new bed. Said it would be a waste of money. But whenever Mom leaves me in charge, I pick her up out of the crib and let her sleep with me.

Little did we know, that at four and six years old, our mom had called social services, effectively landing us in foster care. She just left us, not caring what fate awaited us.

~

Years later

Sitting on the damp cold floor in the back bedroom, I'm huddled with Melissa, my little sister. I hate living here, hate it so much. No matter how many times I tell someone what goes on here, nothing happens. I don't understand why. I even tried telling my counselor at school—still nothing. I feel like no one cares what they do to us, but I keep fighting and staying strong for Melissa. She depends on me. I protect her.

I can't wait until I turn eighteen so I can leave this place, take Melissa with me, and never return. The things they do to us, what they did to me... I can't take it much longer. I'm hoping that, at any moment, those Angels—Angels Warriors, the motorcycle club—will come save us. They help kids like us, get them out of bad homes and protect them.

My friend, Chelsea, finally agreed to call them for us, hoping they'd help. Hoping something, anyways. She said she would do her best.

I have to use the bathroom so bad, but they lock the door from the outside whenever we are in here, only letting us out once a day. I hate to say this, but half the time, I end up using the bathroom in the closet of this little room. I don't have a choice. The smell in this room is disgusting.

It's not long because I hear running feet. Melly tenses around me. "Why are they coming back? They were just here. I don't want to watch you go through that again, Cori," she says, sobbing.

I rub her back and let her know it will be okay.

The door flies open, and our foster parents look completely freaked out. "Get up. Now! We need to all pitch in and get this place cleaned up. We're having visitors coming soon."

They look completely panicked. Melissa and I quickly get off the dirty floor and follow them. As we walk by the bathroom, they stop us and push us inside. "Shower, quickly."

Melissa and I waste no time in showering. She goes first, and I'm next, and as we come out of the bathroom and go down the hall, there is yelling. Lots of it.

"Corinne Treyton?" I hear an intimidating voice shouting my name.

I hold Melissa's hand and walk slowly down the steps, coming face to face with the scariest looking man I've ever seen – tall, fully bearded, tattoos covering his arms and neck, and a leather vest that says Angels Warriors on it. Instantly, I sag in relief and let go of Melly's hands. I rush forward, wrapping my arms around this big guy's waist and sobbing.

"You came," I choke out.

"Darlin'," he says gruffly, holding me tight to him. "Reaper, you check the house, find whatever you can, if you can. These fuckers are slimy. Zippo, get the sister. We're outta here."

"You can't take these kids!" my foster father shouts at him.

I stiffen, scared that I'm going to have to stay here. "That's funny, because we are," the man holding me says calmly. He bends down slightly and pulls me back just a little. "Is there anything here you want to take with you?"

I hesitate. "My baby," I whisper sadly.

He stiffens and frowns. Looking up at my foster family, he growls out. "Where is her kid?"

"She lies. There is no kid. If you're taking her, then do it. Get the fuck out!" my foster mother shouts.

"My name is Angel, darlin'. I'm taking you and your sister with us, and I'll find out what I can about your baby, okay," he assures me gently.

"Okay," I whisper.

We walk out, my right arm around Angel's big body, his left arm around my shoulders, holding me tight to him. He's my saviour. He saved me—Melly too. I will forever be thankful to him for it.

The next few years go by fast. Angel and his boys are there with Melly and I through it all—all the nightmares, helping with school, everything.

CHAPTER 1

Cori

"Cori, can I get you to grab me the files on the Lawrence case?" Blake asks me as he passes the desk, walking toward his office. God, that man looks good in a suit. What I wouldn't give to be fine linen right now. The fabric wraps tightly around his backside, showing off his nice firm ass.

Blake and his friend, Adam, run this entire building. They work closely with a club called the Angels Warriors, the same club that rescued my sister and me years ago. The Angels helped me finish school once they found out I was stripping to earn money for college, and then the club helped me get this job about two years ago. They gave me a chance that I never would have gotten otherwise.

When Angel and Reaper found out I was stripping, though, they were pissed, more pissed than I have ever seen them. Especially since they, at that moment, knew I lied about where I was working. The second they walked into Glitter and saw me on stage, dancing topless, they stormed the stage and dragged me out of there kicking and screaming. I made good money there. I didn't see the problem.

I started working at Lexington Family Services the minute I finished college. The building is made up of five different floors. On the first floor is the main waiting area and where any company party is held. The second floor is a law firm, third floor is the immunization clinic, fourth floor is a small family doctor's office, and my floor, the fifth floor, is child social services, but not the kind that most people think. Of course, I'm just a glorified Personal Assistant now, but I do make better money. And it helps when I get to file some of the closed cases. I smile with relief that my boss was able to help save those children. There are times, though, when it is too late. I try not to think about that. I have to focus on the good Blake does.

I nod at Blake as he walks by. Of course, he never notices me, though... at least, not the way I want him to. It sucks. I've had a crush on Blake for years now, since I first met him, but he treats me as if I'm his little sister. Nothing like being in the friend-zone. Frowning at the thought of never being anything more, I get started with the day ahead. Opening my email, I start checking for tips on his open cases before I bring him his file. Sulking, I notice the newest receipt from ordering flowers for one of Blake's conquests.

Whenever Blake asks me to send flowers to the woman of the week, or call up a restaurant to get a reservation, my heart breaks just a little bit more. Once he's out of sight, I sigh and get out of my chair to take him the file for his next case.

I walk into the office as he's booting up his computer, and I smile. "Hey, Blake, here you go. Do you need anything else?" I ask quietly. He takes a sip of his coffee that I already had waiting on his desk for him. I'm not ashamed to admit, I lick that rim every time he finishes his coffee. That is as close as I'll probably ever actually get to his mouth. Coffee is absolutely disgusting, but it's the only way I can get a small taste of him.

He looks up and takes the file from me, and gives me his signature grin, the grin I go home to masturbate to the thought of. "This is all. Thanks, Cori. You have any plans this weekend?" he asks me, making polite conversation. I don't think he'd care if I ran off tomorrow and got married, as long as I was back in time for work.

I shake my head. "Not really. I think Melly might drag me out somewhere, as usual," I say with a small laugh. My sister is always getting into something. Like that one time we got so drunk, and I let Melissa talk me into baconing

Stacy Ips' house. It was such a waste of bacon, but it was so worth it. At least, it was until, of course, Chelsea had to call Angel because Stacy and I were in a hair pulling fight, and Chelsea was worried someone would call the cops on me.

His eyes narrow. "Don't let her get you into trouble." After the blind date Melly set me up on last week, I haven't heard the end of it from him—Blake, saying I let my sister get me into trouble too often. It's not really that she gets me into trouble so much as she just wants me to settle down and be happy. At the same time, she's fighting her own feelings for a certain bouncer that has been hot for her for years. She uses my love life as a distraction from her own.

"I won't," I answer softly. I'm not normally a pushover, or weak, or anything like that, but whenever I'm around Blake, he reduces me to a pile of goo. I am like putty in his hands, and he doesn't even realize it. Melly is constantly on me to either just show him who I really am or get the hell over him. I can't seem to do either.

"See you tomorrow, Cori," he affirms as I walk out of his office swiftly.

I turn and smile over my shoulder and wink. His face freezes in shock as I realize what I just did. Oh, shit! I did not mean to do that just now. I scurry out of his office and close his door behind me gently, feeling so awkward. My cheeks flush with heat. I fall back in my chair and sigh, wondering, with a scowl on my face, what or whom Blake will be doing this weekend.

I don't know why I let my mind wonder about him and women the way that I do. It is pure torture. Jealousy grips me tightly as I recall all of the dates I have arranged for him. I mentally check the women's names off the list, wishing mine would be the last.

The clacking of keyboards in the background interrupts my pity party of one. Spinning around in my chair, I return to my work. There is always something that needs filed or a case that needs followed up on.

Later, I receive a text from my sister.

This weekend be ready for trouble. ~ Melly

BLAKE

I don't know what is wrong with me. Cori is the only woman that I haven't made a move on, and I don't get why. I want her, have wanted her for years. Even with knowing about her past, in foster care and being with the Angels, I still want her. And that wink she just sent me over her shoulder, the one that she seemed shocked herself by giving me, well, damn. Her flirting was the last thing I was expecting.

I wanted so badly to get out of my seat and pull her to me for a damn kiss. But Cori is my assistant and a good girl I respect. I can only imagine the rumors that would circulate around the office about us. However, would I care?

I can't stop thinking about her now, and I can't keep from wondering what she does when she isn't here. What is she doing this weekend? All I know is, somehow, she is always on my mind.

I grab my phone and scroll down to her sister's number.

Don't get Cori into trouble this weekend. I text Melissa.

Don't worry, big shot. I won't. She fires back.

That really doesn't make me feel much better. Melissa is a good kid, but if she would just slow the hell down on her dating and partying, she would be able to see that she is more than what she thinks. Their mother really screwed them up.

She would pop back in and out of their life for years, according to what Angel once told me. Drilled it into Cori and Melissa's heads that they were no good, no better than scum. It wasn't until Angel stepped in and told her no more that she stayed away. I don't think the girls have seen their mother since Cori was a teen. And good riddance to her.

Twisted Up In You

The woman was a real piece of work from what I have heard and read.

I get busy looking over the file Cori brought in for the Lawrence case. Mrs. Lawrence came to us a few months back, telling us her husband has been molesting her daughter. She discovered it when she was watching the nanny cam she installed in her daughter's teddy bear. Sick fucker. Seems like a slam-dunk case. That's the downside to this job… knowing what these children have to go through before we are called in.

My cell phone buzzes. I swipe the screen and realize it's Stacy, this girl that won't leave me the hell alone. Never before have I given a chick my number, but this one night, I made the mistake of getting too damn drunk and ended up letting her come home with me. Obviously, she got my number when I was passed out.

It's a tit shot, I realize when I look down at my phone. I groan. Really? Why do women do that? Her tits aren't even that great. I bet Corinne would never do shit like that.

"Knock knock," I hear Adam say from my door.

I look up. "Hey, man."

"Hey, we're having our first company party next week. Has Cori finished everything that needs to be done for it?" he asks. We're celebrating one hundred cases solved.

"Yeah, her sister is in charge of the food, and she asked her friend Randy to help out with the booze. He owns that nightclub that opened up downtown last month," I say, my jealousy seeping out.

Adam smirks. "When are you just going to flat out ask her on a date?"

I rub my face and groan. "I don't see her that way. You know that," I lie through my gritted teeth.

He raises an eyebrow. "Sure, then you won't be jealous when I tell you she's bringing a date to the party. Someone that she keeps around purely for sex." He emphasizes the word sex and raises his brows, wiggling them in a suggestive manner.

Anger rushes through me. "What? Cori isn't like that," I say, brushing it off. He shouldn't say shit like that about her. She's our employee, one I'd like to consider a friend.

"Uh, yeah she is. You've just been too blind to see it." His eyes shift to the side, avoiding my icy glare.

Adam is wrong. Cori isn't like that; she's shy and wears clothes that in no way show off the figure I'm sure she has been hiding. I don't believe for a minute she's the type of girl to have a fuck buddy. Her sister, yeah, but not Cori.

"Whatever. Anyway, it's closing time. I have a date tonight, so we'll talk tomorrow about this case I have open," I tell him, getting out of my chair.

"Yeah, later man," he says, walking out of the office.

The thought of Cori with a fuck buddy has the collar of my shirt feeling tight. Loosening my tie, I try to suppress the rage coursing through my body. Hot and angry, I step into the kitchen for a water. The cool liquid sends relief down my throat. Taking a deep breath, defusing my anger, I reassure myself of my opinion—Cori isn't a fuck buddy kind of girl. Or is she? I peek at her as she sits at her desk, modestly dressed, doing her duties with diligence. No, she certainly doesn't get around.

She gives off the appearance of a woman who spends her weekends reading and drinking wine. It shouldn't get under my skin—the idea of her sleeping with someone. I fuck around plenty. I shouldn't want to call her in here to my office right now and demand she doesn't bring a date, or make her so damn busy during the party she doesn't have time to entertain one.

CHAPTER 2

Cori

Melissa and I went to the Calgary Zoo over the weekend. Most people wouldn't think that's something we'd do, but there's something that majorly sucks with Friday and Saturday nights out. Clubs and bars are packed, wall to wall, and no, that's not my thing. Being cramped in a large crowd takes me back to being that helpless child in a small room. I'll never be that girl again. That girl couldn't protect her sister — she couldn't save herself.

Some nights, I dream of my mother. At times, I can remember her face clear as day, and yet, others, she is nothing but a demon face with snarling teeth trying to tear me apart. Those dreams are the worst, the ones where I can't see her to confront her for not loving Melly and me...for leaving us in that shithole time after time.

I wake up, feeling sore all over from walking around all day yesterday, and, of course, I'm slightly burnt. I'm still feeling haunted by my childhood when Melissa knocks on my door.

"Sis, let's go out for lunch," she suggests with a grin.

I groan. "Melly, don't you mean breakfast?" I just want to roll over and go back to sleep.

"No, it's close to two in the afternoon, actually," she informs me.

"Shit, really? I've never slept in this late before." I get out of bed and grab my clothes for a shower. "Lunch sounds good. Where do you want to go?"

"Moxies!" she yells to me as I shut my bathroom door.

The hot water hitting my tender skin makes me wince in pain. Next time, I'll listen to my little sister and put on sunscreen. You'd think she was the big sister the way she tries to look after me. Stiffly, I towel off and get dressed, still unable to shake my nightmare. They haven't been this bad in a long time. Blake is stressing me out. I don't know what to do about him. I think about quitting working for him, but then I wouldn't get to see him and I don't think I am able to give him up. I am addicted to seeing his smile every workday morning.

He has a way of making me believe those smiles are only for me.

I try to shake off my thoughts of him. He is probably out screwing one of his many dates. Not that I have room to talk. I like a good time as much as anyone does. Just the thought of Blake with someone tugs on my heart.

An hour later, we are leaving the restaurant, and Melissa decides she wants to go shopping. "Fine," I groan. "I need new work clothes anyways."

She playfully punches me in the arm. "You're such a guy. What girl hates shopping?" she teases.

"I just don't like people. They bug me, always rushing and pushing and glaring." I shrug. People are rude.

Melly just shakes her head. She is the social butterfly between the two of us. I like people... most of the time.

I head to Garage, and Melly squeals when she finds a pair of faded and ripped blue jeans on sale. I find a few pairs of jeans for myself, and some cute tanks. We later hit up Sears, and Melly really starts complaining when I'm picking out work outfits about two sizes too big for me.

"Seriously, why do you buy this shit?"

I shrug. "I just want to look presentable for work."

"Bullshit. You act ten times different around Blake than anyone else in the universe. I don't get it."

"Nothing to get. It's a workplace, with nurses, social workers, and lawyers. I have to look good. It's called being professional." I kick her swiftly on the butt.

"Yeah, and you'd look just as nice from the nice outfits Suzy Shier has, too. Those would also actually fit you," she snaps at me. "Fine, pick out this gross crap. I'm heading to get an ice cream."

Geeze, someone is cranky today. I finish up in the store and go in search of Melly. She doesn't seem annoyed anymore, so we head home, unload our stuff, and get ready for a night out.

After fighting to get a look at my makeup in the good lighting, we are finally ready to get out the door. The cab has been waiting for five minutes. Tonight, we are both drinking, so it's a cab night.

We end up at Billy Bob's around nine and are let right in. We head straight to the bar and order a few rum and sprites then slink off to find a table.

I spot the Saylor twins across the bar, and the second they see us, they make their way over. Melly pulls me away from the guy I was flirting with, mainly because the girlfriend was about to claw my eyes out. Which, of course, if I knew the dude had a girlfriend, I wouldn't have gone there. That's not who I am. It does make me think way less of the dude now, though. Asshole.

"Melly, Cori, babes, what are you ladies doing here tonight? Aren't you usually at Club Shine with Randy?" Mark asks me. Both men are hot, not Blake level hot, but still hot—dimples when they smile, light brown hair. The only time I can really tell them apart is when they are together because Mark is slightly taller than Lark.

I shrug, take a sip of my drink, and wink at him. "Just needed a little break."

He grins, and his eyes light up. "Good, my lucky night then."

"Melissa, baby, let's dance," Lark says to her, pulling on her arm.

Mark takes the seat next to me, his fingers trailing up my thigh. "Let's play a game. Never have I ever…" He trails off, sucking on my neck.

"Fuck the game. I just want to get straight to the good shit," I tell him playfully.

19

"Now, that sounds like an excellent idea." His fingers are now teasing at what would be my panty line if I were wearing any. Skillful fingers demand my attention, testing my limits.

Just when things are getting good, Melly and Lark come back to the table all over each other.

"Let's take this party back to your place," Lark suggests to Melly and me.

Before I can say yes, Mark is tugging on my hand and leading me out the door, with my sister and his brother following closely behind.

We get to their car, and everything becomes a blur as Mark bites on the shell of my ear, whispering what he plans to do with me once he gets my clothes off.

BLAKE

I don't know why I do this to myself—going out with women I know I feel nothing for. I keep thinking that maybe the next will be the one I feel a spark with, yet every single time I am let down and left drinking my night away, while fucking Stacy.

The second I stepped into The Vat, I knew the night wouldn't go well. I just wanted a few drinks. Maybe I should have just gone to the liquor store and watched a movie at home instead. Nothing good ever comes from my coming here, and yet, here I am.

I am making my way to the bar, debating on just saying fuck it and bailing, when I hear an ear splitting squeal. "Blake!" Stacy shrieks.

Yay. Not.

I plaster on a fake smile. "Uh, hey there."

She beams at me, her bleached white teeth and overly tanned face has me shivering in disgust. Luckily, she doesn't see it. Now that I'm fully sober, since I haven't ordered a beer yet, I'm slapping myself for ever sleeping with this chick and then keeping her around.

She loops her arm in mine, placing her face on my arm. Great, I'm probably going to have to take this jacket in for dry cleaning; her tan and makeup are probably smudging all over it. She pulls me along with her, getting me to sit down at the table she was just sitting at. Her friends instantly light up, all looking just as fake as Stacy does.

"I'll be back, handsome. Getting you a drink," Stacy says to me, leaning in close.

Her friends are like piranhas once she is gone—all jumping for a piece of me.

"So, Stacy tells us you are a real hero, protecting kids," a plastic looking chick croons, rubbing my arm.

"That's so fucking sexy," her other friend says seductively, trying to wink. She is failing miserably.

"You got something in your eye?" I ask, brushing the plastic chick's hand away. Their mouths hang open, gaping at my blunt manner.

Stacy returns, and I am almost grateful for her reappearance. At least she isn't as desperate as her friends, but she isn't too far off. I chug my beer and head to the bar for a second, just to escape the wolf pack of desperation.

Three beers later, I am feeling buzzed. A pretty blonde is making eyes at me from across the room. I smile, holding up my drink. I am debating on going over and introducing myself, but then another guy beats me to the punch. I turn back to the bar, enjoying my buzz.

My peace is short-lived when I smell Stacy's perfume coming up next to me before she reaches me. "I love this song. Let's dance!" She jerks on my hand, pulling me to the dance floor, spilling her drink on my shirt. "I'm sorry, baby. I'll make it up to you. Your shirt isn't the only thing that's wet." She takes my hand, trailing our fingers down her torso. My head says no, but my dick says yes, rising to the occasion.

DAWN MARTENS

The last thing I remember as my temples begin to pound is her going down on her knees in front of me in the men's room.

CHAPTER 3

Cori

"Cori, get up!" Melissa says, nudging me in the ribs.

"Ho be gone," I murmur out, rolling over to smash my face into my pillow.

"Please get your face out of my tits," Melissa says, giggling.

Shit. I get up and look around the room, realizing I was sleeping on her rack. "What the hell? How much did I drink last night?" I ask her, my head pounding. Rubbing my temples, I sigh. As I lay back down, the room spins a little and my stomach churns in response.

"A lot by my guess. That's the only reason I can think of, since you were cuddling my tits all night," she says, laughing. My cheeks would flame red if it were anyone else.

I glance at the clock and notice I'm gonna be late for work. "Shit, I don't wanna go. I wanna sleep," I groan out, wanting to snuggle against my pillow, not Melly's tits and sleep.

"Yeah, yeah, me too. I need to get washed up. All I remember from last night is dragging you off some guy's lap because I swear his girlfriend was gonna kill you, and then we hooked up with the Saylor twins. I don't remember getting home. Shit," Melly gripes.

That bitch never gets hangovers; I don't know how the hell she does it. Always wakes up perky. I still haven't gotten used to her morning cheerfulness, and I have lived with her all my life.

"What Saylor did I bang last night?" I ask Melly, following her to her closet, not that it really matters. I have probably fucked them both. I flop down on her purple comforter and stare up at the ceiling, wishing I could go back to sleep.

"I don't know. They're twins. We got one of each. I'm pretty sure we've done them both at some point," she observes with a sheepish grin, getting out her clothes for work. Melissa goes to school full time to get her nursing degree, but on her non-school days, she works as many hours as she can at a small little bakery that's hidden just behind Michael's.

"Hey, have you talked to Chelsea lately?" I ask her, realizing that I haven't heard from her in a while. Chelsea is a friend I met while I was in school. Both Melissa and I have been close to her for years, and she has this horrible relationship with this douche bag hockey player named Keller. She's been with him since they were juniors, and they have this stupid ass open relationship.

"Yeah, she's actually moving down here in a few months. Her and Keller broke up," she states.

I snort. "Sure they are. He'll show back up after he's done fucking around, lick her snatch, and bam!" I smack my palms together. "They'll be back together."

"You have such a way with words. Too bad Blake doesn't see this side of you," Melly says with a laugh. "Apparently," she snickers, using finger quotes, while standing in her bra and panties. "They had this weird as shit relationship that, when he leaves town to travel with the team, they aren't together. Gives him and Chels an unlimited hall pass to fuck around, I guess. Except, this one girl who lives in town showed up at Chelsea's clinic, saying she was pregnant and gushing about how her boyfriend was a big shot hockey player named Keller. Well, Chelsea lost her shit. I guess him and preggo chick have been fucking around for months when he's in town." Melly shrugs, buttoning her top and smoothing her hands over her skirt.

"Wow," I say, astonished, shaking my head. Poor Chelsea. I begrudgingly get up and start getting ready for work.

Making my way to the shower, I yell at Melissa to lay me out something professional to wear. She screams back at me that she isn't my mother, but I know, when I get out of the shower, my outfit will be laid on my bed.

I'm right. When I get back in my room, a black skirt, red shell top, and black fitted jacket are neatly pressed and waiting for me. I sigh. This stuff is too short and tight to wear, so I switch it out with my baggier clothes. I want to look professional, not slutty.

As I start out the door, Melly chides me and demands I change into the clothes she so graciously laid out for me. Begrudgingly, I change so she will shut up. I will be tugging at this skirt all damn day. I don't dress so revealing for work, ever. Usually, I settle on longer skirts or loose pants that hide my curves. I don't want to leave the wrong impression at the workplace.

BLAKE

My alarm goes off, and memories of last night come back to me. Shit, I hope she went home. I do not want to deal with a pissed off woman this morning. I swing my arm to hit the off button on my clock and slowly get up.

I smell coffee brewing. Shit. She's still here.

Once I'm showered and dressed, I head to my kitchen. I see no sign of her, though when I get to the coffee machine, I notice a bacon and ketchup sandwich on the counter with a note beside it.

Hey, handsome. I made your coffee and some breakfast. Hope you enjoy it.

Last night was amazing, like always. When are you gonna commit to me, huh?

Anyways, I'm just a phone call away. Well, you know that.

Kisses
Stacy

I crumple up the note and toss it in the trash. I'm an idiot. Huge idiot. Why is it, every stupid ass time I'm drunk, I end up hooking up with that bitch, Stacy. She's been on my ass for weeks, and instead of saying no, I get drunk and give in. Giving my head a shake, I eat the food she left me and pour the coffee in my travel mug. Stacy reminds me of the girls I dated in high school. Once I left, I swore I was going to stay away from her kind.

After high school, most of my friends went to university, with scholarships for different sports they were in. I played hockey, but it wasn't a lifelong dream of mine to make a career out of it. I ended up getting a degree in childhood education. Growing up in foster care, I saw how homes were run. There were the odd times I was placed in a good home, but for the most part, it was terrible.

I wanted to be able to make a difference, to help kids that grew up as I did.

I get to the office and notice Cori isn't at her desk. That's odd, but I do see my coffee sitting on mine. I smile. I told her to stop doing that. I can get my own coffee, but she always delivers. I once tried to get her a coffee, and she started gagging. She really hates the stuff.

Adam pops his head into my office as I'm shrugging off my jacket.

"All right, let's go to my office and get to work on this case," Adam says, moving toward his office door. I follow him out and see Cori standing at Clara's desk, smiling widely at her. God, she's beautiful, and she doesn't even know it. She looks different today. Her clothes are more fitted. It's a nice look on her.

Taking a seat, I pull up the file on the Mercer family. "So far, all I have is that they've been investigated six times, each time coming up with nothing. I don't get it. Those kids are terrified, and yet, nothing is coming out about them."

"I know. Something is definitely not right. What's your take on it?" Adam asks.

Twisted Up In You

I lean back in my chair. "I'm thinking abuse, maybe sexual. I don't know, but it's something. I'm thinking we need to give Angel a call, have his club brought in on this."

Adam nods, agreeing. "You make that call. We'll set up a meeting and go from there. Good thing those guys are free because I doubt the government will give us any more cash to fund this investigation."

"They pay us, and they pay us well. We've helped hundreds of kids so far. I highly doubt, if we asked them for more cash, they'd turn us away," I tell him, reminding him what he already knows.

"True, but everyone has their limits, I'm sure."

"Yeah, but this one case is a little more personal," I say, digging through some paperwork on the desk. I hand it over to Adam. "Take a look at this family's last name."

He reads it over, and shock crosses over his face. "Oh, shit. Isn't this the same house you grew up in?"

I give him a grim look. "Yup, and knowing what I went through while living there, I know these people haven't changed, but I also can't figure out how the fuck they are getting away with shit." Growing up in that home, they weren't simply just beating us —they were putting locks on everything. If you had to go to the bathroom, and it wasn't your time slot to go, well, too bad for you. They also only fed us once a day, which was suppertime, and if you got into shit at any time during the day, you would forgo eating. I purposely did a lot of shit, so that, eventually, they would tell the social worker to find me a new home. And they did, about three months before I turned eighteen. Each time I would tell the social worker about what was going on in that home, they would investigate, but nothing would be found.

Adam checks the time. "Shit, I have a meeting in twenty. You make those calls to the club, see how soon they can get down here for a meeting, and we'll go from there."

"Will do. Later, man," I say as he walks out.

I put Cori on speaker. "Get Angel on the line for me."

"You got it." The line clicks, and she buzzes back a minute later. "Angel is on line two."

I hit line two. "Hey, man."

"Yeah?"

"Angel, it's Blake. Got a moment?" I ask him.

"Of course. What's up?"

"Got a case, was hoping I could bring you in on it."

"I got nothing happening for a while. I can do that," he replies.

"Good. How soon do you think you could make it down?"

"Let me talk to the wife and I'll let you know," Angel says with a small laugh.

I smile, thinking of his wife, Eden. "How you guys doing?"

"Just had another kid," he says, sounding proud.

I count in my head. "What the fuck? Six? You're at six kids now?" I ask, shocked.

He laughs. "Yeah, and she's adamant there will be no more."

I shake my head. "Fuck, man. Good luck with that."

"Yeah, yeah, shut up. Wait until you have your own kids. You'll be wanting to see your woman knocked up all the damn time. Anyways, I'll talk with her, make sure she'll be okay without me around to help with the kids. I'll shoot you a text to let you know."

"Sounds good, man. Later." I hang up and set my phone on my desk. I met Angel years ago, when he first turned his club around. It was the same time I started my career, as well, and we helped each other out, both becoming highly successful in what we do.

I never have put much thought into having kids of my own; I don't have much time for a social life, other than an occasional date, with the demanding hours of this job. I wouldn't change it, though. I love what Adam and I do.

I knew what I wanted to do with my life after the horrible, shitty foster homes I grew up in. They weren't all bad, but a few were worse than anything. The worst home I was ever in was my last one, before I aged out. I don't know how the hell I managed to get the grades I did living there. It was literally hell on earth. They would drug our food every weekend. Wouldn't during the week, since they had to keep up the pretenses, letting us go to school and work. But they made sure, if we had jobs, we weren't allowed to on the weekends.

I still don't know what the fuck happened on those weekends, and I wish like hell I did.

Because of homes like those, I work my ass off, wanting to help kids that are just like I was, living in hell.

CHAPTER 4

Cori

I'm typing up the last bit of the latest report for Blake when a shadow looms over my desk. I look up and see it's one of the Saylor twins. I raise my eyebrows in surprise. "Uh, hey. What are you doing here?"

He winks at me. "I heard you were working here. Thought I'd come by and see if you wanted to take a lunch break."

Which twin is this? Oh my God, this is awkward. He must sense my issue because he smirks. "Mark, baby." I blush.

"Uh, yeah." I smile at him, trying to hide my embarrassment for not knowing which brother he is.

"What's going on here?" I hear Blake say from his office.

I jerk back and stare at him, and he looks angry, like mega angry—and mega angry with me. What in the hell did I do?

"Hey, man. I'm here to take this lovely lady out for lunch," Mark says, holding his hand out to Blake.

I notice Blake's hands are clenched. What's with that? "She only has forty minutes," he tells Mark rudely.

Mark shoots him a smirk. "Know that already, man." He turns to me and grins. "Ready to go?"

I give him a small smile. "Yeah, let's go," I say and bite my lip as I come around my desk.

Blake grabs my arm, and I instantly turn around, facing him. "Be careful with him," he quietly tells me with a warning.

I jerk my head back slightly, looking at him confused. "I know Mark. He's fine," I say quietly. I have never seen Blake act this way.

Twisted Up In You

"I'm sure he is, but I just want you to know, if he hurts you, I'll kill him," Blake growls into my face. For a brief moment, I think he might kiss me. His mouth is inches from mine. The tension rising between the two of us is so thick, and I feel smothered under the dangerous glare he is shooting through me with his dark, heated eyes. I swear, if he did do that—kiss me—this whole office would get a show because I would so totally do him on my desk. There is no way I would be able to control myself.

My nipples are diamond hard as his chest rubs against mine. He feels the contact; his ears are red at the tips. My thighs clench, and I could swear my panties just melted.

"You ready?" Mark asks, eyeing the close proximity of Blake and me.

I nod and step away from Blake. I need to get out of here, and I need air.

"Oh, and Cori, when you get back, please make sure you make a reservation for tonight at eight at Tiffany's. And send flowers to Jodi please." And there it is. The reason I need to just get over my stupid crush on Blake. Maybe if I showed him my real side, my wild and crazy side, he would think differently of me.

"I've already done that. Later," I say coldly and walk toward Mark, looping my arm in his.

Screw Blake.

Mark and I make our way to the small little diner a few streets over from the office and get seated. I'm starving, so I order Poutine and cheesy bread, breaking free of my diet, totally cheating. I'm not really on a diet, per say, but I try to limit my junk and fatty foods to weekends only. I don't even bother paying attention to what Mark orders. I like Mark, I do, but this feels too much like a date, so it's weird.

"So what's going on with you and Blake?" Mark asks once my cheesy bread arrives.

Taking a big bite, and not caring about talking with my mouth full, I answer, "Nothing. He's just a good friend."

He winces, watching me eat. I resist the urge to roll my eyes.

"Seemed like more than that," he says finally, shrugging. "Why are you dressed like that, anyways? I almost didn't recognize you."

"It's my work look," I state. I ended up changing in the bathroom at work to my usual clothes, instead of the clothes Melissa made me wear out the door.

He keeps trying to talk to me, and I get fed up. "Look, Mark, I'm hungry. I only have thirty more minutes of lunch left. Can you please shut up?" I say, exasperated.

He gets the message and finally shuts up and quietly eats. I'm half way through my poutine when my cell phone starts ringing. Well, actually, it's been going off since I left the office, but I've ignored it, and now it's just getting beyond annoying.

"Hello?" I say, again with my mouth full.

BLAKE

Watching Cori leave the office with Mark pisses me off. It shouldn't, considering I just had her plan my date with another woman tonight.

I met Mark and his twin brother a few years ago at a buddy's place, and I know how he is with women. I also know he's married, and has been for four years. I didn't think Cori was the type of girl to get involved in that sort of thing.

Storming back into my office, I slam the door, rattling the pictures and certificates that line the wall.

I don't like her with him, not even a little bit. Deciding to try to get her back here faster, I call her. And text. Over and Over again. Why the fuck isn't she answering? The more she goes without answering, the more pissed I get.

Finally, after about forty minutes, she answers, and when she does, I snap. "Why the fuck weren't you answering your phone?"

"Well, excuse me, your majesty. I'm on my lunch break. I'm allowed to have one of those," she barks at me.

I'm stunned for a moment. She's never spoken to me that way. Ever. "I don't like Mark. I wanted to make sure you were okay."

I hear her snort, and as she talks, it sounds like she is chewing food. "I'll be back soon. Just finished lunch."

"Are you eating while talking to me on the phone?" I ask, completely grossed out.

"Of course I am. I'm not gonna stop eating my lunch just because my boss doesn't like my lunch partner." With that, she hangs up on me.

"What the hell?" I stare at the phone in my hand; she's never hung up on me before. What the hell is going on with her lately?

I get back to work on the case that I had opened on my desk before Mark showed up. I grab my phone and dial in Drew's number. Drew is one of the best detectives around, and he's the only person on the police force I deal with because the rest of them don't respect the work Adam or I do. Some even make fun, saying what I do is a woman's job.

"Knight," he answers on the fourth ring.

"Hey, it's Blake. I need you to send a few men to this address." I rattle it off before explaining more. "I interviewed the kid's mother last week, but she's terrified to leave her husband. Apparently, he beats her, too. Gonna need one of your men to take her and the kid to the Angels Warriors' compound. They'll keep them safe until this bastard is in prison."

"Fucking hate sick fucks. I'll send a car. I'm being transferred to Airdrie, anyways, so I'll take them myself to the compound. Need to scout for a house before the move becomes final. This will give me that chance," Drew tells me.

"When did you find out about the transfer?" I ask him, confused.

"I put in for it a few months back. It doesn't start for another couple months, but I wanted to go to a small town. Love the city and all, but I want something a little slower paced."

"Well, man, good luck. Anyways, meet me in about fifteen minutes. We'll get this done." I hang up and head on out, stopping by Adam's office first. "Hey, heading out now to finish up the Lawrence case."

He nods and waves me off. He seems to be doing some deep reading. I hope that the case he is working on finishes up soon because he is gonna end up working himself to death. I offered to take on this case, but he said no.

I close his door and go to Clara's desk. She started as my secretary when she first came here, but when Adam found out she was working here, he came to me, begging to let him have her. Those two have a strange as shit past together.

"Hey, Clara. He's working himself to the bone. In about an hour, could you please order him some food and then you can head out. I have a feeling he'll be working late tonight."

"Yeah, no problem," she says, quickly glancing toward his office, her face looking soft for just a moment.

I head toward Cori's desk, leaving her a note to let her know I'll be out but that I'll see her tonight at the party.

CHAPTER 5

Cori

Tonight is the company party. I'm nervous, considering it's the first party I've ever thrown in my life. Melissa agreed to do the food. I've been telling her for years she should go to culinary school instead of nursing school, but she keeps telling me her goal is to help others. Food is second; she can cook and bake anywhere.

I can't complain because, as it is, only I get to eat her yummy goodies. I walk into the building, looking around, making sure everything looks great and that things are running smoothly. I spot Randy setting up his liquor behind a makeshift bar and walk over to him, giving him my lustful stare. God, he's so fucking hot. Light dark skin—his mother was white and his father black—and full sexy lips. God his lips, so damn hot. And he has the sexiest dreads I've ever seen. I swear, God was like, 'I'm making this dude my sexiest half-black man ever', and bam, zapped Randy with it.

"Hey, baby," he says, greeting me, winking as I come close.

"Hey, hot stuff," I say, biting my lip. Randy is one of my go-to flings. He knows his way around my body better than anyone does. If I want a sure thing, a fun time, and a guaranteed orgasm, I go to him.

I wanted to bring him as my date tonight, but then he wouldn't be in charge of the bar. Sucks because I so friggin' need him tonight. Instead, I'm stuck with my number two, Mark. He's always a sure thing, but I think tonight is the end of us because I'm starting to feel as if he wants more. Especially now, considering he came to my work earlier today to take me out for a lunch date.

I just hope, with my two fuck buddies, Blake doesn't think badly of me. I've never wanted to disappoint him, considering he's helped me so much over the years. And he seemed angry at me when I left the office with Mark.

"Who's your date for tonight?" Randy asks, leaning over his bar.

I sigh. "Mark."

"Saylor twin?" he asks.

I nod.

"You need it good and hard, baby, you know I'll be there."

I groan. "Trust me, I know. After tonight, though, it's done with him. He's starting to get too close."

Randy gives me a soft look. "Baby, it's you. Of course he is. You're you."

I shake my head. "Please don't. I'd hate to end things with you, too."

He captures my hands in his. He has the hands of a working man, warm to the touch but rough and worked hard with lines and callouses. "Cori, you are beautiful, you're funny, and you're smart as hell. Anyone would be lucky to have you as theirs. If I didn't know your heart was already taken by another, you'd be mine," he tells me seriously. His eyes close briefly, and I run my hand over the strong line of his jaw, wishing I could feel differently about him.

I close my eyes and breathe deeply. "I should go," I say softly to Randy. He leans in close and gives me a quick chaste kiss.

"Good luck tonight, babe. You need me, well, you know where I am." He smiles, but his expression doesn't quite reach his eyes.

I smile at him sadly and walk away. I head to the bathroom so that I can get changed. This is the first time Blake will see me out of my frumpy work clothes. Part of me wants to draw him in, make him want me. The other part wants me to show him what he'll never have.

I'm sick and tired of pining away after him when he wants nothing to do with me in that way.

Changing into the black cocktail dress, I smooth the fabric, running my hands down my sides. Twisting to the side, I observe how it does show my curves nicely. It isn't too sexy for a work affair, but it is sexy enough to show I am a full-figured woman. My hair rests on my shoulders in soft angelic waves. *Okay, Cori, you can do this.* I give myself a mental pep talk and prepare to make my entrance.

A brief knock taps against the bathroom door.

"Um, come in," I say hesitantly, wondering who it is and why they are knocking to begin with.

Mark steps in, looking handsome and devious.

"Wow," he says, appreciating my womanly shape.

His hands curve around my backside as a husky growl reaches my ear. I didn't have any intention of sleeping with Mark tonight, but the next thing I know, he has me bent over the counter of the sink, taking me fast and furious from behind.

BLAKE

I walk into Lexington with my date and see Cori coming out of the bathroom, followed by fucking Mark Saylor. Corinne—I never would have thought she would do shit like that. Lately, I've noticed things, things I never have before about her. I've never seen her look so damn beautiful. Her dress is hugging every single damn curve she has. Why the fuck does she wear those baggy as hell clothes then? That's what she's been hiding?

"Put your tongue back in your mouth, man," I hear Adam say. I didn't even realize he was next to me. "She's beautiful, isn't she," he says, clamping me hard on the shoulder.

I feel Jodi stiffen beside me.

"Don't even look," I growl out.

He chuckles. "Don't worry. My eye is on another," he admits quietly.

I look to him and follow his gaze, which is on Clara. I knew it! Love it when I'm right. Clara has worked for us since we started, although I'm not sure why, considering her and Adam have a history. From what I heard, he really fucked her over just after high school, marrying her sister. They had dated all four years of school, but turns out, Adam, for some reason, broke it off. A week later, he came back to town married—to Sophia, Clara's sister.

The marriage didn't last long; about a year later, they were divorced. Clara hasn't seen her sister since the marriage announcement, and even refuses to have anything to do with Adam. She even blatantly ignores him. Of course, she still does every single thing he asks, since she's his assistant, but that's it. It's a strange working relationship.

I look back to Cori and see her in a heated discussion with Mark. I almost want to go over and pull her into me.

"Blake, honey, I'm thirsty," Jodi whines from beside me.

I look at her, really look at her. I shouldn't have brought her. She's one of my only repeaters, besides when I'm stupid and repeat with Stacy. I also know how she feels about Cori. She says she likes her, but at the same time, constantly talks bad about her.

"Then go get something," I say, shrugging.

"Okay then," she says slowly. "How about I just go home? Because if you are just going to be staring at *her* all night, it's not going to be fun for me."

I blow out a breath and glare down at Jodi. "Then leave," I say, not liking how she's talking about Cori, and leave her side. I hear her grumble and then her heels clicking on the floor as she walks away.

Fuck. I want her so damn bad. I walk over when I see her walk away from Mark, making her way to Clara. I'm close enough to hear their conversation, and I'm fighting so damn hard not to storm over there.

"Fuck, Clara, my vagina hurts," Cori complains. Mother fucker.

Clara giggles. "Girl, did you at least get off?"

I stiffen, please say no.

"No, I've only ever come for Randy. Mark is just an itch. I told him it's no more, though. He's not taking it well," Cori informs her. "My vagina hurts because I couldn't even get wet for him. That's never happened to me before. Ugh."

Clara giggles at her.

I clench my jaw. Who the fuck is this Cori?

That's it. I storm over and pull Cori aside.

"Why does your pussy hurt, Cori?" I demand.

She looks up at me in shock. "Why do you think?" she answers with defiance, full of attitude.

I glare at her, and she matches it. "I never realized you were such a slut," I tell her, seething.

Corinne's face pales. "Fuck you, asshole. You are my boss. This is none of your business," she retorts, throwing her hands out in anger.

"It damn well is my business when you are fucking some dickhead in the bathroom of my company party!"

"Oh, fuck you, buddy. Just fuck you," she snaps out, hurt by my accusations, and storms away from me.

What the hell? Am I in some crazy ass alternate universe? Because this is not my Cori. The Cori I know is a shy, sweet girl.

"Hey there, big guy." I hear from behind me. I look back and see it's Melissa, Cori's sister.

"Hi," I grumble.

Melissa giggles. "Let me guess. You've just realized Cori has been playing you big time, pretending to be this shy, frumpy little thing." I turn around, grabbing her arm, and pull her out into the hall.

"What is wrong with her?" I demand.

Her eyebrows shoot up, and then she grins. "This is Cori."

"No, it's not. The Cori I know does not dress or act like that. Hell, she doesn't even talk like that."

"Actually, yeah, this is the real her. She loves sex but avoids serious commitment. She also loves showing skin, the more the better," Melissa tells me, crossing her arms over her chest.

I shake my head. "No way. Cori is always polite and sweet. She's not that," I say, throwing my arm out. I also always thought that, with the way Cori acts, is that she was a virgin. She's sure always acted like it.

Melissa snorts and rolls her eyes. "Actually, she is just like that for you, and only you. She's had a crush on you for years, but no, you don't see that. I kept telling her to let you see her real side, but nope."

I stiffen at her words. "She wants me?"

Melissa's face pales, realizing she gave away something she shouldn't have. "Oh shit. No, no, no, no, no, you can't say anything."

A slow grin spreads across my face, and Melissa slaps herself. "Shit, you aren't gonna let that go now, are you?"

"Hell no," I say and leave her side.

Twisted Up In You

CHAPTER 6

Cori

Everything is going great tonight. Music is pumping through the speakers, Melly's food is a hit, and I'm high on life. Well, I'm kind of hurt, really, because Blake is such an ass. I can't believe he called me a slut. Who the hell does he think he is? I can count on two hands the amount of men I've slept with in my life, and for the last few years, it's only been the Saylor twins and Randy. Blake has a new Barbie every week. I rarely order flowers for the same woman twice.

I see Mark sauntering over to me, and I roll my eyes as he's sidetracked by Kelli-Ann's huge rack. I shake my head and turn around, and instantly smash into a brick wall. I look up and Blake is there. I can't read his expression, and that has me worried.

"Uh, hi," I say quietly and try to skirt around him. He pulls me back and glares at me.

"I didn't think you were this kind of girl, Cori. One that sleeps around, not only that but with a married man," he reveals, his jaw clenching.

I frown. "I've never slept with a married man, or any man that is in a relationship. I do have my limits."

He gives an ugly laugh. "You can't tell me you didn't know that Mark and Lark Saylor are married and have been for years. Even have a few kids between them." It hits me like a blow. Oh shit, I'm a home wrecker. Melly too. Oh no.

"What?" I breathe out in shock.

His brows go up. "You really didn't know?"

I shake my head no, whip my head toward where Mark is chatting up Kelli-Ann, and glare at him. "It's a good thing I planned to break it off with him tonight," I mutter.

"Why are you splitting with him?" Blake asks.

I roll my eyes. "He's getting too clingy, wanting to make more out of what we do. I'm not down with that."

His eyes widen in shock at my answer. "Why did you never let me see this side of you before?" Blake asks me.

I shrug. "I didn't want you to think badly of me. I also knew how your last secretary was, and I didn't want you to think I was anything like her. Angel got me this job, and I wanted him to be proud of me. Didn't want him hearing about me being the office slut because, then, he might look at me differently." One thing I always held in high regard was Angel's opinion. He saved me, took care of me and Melly. I never want to disappoint him.

Blake's last secretary, apparently, was a screaming bitch. I also was told that they threw a going away party for her. She ended up marrying her hockey player boyfriend, so she quit to follow him around. However, she wasn't even invited to her own party because it was more of a 'thank God she's gone' party. According to Clara, she found out about it and ended up crashing said party. I would have loved to have been there for that. Sounded like it would've been hilarious.

Blake's face softens. "Cori, I wouldn't have thought that. It just would have made getting into your pants a hell of a lot easier," he says with a half smirk.

I glare at him. "Whatever, Blake. I have some people to talk to, so, yeah... bye," I say and walk off. What the heck did he mean by that? Did he just admit he has wanted me? Or maybe he just wants me now.

BLAKE

I'm still stewing over the fact that I just found out Cori has been crushing on me for years. I'm also pissed she never showed me this side of her before, because I would have made a move a long ass time ago, instead of getting my dick wet somewhere else whenever I thought about dragging her onto my desk.

I always held off because she seemed kind of shy and skittish. I didn't think she'd ever go for something like that. Or for someone like me, considering she's planned most of my 'dates' over the last few years.

Cori in deep conversation with Mark, and suddenly, I see her slap him across the face. I smile and walk closer, wanting to hear what is being said.

"I can't believe you! You're married? How could you do that to your wife? I was gonna end it with you, anyways, because I told you I don't do relationships, only sex, but now I'm ending it because you're fucking married!" Hearing her cuss shocks me. I've never known her to swear, ever. Usually, she'll say frig or frack, never fuck. And hearing her say 'fucking' has my dick springing to life.

Cori walks away from Mark, and he stands there, looking down at the floor before turning on his heel, walking out of the building. His face is red with white fingerprints where her hand struck him. He is retreating like the dog he is with his tail between his legs.

Turning around, I find Cori flirting with the bartender, downing shot after shot. I shake my head and go to her, grabbing her by the arm, and drag her down the hall.

I take a good look at her, watching her bite her lip, her eyes on my mouth. Fuck, I hope I don't regret this. Wrapping my hands around the back of her neck, I crush my mouth to hers. She gives me a little moan, and I force her mouth open with my tongue, tasting the liquor she just consumed.

I pull back slightly, staring into her beautiful hazel eyes. "If I had known this side of you before, you would have been underneath me a long ass time ago." Apparently, this was the wrong thing to say. Suddenly, I'm dropped to the floor, cupping my balls, while Cori stands over me.

"Asshole," she says and storms out.

Shit, I need to make her mine. It takes me a few minutes for the pain to go away, and once it does, I'm up and off searching for her. I look around the room and spot Adam and Clara yelling at each other. I shake my head. Those two need to get their shit together.

I look to find Melissa smiling as she places more food on the big long table by the far wall. I go to her quickly.

"Melissa," I say, coming close. "Where did Cori go?"

She smiles. "She said she had to go home, wasn't feeling well. Personally, I think it's because she feels guilty about the Mark thing. She never would have been with him if she knew he was married. That pig!" she says, looking disgusted. "I can't wait to see Lark so I can also give him a piece of my mind. I'm also vindictive, because I'm going to find out who their wives are and give an anonymous tip about their cheating." She has an evil gleam in her eye.

Man, does she ever look scary. "Leave it alone, Melly. I'm sure their wives know, or will soon find out on their own," I say, shaking my head. She rolls her eyes at me. "I'm gonna make the rounds, talk to some people, and then we can start clearing out."

I'll talk to Cori at work tomorrow, I decide.

CHAPTER 7

Cori

I woke up this morning, feeling fine. Yay me. No hangover. But I also forgot to let Melly know about what all happened last night. I was asleep when she came home, and she didn't wake me up. Then this morning, I realized I was running late so I didn't get the chance to fill her in on how Blake spoke to me.

Sitting at my desk, I lean back in the chair and sigh. Today looks like a full workload.

I swivel around in the chair with my eyes closed. Yes, that is something a five year old does, but I do it when I'm bored. It's fun. My chair stops abruptly.

"Hey there, beautiful," Blake says, grinning down at me.

I stiffen in my seat and glare at him. "I'm not doing this."

"We're doing this," he says firmly. Right, sure we are.

"Let the chair go," I snap at him. He never once looked at me before, not the way he's looking at me now. Why wasn't I good enough before? Was it just because he couldn't see what was under my baggy clothes? Or is it the fact that he now knows I'm easy.

"No." He is smiling smugly. I used to go weak in the knees for that smile.

"Problem here, Cori?" I look up and see Mark Saylor glaring at Blake. Oh, great. Guess my talk with him last night didn't work.

"What are you doing here?" I ask, standing up and stepping back from Blake.

"You free this weekend?" Mark asks, holding out a bouquet of Lilies.

"No, she's not," Blake growls out, interrupting, then stalks over to me and pulls me into him.

I try to move out of Blake's hold, but he doesn't let me budge.

"I think you should let go of my girl there," Mark says with anger.

"Your girl?" he says, snorting. "Don't think so."

"Where were you the other night when my dick was in her?" Mark says with a smirk.

There is gonna be a fight here—I know there is.

"Mark, please, we talked last night. You shouldn't be here," I butt in.

"Cori, come on. You can't be serious about that," Mark whines.

I shake my head. "I told you. I don't do married men. Ever. So it's over."

"Whatever, Cori," Mark says, looking pissed then walks away, throwing the flowers in the trash can by the elevator.

I let out a sigh and stiffen when Blake's hands tighten on my arms.

"Your days of fucking around are over," Blake says, anger dripping off him.

"You can't tell me who I can and can't sleep with." He might be the boss here, but he can't dictate shit about what I can and can't do on my personal time.

"Yes, I fucking can," he says into my hair. "I'll let you get to work. Don't leave after. We'll go out to get some supper."

"Fine," I lie. I do not intend to be here by the time he gets off.

He kisses my temple and walks away. Just wait until I get home to tell Melly about this.

The day passes by fast, but I'm constantly checking the area to see if Blake is around. Luckily, he's been swamped so he hasn't made an appearance. I have been sneaking and looking at other wanted ads in my spare time.

Four-thirty hits, and it's leaving time for me. I switch off the phones so all calls go directly to the machine and walk out, locking the door behind me. The staff upstairs don't leave for another hour, but they all have keys to close up behind them.

I get home fifteen minutes later, and Melly is already home, starting supper. "We need to go drinking tonight," I shout as I close the door.

"Uh oh. Bad day?" she asks, coming out of the kitchen.

"You will not believe what Blake said to me today. Ugh. Damn that man. I pine for him for years, but he never friggin' notices, and then, finally, he does, and now he just expects me to jump into his arms." I snort. "Fuck him."

"I really don't see what the problems is," Melissa says, biting her lip.

"The problem is, he never wanted me before, but now suddenly he does. Pfft. Probably just wants an easy lay instead of going out and searching around for it."

"Or it could be that he's always liked you and you were too blind to ever see it. Maybe him seeing you in your real element last night made him realize that he just needed to be the one to make the first move," Melissa says, sounding so damn sure of herself.

"Whatever, I don't even want to think about this right now. I'm not going to let him do to me what he's done to so many others. I'm going out tonight."

"Ugh, but it's Friday. Every club and bar will be swamped," Melissa points out. She hates going out on weekends because she hates crowds just as much as I do.

"Yeah, but at Randy's club, we get V.I.P."

"Well then, Club Shine it is," she says, sitting next to me on the couch.

"Hell yes!"

I sink back into the leather, already craving a drink and to get laid. As I said, I know what I like and what I want. And tonight, I need to get drunk and have sex.

"What's for dinner, bitch?"

"Burgers and Fries," Melissa says, knowing I try to eat better than that.

I glare at her.

"Oh, come on. Live a little. One burger won't kill you."

"No, but it will cause me to die one day of heart problems." I already had a friggin' greasy meal this week when I had lunch with Mark.

Melissa smacks me and laughs. "Live a little."

BLAKE

I check the time on the computer as I shut it down. Five forty-five. Shit. I'm pretty sure Cori isn't still here. No way would she stick around over an hour to wait for me. I shut down my office and walk out. Monday, I have a meeting with Angel, Reaper, and Zippo of the Angels Warriors. They are gonna help stake out a foster home that I have a bad feeling about.

I get into the elevator when Adam joins me. "Hey, you up for the club tonight?" he asks me.

I raise an eyebrow. "Ugh, you know I hate going out on Friday nights." Normally, it's the one day that Stacy seems to stalk me, and I end up drunk and fucking her.

He shrugs. "Yeah, I know, but I also heard Cori is going there tonight. Something about her getting free drinks there because she's always screwing the owner."

"How do you know this?" I say, my jaw instantly clenching.

"Melissa texted me, told me to bring you. You know, the guy Cori hired to do the drinks, the one I told you about who's her fuck buddy? Yeah, it's his club."

"I'm in," I say instantly.

"Stacy knows her," Adam confides.

"How the fuck does she know her?" I ask confused.

Twisted Up In You

"They got into a fight at the club last year, I guess. Randy has her banned from the club so she can't bother Cori again."

"Well, at least I know if I wanna get drunk and not worry about fucking Stacy, I can go to his club."

Adam bursts out laughing. "You hook up with her at least once a month. You really sure she means nothing to you?"

"Trust me, she's an easy fuck, but that's the only thing good about her."

He shakes his head.

CHAPTER 8

Cori

Dressed to the nines, both Melissa and I are ready to go. My hair is down with nice waves. I have on a black skirt and a green open back halter, paired with my favorite black leather studded fuck me heels. Melly looks awesome in her navy blue wrap dress. She looks amazing in navy. It goes great with her complexion and blonde hair. I called Randy and told him I needed a night, including a possible fuck in his office. I'm not picky. He told us to be there at least an hour before open.

Randy is a cool dude; he owns the club Melly and I frequent often, Club Shine. He knows I don't want anything serious, and he enjoys sex as much as the next man. So why ruin a good thing by complicating with stings, feelings, and labels?

Melly and I fill up on greasy burgers and fries and are off. It helps us to not throw up. We have a cab drop us off. No way will either of us be able to drive.

"Holy shit. There's a line already," Melissa says, shocked.

I stare at the line-up. "It's a Friday. So duh."

"Oh, shut up," she counters, laughing.

We walk to the front of the line, and everyone starts yelling for us to go back. "Hey Monster," I say, smiling at the bouncer.

"Cori, baby!" he bellows with a loud boom. "Melissa." He greets her, smirking seductively at her.

"Dray," Melissa says quietly and turns her head from him.

I swear, he has a serious thing for her, but she won't give him the time of day. The way Monster is, I bet you anything, at some point, he's gonna make his move and she won't be able to dodge him anymore. His real name is Drayton, but he usually goes by Dray. I started calling him Monster as a joke a few years ago because he is fucking huge and he took out four hockey players once in one go.

"You gonna let us in?" I ask sweetly.

"Yup, boss man says go right in. Take your VIP room and make yourselves at home." He unlocks the door, letting us in. A few patrons in line are grumbling because we bypassed them.

The place is a ghost town. All the servers and bartenders are bustling around, getting the place ready. Gloria comes over with a bounce in her step. "Hey, it's my favorite costumers." She winks at Melly and nods at me.

Randy always sends her to us each and every time we are here. She's become a friend, a strange friend, but a good one. Plus, half the time, she sneaks us shots, although she doesn't have to, since Randy says it's all on the house. I think she feels like she is doing us a friendly favor. Whatever. Free booze is free booze.

"Hey, babe!" Melly and I reply in unison.

"Drinking hard tonight, huh? Must have been a shit day," Gloria makes small talk.

"Yup, like you wouldn't believe. Start us with double vodka and sprite, no ice, and use the good shit that Randy has. Don't want any of that watered down vodka he's got," I tell her, ready to get my party on.

She grins. "Sure thing. Actually, Randy must have known you were coming because he already brought out the good shit and put it under the bar." She walks away to get our drinks, and I sink back into one of the clubs seats. The vibe here is cool. The seats are leather, not that vinyl shit. Neon lights line the ceiling around the dance floor. The walls are painted a deep purple, and everything is black or chrome.

"You gonna be screwing Randy tonight?" Melly asks me, taking off her jacket. Randy and I met when I got rip roaring drunk one night and started trying to strip on his bar top. He pulled me down, yelled at me in his office, and then told me if I remembered him when I was sober to come back to see him. I did, and well, the rest is history. I go to him if I'm feeling up for a bit of kink. Sometimes, I just want to be tied up and spanked. Yum.

"Probably." I waggle my brows at her, shrugging my hoodie off.

Gloria comes back over with a tray full of booze and shots and places them on the table. "Enjoy. I put a trash can under the table just for you, in case you need to barf. I'm so not cleaning it up next time." She gives me a pointed look, laughing as she walks away.

I pick up a shot and clink with Melly. "Cheers, whore."

"Fuck yeah, bitch!" She downs her shot.

The club begins to get crowded. I can't believe this many fuckers are out tonight. I lead Melissa to the dance floor, and we shake it and grind on each other, not caring who is watching or what they think of us.

BLAKE

We arrive at the club two hours after opening. When we got here, the line for the club was huge. I didn't want to stand in the line, and likely not get in. I went up to the bouncer at the door, told him who I was and why I was there, and he smirked, letting me right in.

"That guy back there said they were up in the VIP area," I yell at Adam over the music.

We go to the stairs and walk up. I spot Melissa, slowly sipping a drink.

Her brows raise, almost surprised I would actually show up. "Uh, hey there, Blake."

"Where is your sister," I ask her.

She gives me an almost sad look. "Um..."

A bubbly waitress bounds up to the table and looks at Melissa. "Where's Cori?"

Melissa's face twists, and she pales slightly. "Uh, she's busy," she says softly.

"Oh, you mean busy with Randy, right," the waitress says, giggling loudly over the music. "I wish I could be like you two, carefree, fun. But, nope, I can't do it. My heart always gets in the way," she says, sounding envious of Cori.

I clench my hands and my jaw. Cori is fucking mine, and I'm standing here while this bitch basically blurts out she's fucking Randy right now.

Melissa looks over my shoulder and shakes her head.

I turn around to see what she was looking at, and there she is. I'm gonna fuckin' kill someone. Jealousy rages through me as my nostrils flare in anger.

She's against the wall, skirt hiked up, her legs wrapped around some dick. She looks up mid moan and stiffens at first when she makes eye contact, then goes back to sucking that fucker's neck. Her nails are clawing up the back of his shirt. As pissed off as I am, I can't help but wonder how it might feel to have her nails scratching down my back. A deep moan escapes her throat once more, and it is so damn erotic sounding. It is killing me that another man is bringing that reaction out of her.

"Whoa, I never would have thought she'd just have sex right there, in a club," Adam says, shocked, from beside me.

I hear a snort behind me. "She does this all the time," the waitress says, like it is the most natural thing in the world for Cori to be pressed against the wall getting her rocks off.

My blood soars. I'm definitely gonna kill someone tonight.

"She's not having sex, though. He's just fingering her," Melissa says, as if that would be any better.

Still, fucking pisses me off. I'm about to go over and rip the fucker away from my woman when she walks over, looking flushed. But she doesn't stop. Nope, she keeps walking right past me.

The fucker that had her pinned to the wall comes over to us, smirking. "Hey, man," he says to Adam.

Adam's face pales. "Uh, hey, Randy."

This is the guy from the company party, the bartender. Shit. I can't start something now. But I can say something.

"You fucking her?" I ask him angrily.

He looks at me in shock. "Yeah, have been for a while." He glances at Adam like he wants to ask what the hell my problem is.

"Not anymore you're not," I threaten, stepping into him.

"Back up, man. What the fuck?"

"She's mine," I say, leaning in close to him, making sure he gets the point. I step back and walk to her table, sitting right beside her so she can't move. "That shit over there just now is done. I see it again, you'll be responsible for when I end up in prison."

"Screw you, Blake," she spits out at me, blowing off my threat.

I grab her by the back of the head. "Try me, Cori. Just fucking try me." I crush my lips to hers, roughly, bruisingly.

When I pull back, I stare at her shocked face. "Tomorrow night, we're going out." I get up out of the seat, not waiting for an answer. Adam follows closely behind me.

"So, uh, I take it you finally are moving in on that?" Adam asks me as we walk out to my car.

"She's going to be mine," I say, shrugging.

He shakes his head as he gets in the passenger side. I drop Adam off at his place and head home myself. I keep seeing flashes of Cori pinned against the wall, but now, in my mind, it's me making her cry out in pleasure.

I get home soon after leaving, and it's not long before my phone goes off. I check it and see that, once again, Stacy has messaged me. When the hell is she going to take the damn hint?

BLAKE, text me back or call me. Why are you
ignoring me? – Stacy

Groaning, I text her back.

Stacy, don't contact me again. Lose my number. –
BLAKE

Instantly, a text comes back.

**Don't be like that. We're good together. I'll come
see you at work tomorrow. – Stacy**

Come to my work, we'll have problems. –
BLAKE

She shows up there, I swear to fuck, I'm gonna lose it.

She doesn't text back, so I throw my phone onto the
counter top and head toward my shower.

I start it up, letting the shower warm up while I strip
my clothes off. I still can't believe the Cori I've come to
know is anything like the way I've seen her the last few
days. It doesn't sit right with me. Not even a little bit.

I always told everyone I didn't want her, that she was
like a sister to me, but everyone knew I was lying. I've
wanted her since I first saw her. Her beauty, the way she
carries herself... I was drawn to her. Something about her
just made me want to be near her.

Thinking about Cori as I lay in bed has me rock hard.
I am almost tempted to have Stacy come over, but I need to
put a stop to that shit if I want a chance with Cori.

CHAPTER 9

Cori

"Oh shit, that was hot," Melissa says in shock. "I had an orgasm just watching that. You sure you won't just give in and be with him?"

I shake my head, still stunned. "I'm sure. Remember, he has had years to notice me and he never has."

"Cori, babe, I think you should just go for it!" Melissa shouts over the music.

"I'm ready to go home. He totally ruined my vibe for the night," I shout to her. This side of Blake is hot, sexy, but I can't. That kiss... that kiss is still touching me deep inside. I know sex with Blake would be out of this world. Too bad I'll never allow myself to experience the sensation.

She nods and we leave. Once home, we get comfy and sit on the couch watching Dance Moms.

"This show is so stupid. All these moms bitch and bitch, yet they don't do anything about it. If they are really that unhappy, they should just quit it. Gee," Melissa points to the TV.

I snort. "Yeah, no shit. I watch it for the drama, though. I bet you anything it's all played up for views."

"So what are you gonna do about Blake, huh?" she asks.

"What are you gonna do about Monster?" I shoot back.

"Nothing," she says defiantly. Her brows are scrunched up; I know she thinks about it. She likes him more than she cares to admit.

I raise my eyebrows at her questionably, waiting for more of an answer.

"Fine! Gee. I like him, like a lot a lot. But I also know he's known for cheating on women he's dating, with chicks from the club. I've survived this long without any serious attachments so I wouldn't get my heart broken, and I'm not diving into his shit storm," she says quietly but openly.

I place my hand on her knee and squeeze. "Babe, you never know. He could change for you. And last I heard, he's been turning down women at the club. Randy was telling me that Monster is like a born again virgin."

Her head whips around to face me so fast, I swear she was like the chick from that movie *The Exorcist*. "Really?" she asks in shock.

I shrug. "It's what he says."

"Huh."

"Yeah, huh." I nudge her shoulder, hoping she will think about it.

"Okay, back to you. What about Blake?"

"Nothing, seriously. He's gone all weird and shit, saying I'm his, but I'm so not." Dude has to be mental, staking his claim like a damn Neanderthal.

"Don't get pregnant," she breathes out. "Because then you are fucked."

I give a forced laugh. "Don't worry. I don't want kids, ever. Kids will never in a million years happen for me." Is she bringing that shit up just to hurt me? She knows what happened in that damn foster home we were in before Angel saved us.

"I want kids, one day," she admits, shocking me. Why did I not ever know this about my sister? "I want to be a better mother than our mom ever was," she says quietly.

"Wow, well, looks like I can have the best Auntie in the world duties, and just pass 'em on back when they cry or need changing."

"You really don't want kids, Cori?" she asks me softly.

"No," I say, giving her a look to shut up. Thankfully, she gets it and backs off.

"You should know, I thought he was gonna kill Gloria for bragging about you and Randy together. I really do think he likes you, Cori. I think he has for a long ass time." She shakes her head, frowning.

I laugh. "Whatever."

"Cori..." she starts.

I shake my head. "I'm not doing this, or him, Melly. I highly doubt I'll ever get a reason for 'why now?'. He'll probably just screw me and then fire me so he can move on."

Melissa sighs on the couch next to me but says nothing.

We end the night watching a bit of TV before passing out on the couch.

BLAKE

I walk in the front doors and head up to my office, expecting to see Cori sitting at her desk. Instead, the seat is filled with someone I don't know. "Who are you?" I demand. I haven't seen Cori since Friday night. I tried calling her phone, but she never picked up.

The small, scared looking girl's eyes widen in shock. "Um, I'm the temp," she stutters out.

"Where is Cori?" I ask.

"I-I don't know who that is. I-I'm sorry."

I shake my head and walk down the hall, and see Adam on his phone through the glass walls of his office. He quickly ends his call and looks up as I step inside.

"Where is she?"

He leans forward and pushes a letter toward me. Her fucking resignation. I rip it up and toss it in his trash. "She's not quitting. Give me her address," I demand.

Adam shakes his head at me. "Never seen you like this in my life. Crazy fucking shit, man."

I jot down her address and realize she's only two floors down from my condo. How long has she been living there, and not once did we see each other.

"Don't forget to be back by one! Angels Warriors will be here for the meeting," Adam calls out as I get to the elevator.

I send him a wave over my shoulder as I get into the elevator. If Cori thinks she can get away from me, she's got another think coming.

I arrive home and park in my spot, still not believing that she has been living in the same damn condominium building as me. We have underground parking, and every floor in the building has their own area. In a way, I guess it's not a surprise I didn't see her car here before.

"Hello, Mr. Lexington," Gary, the doorman greets me.

"Gary, my man, what did I tell you about that Mr. Lextington thing?" I say, smirking.

He laughs and smiles, shaking his head as I walk past him.

The elevator reaches Cori's floor, and I step out, walking down the hall to her condo. After knocking, I wait.

I knock again when there isn't an answer. Finally, after my fourth knock, the door is thrown open, and a highly hung over Cori stands there glaring at me.

"Well, hello, miss sunshine," I greet, shoving her out of my way to enter.

"I didn't invite you in," she says, slamming her door shut.

"Why aren't you at work?" I ask her, making myself at home on her couch.

"I quit."

"Yeah, no, that's not gonna work for me."

"You really don't have a say in it, so you should just leave," she says, getting irritated.

"Wanna know what's funny? I live in this building. Have for three years. How long have you lived here?" I ask her, watching her eyes bug out in shock.

"You've got to be kidding me. We moved in here our second year of college. Lilly helped us get it." She rolls her eyes. Even pissed off and hung-over, she turns me on. She is dressed in a thin white tank top, no bra, and boy shorts. I can see her nipples clear as day, and I am trying not to get a hard on. Her body is smoking hot. She clearly takes care of herself. Her arms are toned as well as her legs but not in a manly way.

"Wow, so a bit longer than me, huh? I'm surprised we never saw each other."

She doesn't say anything, just stands there staring at me. Growing frustrated with my presence, she goes to the kitchen and takes a banana from the counter. She peels it quickly and takes an angry bite.

"Look, you need to leave," Cori demands.

I shake my head no. "Not until you agree to resume your job at Lexington."

She clenches her jaw. "If I work for you, will you leave me the hell alone?"

"Not a chance in hell."

"Then no."

"Fine, I'll stay right here then," I say, slowly kicking off my shoes to lay on the couch.

She lets out a loud growl and stomps from the room. Ten minutes later, she comes back out, dressed and looking better than she did before.

"Fine," she snaps, stomping past me, grabbing her purse.

I grin as I put my shoes back on. That was easier than I thought.

We get down to the parking lot, and she goes to walk toward the street. "Where you going?" I shout at her.

"Bus. Melly has my car today," she shouts back, not breaking her stride.

I jog to catch up with her and grab her arm, pulling her back. "Let go of me, Blake," she says, trying to get loose.

Twisted Up In You

"You can ride with me. No point in taking the bus when I'm going there myself." She stops fighting me and sighs heavily.

During the drive, my hand itches to touch her, feel her. I reach over and place it on her thigh.

Throwing my hand off, she glares at me. My hand goes back to her thigh, and this time, I don't let her move it. She tries, but I manage to get under her skirt and begin playing with her pussy through the thin material of her panties. She's already fucking wet. A whimper leaves her throat, and fuck me if it isn't the sexiest sound. I want her screaming my name, writhing beneath me in ecstasy.

My free hand grips the wheel, white knuckled. Fuck. She is so turned on. If I didn't have that meeting to get to, I would pull into an empty floor of the parking garage and ravish her pussy with my tongue. I bite down hard thinking of doing it. The salty taste of blood from my bleeding lip, from biting down so hard, coats my tongue and I swallow hard, wanting her.

I park in the staff lot, and before the car shuts off, Cori gets out of the car quickly and runs into the building. I smile. She thinks she can run from me, but it's not happening.

CHAPTER 10

Cori

Blake is completely insufferable the whole damn ride over. He kept trying to cop a feel. I end up back at Lexington, but I am not in a good mood, and everyone that comes in the doors and up to me knows it.

Ten minutes before one o'clock, I see Angel from Angels Warriors MC walk through the doors with his friends, Reaper and Zippo.

"Well, hey there. Any of you single?" I say, smirking.

Angel smiles at me. Oh shit, I think I just came in my panties. Angel has always been hot, but I can't flippin' believe he has gotten even hotter. Married life suits him.

"Sorry, darlin', all of us are married."

"Well, shit. Oh well, didn't hurt to try," I say, sighing dreamily.

Vinny gives a small laugh and shakes his head. "Awe, man, Zippo, lose the damn beanie already!" I say, pointing at him.

"You are just a bag of trouble lately, aren't ya, darlin'?" Angel says, grinning at me.

"Yeah, yeah," I say with a wave of my hand.

"Club is having a family thing next weekend. You and Melissa should come," Angel says.

"Really?" I ask him, smiling widely.

"Yeah, and my six kids will be there."

"Holy fuck! Are you kidding me?" I ask in shock. Last time I talked to Angel and the boys was when he was sitting at five kids. Hell, I even just talked to Eden a few months ago, but she didn't mention being pregnant.

"Not kidding. Text me if you can't make it," he says, giving me a smile.

I shake my head. "Wow, anyways, you can go on in," I tell the guys, waving toward the boardroom.

I watch as they walk away, and, holy shit, they have very fine asses. I've never once checked them out before, because I never had a reason to. They helped Melissa and me, saved us from hell, but watching them walk away from my desk... Hot damn. As I'm watching them wait for the doors to open, my phone rings.

"Thanks for calling Lexington. Blake Lexington's assistant, Corinne speaking. How may I help you," I greet the caller.

"I see you doing that again, I'll come out there and spank you," Blake barks at me.

"Uh, what?"

"I watched you through my damn window, you flirting, checking out the men that just came in. That shit stops," he growls and hangs up.

"Well then." I'm half-tempted to flip him off, but I think better of it.

The guy is making me rethink everything. I don't get him and what he is trying to prove.

I watch him from the corner of my eyes as he gets down to business talking with Angel. I wonder what this is about. After the last two days, with things getting weird with Blake, I'm worried that he called them down to ask about me. Those three boys know everything, every horrible fucking detail of what happened to me growing up—what I lost, all of it. I've always been terrified that Blake would see my slutty side, but the thought of him finding out about my childhood is worse than anything.

BLAKE

After hanging up on Cori, I stomp to the boardroom and settle into my chair. Adam comes in moments later with

Angel, Reaper, and Zippo following behind him. I stand up to shake their hands.

Angel rubs his hands together. "Whatcha got for me?" he asks, taking a seat.

I let out a breath and pass him the folder. "I've gotten many reports about this home, and I've been there to follow up on them, but haven't seen anything wrong. Neighbors have even called the police. Hell, the children were even removed for a few days to further investigate. Still, nothing, so they were returned back. Last week, I saw a kid walk up to the house. Pretty sure he's one of the kids living there. He looked like he didn't want to go in. He was shaking, looking scared. I waited. Took him fifteen minutes to get the courage to finally open the front door."

Reaper's face goes dark. "What do you want us to do?"

"We're hoping to get you to recon the place, stake it out. Watch it closely. Get cameras set up inside, outside, anything. I'm positive these bastards are hurting those kids, and I want them finally brought down. I have no fucking clue how they keep passing all inspections, but I know something is happening," Adam says from his seat beside me.

Angel nods, and Zippo speaks up. "I'll get on that. I have some equipment in my garage, so it won't cost shit, and I'll have all surveillance sent back to the club house for T-bags to monitor."

"I don't know how well that shit would hold up in court, but Zippo's father-in-law is a damn good lawyer. I'm sure he'd help out," Angel tells us.

"Sounds good, man. I want those kids safe."

We finish up the meeting, and I give them the address of the home. As they are about to leave, Angel stops and sits back down.

"What?" I ask.

Zippo and Reaper both flank him, both looking worried. "Have you ever met Cori and Melissa before Cori came to work here?" he asks me, his face carefully blank.

"No, you are the one that got Cori the job," I tell him. He knows this.

"Fuck," he says, rubbing at his beard. "Are you positive?"

I frown and look at Adam, who looks just as confused as I am. "Yeah, I am."

"I should have recognized this last name and address right away. This is the home that we rescued Cori and Melissa from."

"That's not possible. I lived in that house," I tell them.

"Which is why I'm asking if you knew her. Melissa and Cori were in this house until I got them outta there when Cori was seventeen. You would have been in that home with them. Cori would have been sixteen when you were in your last year at this place."

What the fuck? I don't remember a Corinne or a Melissa living there with me ever. Hell, there were no girls at all in that house. "Man, you've gotta be wrong. There were no girls living there."

Angel shakes his head, giving me a grim look. "There were four girls living there when you did, Blake."

A silence comes over the room. I have no idea what to say.

"Blake, that home has a secret basement. That's where the girls were kept. The day we saved Cori and Melissa, we brought cops with us, but it was like they knew we were coming and had it all sealed up with the girls in the main house. Corinne was seventeen, just a few months away from being eighteen, and social services let us take her and Melissa. But there wasn't anything else we could do. That family is highly respected. Dane Mercer is a hot shot family Lawyer. His wife, Hilda, is a nurse at the local hospital, and their family ties stretch far. No one believed, ever, they would hurt anyone that lives there," Reaper says quietly.

"Corinne used to have these awful nightmares. Scared the shit out of anyone that was around for night watch. When we finally got her to talk, it wasn't good, man. There are still some things you don't know about her, and I can tell you, what you think you know about the case the investigator gave you about Cori doesn't even scratch the damn surface." Angel says darkly.

Fuck.

"We watched them for a few years, but I'm thinking maybe we shouldn't have stopped, considering this new information you've got in this file," Zippo says.

"We'll contact you soon, man. Send us a copy of that file. We'll want all of the details, every last one. When you're ready, I'll also fax you over the Intel we have from when Melissa and Corinne stayed there. This way you know everything you're up against," Angel says, getting up to leave the room. He says that as if he knows I want Cori as more than my employee.

I watch them walk out, feeling completely lost. How the fuck did I not know about Corinne living in the same damn house as me? That house was the worst fucking house I've ever been in—abuse, neglect, drugging, all of it. Deciding to check on Corinne, I see her through the office window and catch her in a showdown with Stacy. And Angel and Zippo are trying to calm them both down. Fuck.

CHAPTER 11

Cori

Sitting at my desk, I'm popping some gum. My lips smack as I twist my tongue around the strawberry gum. It is starting to lose its flavor. I'm bored out of my damn mind when I see a shadow come over me.

"What the fuck are you doing here?"

I look up and see fucking Stacy Ips. "I work here, bitch," I sneer out. If she wasn't such a screaming bitch and a whore, I would admit she's beautiful—long brown hair, blonde highlights, and a fantastic ass and rack. I used to be jealous of her looks, but that was before she tried pulling shit with Randy.

"You won't be for long. Once I go talk to my man, you'll be gone," she fires back.

"You're man? Which one would that be?" I ask.

"Blake. Duh," she says flippantly with an eye roll. She flicks her tongue out over her top lip, thinking of saying more, but hesitates when she sees my mock expression to her claim on Blake.

I burst out laughing. "That's funny. I've been working here for a few years now, and when I tried to quit this morning, he stalked me and forced me to be here. I highly doubt he'll fire me. He wasn't yours when he was trailing his skillful fingers up my thigh this morning, or when he rammed his tongue down my throat last night." I cock my brow in satisfaction at seeing the horrified twist of her lips as her face scrunches. My cheeks flush as I remember that damn kiss and the way Blake teased my clit earlier.

"You stupid bitch!" she yells, surprising me as she comes around my desk. "You tryin' to steal my man?"

I stand up, ready to face off. "You really want to do this? Again? Really?" I swear to God, I will knock this chick out again if she steps any closer to me. I took classes to defend myself once I started college. I don't chick fight. She found that out when we got into it before. I punched her square in the face, and all she did was pull my hair and try to scratch me. Last year, Randy and I started getting somewhat serious, and I gotta say, I have an ugly jealous streak. I went to see him at work and found Stacy spread across his desk.

It was the sickest thing ever. Randy wasn't even in the room. He didn't even know she'd be there. He was pissed she was, so I took care of it. After that, the feelings I was getting for Randy were way too serious, and I backed away from him for a few months. Now, we're strictly friends with benefits. It works for us. Feelings get ugly, especially with him working in a club. My jealousy would be on constant play, and it would kill us in the end.

"Ladies, calm down. Back down." I hear someone say. I look over Stacy's shoulder and see Angel. He looks large and in charge.

"She needs to leave," Stacy says, pointing her boney finger at me.

"You need to leave. You can either go on your own, or, I swear, I'll force you outta here by your hair," I tell Stacy, getting into her face.

"Screw you, Corinne! You're still just pissed off that I fucked Randy. Get the hell over it," she shouts at me. "Your pussy is so used up and loose, he was so damn thankful to have mine."

I've had it. I grab her by her hair and bring her face in close. "You speak to me like that again, you'll need reconstructive surgery."

I am yanked back by a large muscular arm around my middle, but I also didn't let Stacy's hair go, so she comes with me, letting out a shriek of pain. I yank harder, and a husky voice grits in my ear, "Let go, babe." I let go, and she shoots backwards, landing on her ass.

"What the fuck is going on here?" I hear Blake shout as he jogs down the hall.

I look up and see it was Reaper who pulled me away from her. The man is a towering wall of sheer muscle and power. He is hot and married. All the hot ones are, it seems... well, other than Blake, but he doesn't count. I think of Mark and how he lied to me. Married jerk.

"Blake, honey," Stacy starts. She goes over to him, trying to saddle up to his side like a wounded cat.

"What did I tell you about coming here, huh?" he says to her, stepping out of her unwarranted embrace.

Stacy stumbles on her too high heels. She looks stupid trying to walk in them. Looks like a newborn giraffe. She falters, going down on her ass again.

She looks down at her shoes once she stands up and fixes her hair.

"You were a fuck, woman. That's it. And each time I was with you, I was drunk out of my mind." Blake doesn't hold back the brutal insult and honesty of how he feels about her. His jaw clenches so tight I can make out every bone in his jaw and his neck as his shoulders roll with anger.

She whips her head up and looks at him. "But it's been months. I thought we were finally going to take this to the next level," she whines.

He gives her a disgusted look. "Yeah, not happening, ever." He snorts, seeming amused by her assumption of where their 'relationship' was headed in her delusional eyes.

"Fine. Next time you want a hot tight pussy, I won't let you back in it. You'll be sorry," she says as she stomps off, her heels clicking across the floor in a hurry.

"You were never tight, woman. Trust me," he shouts to her retreating form.

I almost feel sorry for her—almost, as Zippo laughs quietly.

Blake turns and stares at me as Reaper lets me go. Blake's angry face softens, and a grin forms.

Narrowing my eyes at him, I ask, "What the hell are you grinning about?"

"You were jealous. Knowing I fucked her, that she showed up here to see me, you were about to lay her out," he says smugly.

I snort. "Pfft, bitch, please. I wouldn't care. Why don't you go after her? My car is unlocked. Just don't get the fluids on my leather seats. Plus, it wasn't you we were fighting over. She threw in my face about fucking Randy, which wasn't true. Randy never fucking touched her. That was why I was in her face," I tell him snottily.

His face turns dark. His eyes narrow in on me menacingly. Other people from the office are beginning to stare and whisper about the outburst.

"Well, I think we'll be taking off now. Enjoy this lover's spat. Blake, we'll get in touch soon. Corinne, really do hope that you and Melissa can make it down soon," Zippo says, giving me a small smile, and then they leave.

I keep my eyes locked on Blake's, watching his face fuming. Damn he is hot, even more so when he is angry.

BLAKE

I'm seriously about to strangle her.

"You want me to fuck her?" I ask her, my voice low.

She rolls her eyes. "Seriously, what would I care? Although, I must say, that's pretty disgusting. Stacy? Really?" She shivers in disgust.

"In case you didn't hear. I've only fucked her while drunk. It's like she has a fucking radar for it or some shit."

"Again, I really don't care. You fuck whoever. I'll do the same. Gee," she says, sighing, sounding bored.

I've had enough of this shit. I walk to her, bend low, my shoulder going into her stomach, and lift.

"What the hell!" she screeches.

I walk fast into the staff lunch room with Cori still pounding away on my back. A few people are hanging around, and I bark out, "Get out, now. Close the door."

Everyone scurries out of the room, shutting the door behind them. Cori is fuming when I toss her on the couch.

"Shut up," I growl, forcing her to lay down on her back. I come down over the top of her and thrust between her legs.

"What are you doing?" she says breathily. Her chest heaves in excitement. I know she is turned on.

"I'm gonna fuck you, and you're gonna love it. You'll be ruined forever. No man will come close to what I can do to you." I crash my mouth down on hers, forcing her to open her mouth.

Pulling back, I lift her skirt and move her panties to the side, trailing a finger between her lips. "You are fucking soaked," I growl out.

She moans and moves her hips against my hand. "Oh, fuck."

Using my other hand, I unzip my jeans, pulling my cock out. Her eyes go wide as I push the tip of my cock against her slit. "You want me?" I ask her, taunting her with my dick. My cock is straining, needing to be deep inside her slick heat.

"Yes. Please, God, yes," she assures me, breathing hard. Her smooth legs spread apart, giving me more room.

I shove in to the hilt with one hard thrust. I pause, leaning over her to look in her eyes. "You're fucking mine," I claim before capturing her mouth. Pulling back, I look at her as I slowly thrust inside her. "I hope to fuck you're on the pill because I will never wear something with you." I kiss her again before she says anything.

Our kisses are rough and frantic. Nothing sweet about it. It's lustful want. It doesn't even matter that we are at work. The need to have her is driving me mad. Her nails dig into my back, drawing blood. The pain feels good, knowing I drive her to that.

She bites on my neck, pushing her hips into mine. My pulse quickens under her lips.

"This changes nothing," she grits out between pants.

"The hell it does." I pull out to the tip and slam back into her hard, gripping her hips roughly.

Her muscles clench around me, milking my cock. I know she is close by the way she is breathing heavily in my ear and from the fast beat of her heart thumping against her chest.

CHAPTER 12

Cori

Blake finally moves off me and zips himself back up. I don't move, still laying on the couch he threw me on. Shit. I can't believe I just had sex with him. But fuck, it was amazing, so heated and passionate. God, the way he felt inside me was unlike anything I have ever felt before. It was everything I have ever imagined and then some.

"Tonight, seven, we're going out. You try to hide from me, you'll be sorry when I finally catch up with you," he tells me, placing a soft kiss on my lips before walking out of the room.

"Fucking hell," I murmur through swollen lips. I sit up, fixing my undies and skirt.

The door opens to the lunch room, and in walks the new girl from the second floor, a Malibu Barbie type. Great. These types of chicks are such bitches. Short blonde hair and a dazzling smile greets me.

"Hey," she says happily.

I look up and see she is genuinely smiling at me.

"Uh, hey," I say, hoping I don't look like I just fucked in here.

"Blake seems to really like you," she states, smiling.

"Uh, yeah."

"Why're you giving him such a hard time?"

"I'm not," I retort.

She stares at me for a while longer. "Word around the office is that you've had a thing for him for years, and more word around the office is that he's wanted you for just as long."

"Most likely not," I tell her, standing up to check myself in the mirror.

"When Blake wants something, he gets it. Trust me."

"Look, I'm sorry, but I don't know you," I tell her, trying not to be mean. I don't want to hurt her feelings, but I'm not giving her information on this Blake stuff.

She shrugs. "I don't know you either, but if you need someone to talk to, I'm here." She gives me a small smile. "He's a good friend, a nice guy. I think you should give him a chance."

I clench my jaw and take in her figure. "Did you sleep with him?" I ask, suddenly feeling jealous.

She bursts out in laughter. "No. I don't screw around where I work. He's a great looking guy, sweet on the inside, but I wouldn't go there. Not my type," she says with a wink.

"What's your name?" I ask her.

"Marcy. And you are Cori."

I nod.

"A bunch of us are going out this weekend for some food, drinks, maybe a little dancing. You should come with us," she offers.

"Yeah, that sounds good. Mind if I bring a friend?" I ask.

Her eyes narrow. "What kind of friend." Wow, she is overly protective of Blake.

"My sister Melissa," I say, trying to hide my smirk.

She grins. "Perfect."

She walks to the fridge in the staff room and pulls out her lunch.

"Uh, so… Yeah, I should get back to work. Later," I say as I walk out of the room, back to my desk.

I should feel really weirded out that Blake and I totally just fucked like animals in there, but damn, he does fuck well.

BLAKE

Walking away after I had Cori had me feeling both proud and angry at the same time. Angry because I know I still haven't gotten through to her, but proud because I was able to get that out of her. At least I know she wants me, even if she is trying to convince herself she doesn't. I should have taken her when I wanted her the first time I met her.

It's not long before there is a knock on my door. "Come in."

Marcy, one of the new nurses that works on floor two comes in.

"Hey there," she says, smiling.

"Hey, what's up?" She's a beautiful woman, but she doesn't swing my way. Trust me, I've tried. First day I met her at the university we attended, I used all the lines I could think of, but she kept laughing in my face. That pissed me off, so I tried kissing her. Afterwards, she laughed even harder and told me to follow her. I did and ended up just outside her dorm, where she yelled at another woman and smiled huge. When the woman got close, she pulled her in for a long lingering kiss and then looked at me, smiling, letting me know that was why my shit didn't work on her.

"Had a chat with your woman just now," she informs me, grinning.

"And?" I ask, arching a brow.

"I'm going to help you get the girl because, honestly, watching you fuck your way through all the women in town, and repeatedly with that horrible wench Stacy, is getting on my nerves," she says, taking a seat at the edge of my desk.

I roll my eyes at her. "I really don't need your help."

"Sure you do. It's going to take a lot more than your force screwing on the couch in the staff lunch room to get her to be with you," she utters, chuckling.

"How'd you know about that?" I ask. I didn't think Cori was that loud.

"Once everyone came running out, fearing for their safety because they said you were extremely pissed, carrying a woman over your shoulder, I put my ear to the door and heard it all. That woman is hot. I swear, if she was even a little bit gay, I'd be fighting you for her," she teases, winking.

"You've already stolen three of my dates before. Keep away from Cori. Don't you have some poor child to prick with a needle?"

She laughs as she hops off my desk. "I invited her out Friday night for some fun. You should, oh, I don't know, randomly show up," she says, winking as she shuts my door behind her.

I hired Marcy after she finished her nursing degree. I met her through some mutual friends and told her the minute she was done schooling to come work in my building.

Instead of forcing Cori to be with me, I'm going to give her a little break. Maybe pushing her the way I did today was wrong of me. I'll give her a few days to come to terms with an 'us', but after that, I'm moving in and nothing will stop me.

CHAPTER 13

Cori

The rest of the week goes by pretty fast, and I'm almost disappointed when Blake doesn't try anything else with me. I actually haven't even seen him since he screwed me on that couch. Hell, the bastard didn't even follow through with his plan to take me out the other night.

I shouldn't be surprised. Once an asshole, always an asshole. I check the time when I notice most of the staff leaving.

"Hey, Cori, it's Friday. Let's go," Marcy calls out as she walks toward the desk.

"It's only three," I say, confused.

She shrugs and grins at me. "Yes, but it's Friday. We are going to close up early today."

Well then. Wicked. I grab my purse and clock out, following behind her. "Do you have a car?" she asks me.

"Yup."

"Mind if I catch a ride? I walked here today because I didn't want to chance you bailing on me," she says, winking.

I burst out laughing. "Yeah, come on. We'll go to my place and get ready while we wait for Melissa, and then we can head out."

"Perfect!" she says happily.

We make it to my condo, just talking about randomly weird shit. I also found out she loves women, which makes any jealous thoughts I had about her and Blake disappear. She even told me about a time she stole Blake's date to some party right from under him. I thought that was awesome. Apparently, Marcy got one look at Blake's date, got her drunk, and took advantage of her in the coat closet.

Blake walked in, fuming about how it wasn't fair, but then later laughed it off, saying he was glad his date ditched him for a pussy instead of a dick.

After getting into my place, I shut the door behind her, and she makes herself comfortable on my couch.

"Melly should be here. Be right back," I tell her and make my way down the hall to Melissa's room.

"Cori, is that you?" Melissa asks, opening her door.

I smile. "Hey, got a friend out in the living room. She invited us out tonight."

When we get out to the living room, Marcy smiles brightly. "Hey there, you must be the sister."

"Sure am, but I'm also the best-friend," Melissa says just as happily.

"Awesome. Now sit here. Got a question. Why don't you tell me why your girl here won't give Blake a chance?" Marcy asks.

Melly raises a brow. "Because she is stubborn."

I sigh and sit on the chair by the couch.

"I can tell," Marcy says, giggling.

"Look, okay, I've liked him for years. Wanted him for years. But he's never once noticed me. I was always like a sister to him. I've arranged his dates for years and everything."

"Yes, and you also always acted shy and reserved around him. Plus, with the baggy clothes..." Melly points out.

"That shouldn't matter, Melly! So what? One company party, he sees me in form-fitting clothes, attached at the vagina with Mark Saylor, and bam, he wants me? That doesn't fly with me. I'm sorry, but no. It will take an awful lot for him to convince me he actually wants me for me, not just because he sees this different side of me," I tell the room.

"Look, I've known Blake since we were in university together, where he tried to hook up with me. He would never purposely set out to hurt you. He's always upfront with the women he's with. They've always just been a little, uh, psycho, afterwards," Marcy says, leaning in.

I shake my head. "Not doing it." I look to Melissa, and she looks at me with sad eyes. "You know what growing up was like. You know what I went through. What our mother constantly says when she shows her face around us. This situation with Blake is exactly like that," I tell her.

She hangs her head down.

"Um, I'm kind of lost here. What's this about your mother?" Marcy asks. I totally forgot she was here for a moment.

"Well, she wasn't a good person," I say, shrugging.

Marcy clasps my hands and squeezes. "Tell me. I'm here. Maybe getting an outside ear will help."

I look to Melissa, and she nods. "Maybe it will be good."

Sighing, I start our story. Marcy cries a few times, gets angry, and by the end of it, vows to kill our mother and the foster family that had us. By the end of it, she leaves our condo, giving us both hugs, saying we have to hang out soon, saying now that she's heard all of this, she's not really up for going out.

Melissa and I both decide we still need to get out, so we get dressed and head off.

BLAKE

Just as I'm about to close up my office for the day, Adam comes in, looking jumpy. "What's up, man?" I ask him.

"Zippo just called me. They have something they need us on. Local kid was reported to have had bruises on her arms and back. Girl's only ten years old. Zippo says the girl lives with her mom, and her mom is a known addict," Adam explains.

I frown and clench my fists. I fucking hate when kids get hurt. "What does he need us to do?"

"Needs you to do a surprise visit. Angel and Reaper are both waiting just down the street. They follow in behind you, assess everything, and if it's what we all think, you take the kid out of there."

I rub my face. "Why can't you do this?"

"I still haven't finished going over the police report for that Zambini case. Been working on that shit now for a week straight. Once I finish, I can let the police know what I think and then call in Angel and his boys on that one, too."

I nod. "Okay, man, cool. I'll head out now." He hands me the address and leaves my office. I get up from my chair, grab my sweater, and head out.

Twenty minutes later, I pull up beside Angel and Reaper and roll down my window. "Hey, guys. I got here as fast as I could. Wasn't able to get a call in to the station, though. Any of you do that?"

"Yeah, called about half an hour ago. They are on standby if we need 'em, but since we're here, we won't." I nod and roll my window back up. I drive down the street and pull into the driveway.

Lights are on and music is blaring. I step out of the car and look to the guys, who are getting off their bikes. "She having a party?" I ask them.

"Yeah. And the kid is in there, too," Reaper reports, pissed. "Called in for back up when we saw that shit. Got a bunch of members scattered around the area, waiting for the signal, in case shit gets bad."

I nod, go to the front door, and knock. The door opens, and a seriously strung out woman answers. Her hair is greasy and stringy, appearing not to have been washed for days, maybe longer. Her shirt has holes in it and is covered in stains from old food. "What ya want? You a cop?" Smoke hits me in my face. The smell is so strong it nearly knocks the breath out of me.

I shake my head and sigh. "Child protective services, ma'am. Need to step in and have a chat." Her face pales.

Then she steps back from the door and screams into the room. "Fucking CPS is here! Shut that shit down and get out! Delia, get fucking out here now!" Everything immediately quiets down, and a little girl who looks scared shitless comes down the stairs slowly. She is so tiny and frail. Her eyes have dark circles under them; her ribs are poking out of her t-shirt.

"You fucking brat! You open your fucking mouth? Who'd you fucking talk to, you little bitch?"

"Ma'am, need to you stop talking to her that way," I inform her.

"Fuck you, man! She's my fucking brat. I can talk to her how I want." I go to reply again, but Reaper moves, and he moves fast, leaning into her face. I watch her shrink from his glare.

"Never fucking talk to her like that again. Do you fucking get me?" Reaper growls.

"Oh, shit. There's bikers. This will not go well," some scrawny guy peeking around the corner says.

I almost smirk but catch myself. In these situations, I have to remain calm. I can't have the children see me any other way than professional.

I look back to Reaper and then the woman, who now looks scared shitless. "Blake, do your thing. We'll keep Ms. Renee here," Angel tells me as he walks over to the little girl. He crouches down and smiles at her gently. I'm not sure what he says to her, but she starts sobbing and throws her arms around Angel's neck, hugging him tight.

At that, I move, walk around the house, spotting beer, vodka, and dirty dishes all over the kitchen. Living room is much of the same, with the added overfilled ashtray. I pull out my binder, flip it open to a clean page, and jot down my findings. So far, everything looks unsafe.

As I'm finishing up what I found in the living room and kitchen, I turn and spot white powder and a huge amount of marijuana on the desk by the computer. That right there is enough for me to remove the child, but before I do that, I inspect the rest of the house. Everything is the same.

When I reach the kid's room, I get pissed. "Angel!" I shout.

I hear his feet come up the stairs, and he finds me in the room. "What the fuck?" he growls, seeing the state of the bedroom.

The only thing in here is two outfits and a blanket. Nothing else. "Get the kid out of here. Have Reaper escort Ms. Renee to the police station. I'm going to grab my camera, and then I'll be there shortly. Take Delia with you," I instruct him.

"Yeah, T-bags has the SUV. I'll switch with him. He can ride my bike. Not sure how it's gonna work with Ms. Renee, though. Reaper won't have her on his bike."

"Call Drew. He'll send someone for the mother. Reaper can follow. I'll get in touch with some people and hopefully put Delia in a good home."

"Sounds good. There are times I really wish Reaper was his old self, because honestly, I want that woman to pay, and I mean more than just getting a fucking cushy jail cell," Angel grounds out.

We walk out of the room and down the stairs. Ms. Renee is completely losing it—yelling, screaming, putting up a fight. Reaper has her somewhat controlled, with her hands cuffed and his hands on her shoulders, keeping her pinned in her seat. I look around for Delia and see her sitting on the filthy couch, arms around her knees.

I walk to her and crouch down. "Hey, sweetheart," I say quietly, approaching her with caution.

"Hi," she whispers.

"Do you mind if I talk with you for a little bit? Or do you want Angel instead?" I'm not surprised when she says she wants Angel. So I stand back up and smile down at her, nodding to Angel. "She wants you, man. You can talk to her once you get her to your compound. Just fax me everything."

"Sure thing," he says with a nod and goes to gather Delia up in his arms, carrying her out of the house.

"Bring that little bitch back here! You can't take my daughter!" Ms. Renee screams.

"Ma'am, you need to calm down and shut up. The police will be here soon. You'll be booked and locked up for a long ass time. One thing to know is you will never see your child again." That, of course, doesn't calm her down, and she thrashes wildly, trying to get out of her cuffs and seat. Minutes later, two cops come in and take her to their car.

I pat Reaper on the shoulder and nod at him. Sometimes, this job fuckin' sucks.

CHAPTER 14

Cori

I came home early tonight. Normally, I'm at the club till closing, but I just wasn't feeling it. Melissa got extremely drunk, and I don't know if she's realized it or not, but she went home with Monster tonight. I'm sure I'll hear her rant about it when she wakes up. Thinking about it has me laughing to myself. I don't get why she fights it. Yeah, Monster is a giant player, but I also know he wants Melissa, has for a long time. I know he'd treat her right.

As I finish changing into my fuzzy pink jammies, a knock comes at my door. Frowning, I go to it. Who the heck would be knocking at ten at night?

I should have checked the peephole, but nope, I didn't do that. The second I open the door, Blake comes in, shoving me aside, slamming my door, and pins me to the wall. Before I know it, he's kissing me.

I pull away, breathing heavy. "What are you doing?"

"I need you. I need you to erase my night," he declares, breathing heavy. I don't get a chance to respond before he's kissing me again.

I know it is a bad idea, but my body has other ideas. I tear at his clothes and lead him to my bed. His mouth is hot and needy, taking what it wants as he nips and sucks on my lips. Strong hands cup my rear, caressing the round globes of my ass cheeks. We fall into my dresser, knocking over a picture. Blake doesn't even pause in his attack as I pull my shirt over my head. Greedily, his mouth finds its way down my body, latching onto a nipple and biting it gently.

My slender fingers work on his zipper as he leans down over me on the bed, resting on his elbows. "Fuck, Cori. You make me crazy."

"I see," I tease, taking his hard length between my palms and wrapping my fingers around the head of his cock. His lips feather kisses across my stomach, and my stomach flutters in excitement. His fingers tug my shorts off, exposing my pussy to his greedy tongue.

With my hands in his hair and his mouth working my clit, I moan loudly, arching my back up off the bed. His hands grip my hips to hold me still. His tongue flicks against my clit before he sucks it hard, his teeth grazing my tender skin.

This time, with him, it's different. It's more intimate as he gets to know my body in ways I never thought he would.

BLAKE

I wake around four in the morning, over heated, a firm body wrapped snuggly to me. I then remember where I'm at—with Cori. Fuck, she was amazing. After a shitty day, I usually go to the dive bar downtown and hook up with whomever I can to bang out my issues. Tonight, I chose Cori.

My dick already got a taste of her before, and tonight, my dick didn't want anyone but her. I don't want anyone but her. So instead of going to the bar, or even straight to my apartment, I went right to Cori.

I move gently away from her and out of the bed. Grabbing my clothes, I leave her room. I don't want to hurt Cori, not ever, but I also know that, when she wakes up, she might regret last night, and I do not want that look in my brain. I care about her more than I've ever cared about anyone. I always knew that, when I found the right woman, I would never let her go. I knew I'd hold on to her, have a family, all of it. But, Cori... There is something lurking inside her, and I just hope I'm strong enough to stand by her when she finally explodes.

As I'm walking down the hallway, the condo door bursts open, and I see Melissa barely walking through it, mumbling about someone named Dray. She stumbles, falling to her knees. I rush over to help her up, and she looks at me, confused.

"Hey, Blakey poo. Finally get some outta my sister?" she slurs as I hold her tight while closing the front door.

"Come on, Melly. Let's get you into bed," I say gently.

"My sister loves you, you know. Has ever since she met you, but you are such a player," Melissa slurs again. "She can't be with you, though, because of how dirty she is, and you are so clean and amazing." I have no idea what she even means by that.

I get her into her room, and the second she hits the bed, she passes out. Running a hand over my face, I walk out, closing her door, and go to the couch in the living room and sit, contemplating on whether or not I should just leave. But if I do that, she might hate me for real. I lie down and grab my cell, turning it on. I notice a few texts from the Angels and see they invited me to the clubhouse tomorrow for a BBQ.

Both Melissa and Cori will be there. That, at least, will give me more time with her. I'll be able to see the girls in their 'home' and get to know Cori better, the Cori she truly is and not the girl I've come to know.

It takes me about an hour, my brain going into overdrive, before I finally fall asleep on the couch.

CHAPTER 15

Cori

I wake up and stretch out in the bed. I instantly remember last night, Blake coming over and making love to me. God, it was amazing. I roll over to watch Blake sleep, but he's not there. Feeling his spot on the bed, it's cold.

I should have known. So fucking stupid. I throw the blankets back and get out of bed, checking the time. Shit, Melly and I will be totally late now. Angel and the guys invited us out this weekend for a family thing at their compound, and I've been looking forward to it. I will finally meet Angel's wife and his children, and I'll get to see Lilly again. I've only met her a few times, but she was pretty great.

Reaper always scared me, though I'm not really sure why. I only ever got bits and pieces to his story, something about his wife running away from him or something like that. So this weekend will be nice to catch up, since these guys are practically family.

I grab my Sons of Anarchy robe and head out of my room to wake up Melissa so we can hurry up and get ready to leave. As I walk down the hall, I hear someone in the kitchen. I frown, because I know Melissa, and unless I remind her the night before, she is never up this early.

"Cori, where is your coffee maker?" Blake is here. Holy shit. Why didn't he leave?

I'm stunned for a moment before I finally answer him when I step into the kitchen. "Uh, we don't have one."

He closes my cupboard and turns around, glaring at me. "Why don't you have a coffee maker?"

I roll my eyes and throw him some attitude. "Because coffee is disgusting, of course. Both Melly and I hate it, so why would we have one?"

Amusement floods Blake's face. It's like he is loving the real me, the me that is sassy and all attitude. It's weird.

"You're gonna have to go, so you can get coffee when you leave," I tell him.

"Why would I go?" he asks, voice edging in the danger zone.

"Because Melissa and I have a family thing, and we're already going to be late," I convey to him, leaving the kitchen to go back toward Melissa's room.

"It's at the Angels compound, isn't it?" Blake asks, following me. Why is he following me? "Because, if so, we can just drive down there together." That stops me in my tracks.

I'm not surprised he would be invited, but I was hoping he wouldn't be. Yay, lovely, just great. Should be fun. Ugh.

I continue to Melly's door and walk in without knocking. I look at her passed out on her bed, not even under her covers, and she's still in last night's clothes. "Great. Hungover Melly," I mutter. She never gets hung over. It's only happened once, and it was bad. And by the looks of this, it's bad. Her hair is sticking out in every direction. One foot hangs from the bed, and her head is turned in an awkward angle. That is gonna hurt when she wakes.

"Why don't you go get ready so you aren't even later? I'll help get Melissa up and going," Blake says, touching me on the shoulder. Well, that's, uh, sweet. Damn it. Why can't I shake him?

"Um, sure. Okay." I walk away and go to my room, take a quick shower, and blow dry my hair. If I didn't have to blow dry, I could have been ready a long ass time ago, but nope, my hair is so damn thick and would look extremely bad if I dried it naturally.

I grab a pair of my black yoga capris and a simple t-shirt and put them on quickly, checking the time. Crap, we are so, so, so late. I rush out of my room to see how Blake made out with Melissa and see that she's ready to go. I wish I could get ready as fast as she can. Of course, she has super thin blonde hair, so she doesn't need to do much to it.

"Ready?" I ask, grabbing my Old Navy hoodie off the back of the kitchen chair and shrugging it on.

"Yup," Melissa mumbles.

Blake just grins and shakes his head at Melissa.

"I haven't seen you hungover in years. What the heck did you do last night?"

She puts a hand up. "Don't, okay. Not right now. I'll talk to you later," she says, pleading with me.

I grimace and nod.

BLAKE

We all climb into my car and head off toward Airdrie. Getting Melissa up was brutal. She kept dry heaving, but finally, I was able to force some leftover pizza into her that I found in the fridge, and she seemed to be somewhat okay after that. Still looks miserable, but she's not so green anymore.

The drive is quiet and somewhat awkward. I can feel Cori vibrating with the need to talk to Melissa about what is bugging her so much. However, she knows Melissa will shut that down right now. I flip on the radio and try to find a good station, when Cori slaps my hand away and puts what she likes on.

I groan when the tunes of Maroon 5 come through the speakers. "You like this?" I ask.

Cori smiles at me. "Duh, Adam Levine is so hot. God, if I could meet him in person, I'd end up in jail because I'd lick him all over." She bites her lip, and her eyes roll back. What the hell?

"Well, it's a good thing you never will then. That tongue of yours is only for me," I say, grinding my teeth together. I know I'm being irrationally jealous, but right now, I don't care.

I hear Melissa snort. When I look in the rear-view mirror, she is looking at Cori, amused.

"Someone has a jealous streak," Melissa says with a giggle.

"Damn right I do," I state.

About ten minutes outside of Airdrie, Cori turns in her seat to look at Melissa, her eyes lit right up. "I can't wait to see everyone," she says excitedly.

"Gah, yes! I can't wait to see Lilly, Eden, and Moira again," Melissa replies back.

"Yeah, deffo. I only wish I could have met Hilary, too. Sucks the way she passed," Cori says, sounding a bit sad. She turns to me and tells me, "We moved in with the guys when Mason was still married to Hilary, and when she finally came back to town, I was in university, and Melly was still living at the clubhouse, going to school. Though, she said she never got the chance to meet her." Finally, she's opening up to me a bit.

"Yeah, but from what Lilly used to say about Hilary and Reaper's marriage, it wasn't good. They obviously weren't right for each other," Melissa points out.

"I'm glad I didn't know the Reaper he was before. I might not have liked him much." Cori pauses and then grins. "I can't wait to see T-bags, though," Cori says.

Melissa bursts out laughing. "I can't believe that name stuck."

I'm obviously missing something.

"I know, right. But it was well deserved, and I won't ever let him forget how he got it, either," Cori alludes, snorting.

The girls continue chatting back and forth about the members of the club, laughing and giggling. I stay out of it, mostly because I love hearing Cori so carefree and laughing.

I see the turn off for the compound, so I interrupt the girls. "We're almost there, ladies." Both girls immediately squeal.

CHAPTER 16

Cori

The second Blake stops his car, I bolt from it and run inside the clubhouse, searching almost frantically for Momma B. During my time here, she was so damn amazing and even cuddled me after a horrible nightmare. But then I remember that she's gone. She betrayed the club and paid for what she did. Every time in the past six years that I've been to visit, I always forget. I don't know why I do, but I do. It sucks. I deflate until I hear him.

"Who ya lookin' for, Rin?" I smirk slightly, hearing T-bags' voice.

"Just your balls," I shoot back at him before turning around to face him. I have always thought he was hot. A little on the skinny side, he dresses like an emo, but the tattoos and piercings he's decorated his skin with make him extremely hot. I've always been a sucker for heavily tatted men.

I came up with the nickname T-bags when I was just eighteen. He was really drunk one night, as was another guy who I think they called Breaks, and I walked into the bathroom to see T-bags' balls on Breaks' forehead while he was taking a piss. Breaks was passed out, lying with his head on the toilet—gross—and T-bags didn't even realize he was there.

The name stuck after that. He also has called me Rin since he met me. Not sure why, since my nickname has always been Cori.

I squeal and he scoops me up, hugging me tight. "Missed you around here," he says quietly in my ear.

I pull back. "Yeah." I haven't visited in about nine months. He moves away from me, grabbing a beautiful dark-headed pixie around the waist that was walking past us, and brings her in close.

"Rin, this is Tori," T-bags says proudly.

Tori blushes and sticks out her hand. "Rin? Nice to meet you," she says quietly.

"You too, but everyone calls me Cori. This loser here is the only one to call me Rin," I boast, smiling back at her. I look back to T-bags.

"Cori!" I hear Angel shout across the room. He looks happy, his face filled with joy, carrying two children in his arms. Two more are attached to his legs, and someone that looks nothing like him is on his back. I shake my head. It's like he and Eden are trying to become the next Duggar family.

"Nice brood you got there," I compliment him.

"Wanna hold one?"

"Oh, hell no," I protest, taking a step back.

"Oh, come on. You can't still be freaked out about kids," T-bags quips, sounding amused.

Before I know it, he swings his youngest son, Harley, my way, and I catch him, because duh, if I didn't, he'd get hurt. The second he lands in my arms, he makes a weird noise and I look at him.

"Oh, shit!" Angel says suddenly.

And then it happens. The little shit pukes all over me—my hair, my shirt, everywhere. I try to hold back, but the second Angel takes Harley out of my arms, I start gagging. Next thing I know, I'm hunched over and puke is spewing outta me.

This is why I don't like kids.

BLAKE

I watch Cori run from my car into the clubhouse, looking happier than I have ever seen her. What I wouldn't give for her to light up like that for me.

"Blake?" I hear Melissa say from the back seat. I'm shocked she's still there instead of running behind Cori, since she grew up with these guys as well.

"Yeah?" I say, looking back at her.

"Do you really care about my sister?" she asks quietly.

I narrow my eyes at her. "Of course I do."

She bites her bottom lip. "Like, actually, and not just doing this thing because you now know what she's really like?"

I clench my jaw, calming myself down before I lash out at her. "I've liked Cori for years, even when I thought she was this shy, sweet, good person. Her revealing her true self just meant I could make my move. A move I've been trying not to make because I didn't think Cori would go for that shit."

With that, Melissa lights up and gives me a huge as fuck grin. "That's so awesome." She bounces out of my car and heads inside. She must not remember what she said to me last night.

I get out and follow her in but stop suddenly, watching Melissa go stiff, and stop in the doorway. I look over her and see Cori hunched over, puking. I go to her swiftly.

She empties her stomach on the floor, and when she's done, after I growl at Angel, I walk her down the hall and into the bathroom to clean her up.

"I never want kids. This is just wrong," Cori blubbers, sobbing slightly.

I chuckle slightly. "Just get cleaned up. I'll go see about getting you some clothes while you take a shower. You reek." Cori's head snaps up to me, and she glares.

I leave the bathroom and spot Melissa, tears in her eyes from laughing so hard. "Go see if you can find her some clothes, and she needs a shower." Melissa, still laughing, nods and takes off.

"Sorry about that. It's probably all of the candy that Moira keeps sneaking him," Angel confirms, his mouth twitching, trying not to laugh. "I wish I was here to see the whole show in action," I admit, chuckling, thinking of my puke-covered woman.

"It was like something out of *The Exorcist*, man," Trevor speaks up. "I can't believe she still does that, the whole gag and puke thing, if she sees puke," he says, then burst out laughing. Angel and I following.

"Tori went to go get a few cleaning supplies so the mess can get cleaned up," Angel says when he calms down.

"She's gonna be so mad when she comes back out here and sees us laughing," I tell the guys, so we can try to get a lock on it.

"The girls can't wait to see her again. They haven't shut up about it, actually," Angel says when the laughing dies down.

"Yeah, she was chatting in the car on the way here about them."

The clubhouse is quiet, but outside, you can hear kids laughing, squealing, and some even crying. It's not until a really loud scream cry that Angel moves fast.

"Shit! That's Hilary." He runs off and out the doors.

Not long after, Cori and Melissa come out of the bathroom, arms looped in each other's, and Cori gives me a glare. Melissa is still trying hard not to laugh.

"Keep the kids away from me, and today will be awesome," Cori announces as she walks out to the yard.

CHAPTER 17

Cori

In the bathroom, I manage to get a shower and clean all the disgusting stuff off me, and I do it without actually puking again. I just gag, a lot. Melissa comes in with some clean clothes and chats with me as I'm finishing up about how cute Angel's kids are. Bitch. We both walk out of the bathroom, arms linked, and I glare at Blake, because I can still see the stupid smile on his face from when he was laughing at me.

We walk out to the yard, Blake following behind us. "Corinne!" I hear yelled. I look to the picnic tables and see Lilly running toward me. My face hurts from smiling so huge. I run and meet her half way.

"Oh, God, I missed you! How are you, sweetie?" she asks me.

"I'm good, Lilly. You?"

She smiles brightly. "I'm amazing."

"I'm glad." I smile at her. I fill with joy at that, because she and Zippo were crazy together, but now she's happy, married to him, and her light is shining so bright, I feel blinded.

"You have to meet the others," she says, pulling me along, her wild curls blowing with the gentle breeze.

"Melissa!" I shout behind me, and she follows. Melly might not be as close to everyone as I am, but I think it's because she's looking for someone. "Who you looking for?" I whisper as Lilly drags me along.

"Gilvaja," she says.

I smile. "Lilly, whatever happened to Gilvaja?" I ask her.

"Oh, he ended up retiring and moving away with his wife. I know he calls Jasper sometimes, to see how you girls are doing," she says, looking at Melissa.

He was the one guy that Melissa bonded with. He was never part of the club, but he was like a grandfather to her. I never was close to him; I had that bond with Angel, though. Melissa was close with the guys, too, but not in the way I was.

"Eden!" I shout. She turns around, her hair still short, blonde, and she's finally stopped hiding the scars on her face.

"Oh, Cori and Smelly!! So happy you're here!" she jokes, coming to us, hugging us one at a time awkwardly so she doesn't squish her baby.

"Why do you still insist on calling me that?" Melissa snaps at her, laughing.

"Well, let me in. Gee." I hear said. I look behind Eden and see Moira. I always felt like a midget next to her because she's so damn tall. Her dark brown hair is flowing down her back. She could be a model, but instead, she chooses to wipe old people's asses for a living. Well, I think anyways.

"Moira," Melly says, stepping close for a hug.

I look to the baby she's carrying, and I'm so confused. That kid looks nothing like her or Mason.

I look back to Eden after hugging Moira and narrow my eyes at her. "Why didn't you tell me you were having another?" I demand.

She just smiles. "Because I know you have a fear of kids, and if I told you I would now officially have six, you'd run away and never come back."

I shake my head. "You're nuts. You know that? At least Lilly is smart. Two kids, done. Bam. That's it."

Lilly bursts out laughing, and I laugh along with her. I don't know how the hell this happened. Angel was always a stand-up guy, when I was around anyways. I saw how he was with kids, always knew he'd make an amazing father.

I smirk, looking to Moira, asking her the same question I ask her every single time I'm with her. "How can you put up with him? I swear, the guy is a moody prick most of the time."

Moira throws her head back, laughing. "You got that right. He sure is. But he's my moody prick," she declares, smiling warmly at me.

After chatting for a while, Eden leaves with the baby to where Angel and five other kids are playing on the playground. I watch the interaction. Angel pulls Eden in close to him, smiling down at her, kissing the scarred cheek, his kids all squirming to get close, while one of the younger kids fights with two of the older ones. They look so happy, so at peace.

Moira leaves just after that with her son, to go to Reaper, who is seated on a swing, his daughter on his lap, while his little boy is next to him on the other swing. Another boy is playing in the sand just off to the side of the swing set. I look at him for a moment, and realize it's Hunter, Hilary's son. Moira hands the new baby to Reaper as his daughter hops off his lap and takes the other swing. Moira walks over to Hunter playing in the sand, and starts helping him with a sand castle.

Lilly says from beside me, "Sucks Hilary isn't here, watching him grow up, but Moira is damn good with him."

"She really is. I don't know how some people do it, raising someone else's child, but Moira is amazing that way," I say.

"It's sad, ya know. I always thought Hilary was Mason's one, but seeing those two, I know now that Moira is his one. And before you question it, since I saw you looking at the newborn baby Moira was holding, they just adopted her. She came from a home that the guys were checking out. Moira went along, took one look at her, and told Reaper to get papers done because she was theirs."

"That's so sweet." Melissa says, finally speaking.

Lilly giggles. "It is. Through all the bad things we've been through, life is looking up, way up."

"Makes me know even more now, seeing this, I can have it all, too," Melissa states quietly.

"Sweetie, trust me, you will. You more than deserve it. You both do," Lilly says, squeezing Melissa's arm.

"So who was the girl that was with T-bags?" Melissa asks.

Lilly laughs. "Would you stop calling him that? We haven't called him that in years now, and you both know it. And, Tori, or Victoria, is my cousin. She's gone through some bad shit, came up here about a two months ago to get away from her husband. We just keep praying every day he doesn't find her. Bad man that guy is. Worst of the worst," Lilly informs us, looking worried a bit over to where Tori is, standing next to T-bags by the grill.

"Mom! Hunter keeps pulling my hair," a little girl yells, running up to Lilly. I smile. I look to where I just saw Hunter playing and see Moira is up and standing next to Mason now. Hunter is nowhere in sight.

"Did he? Did you do anything to him?" Lilly asks with a hand on her hip. The little girl puts her head down. "Elizabeth, answer me."

Elizabeth looks up, chewing on her bottom lip. "I put sand down his pants," she says, but hurries to finish, "but he kept stealing Hilary's cake."

With that, Lilly bursts out laughing then yells to Eden. "Stop telling Elizabeth stories about the boys! She's doing it to Hunter!" Eden throws her head back and laughs.

"I swear," Lilly starts. "Thursday, Elizabeth punched Hunter in the face because Hunter wouldn't stop throwing mud at Hilary, and today, she's putting sand down his pants. I swear, Bethy is so much like Eden it scares me sometimes."

I chuckle. "Sounds like it."

Lilly's smile fades slightly, though. "It would be weird, though, Hunter and Hilary getting together when they are older. Hunter is so much like his dad, and Hilary is so much like her namesake, that it's like watching Mason and Hilary when they were kids."

Eden comes back over to us, dragging Tori along with her. Everything seems to be going well until Tori's face pales as she looks at Melissa.

I frown. "Everything okay?" I ask.

"H-how old are you?" she asks Melly.

Melissa's eyes widen slightly. "Twenty," she answers hesitantly.

"Who is your father?" Tori whispers out haggardly.

I speak up then, "We don't know who our father or fathers are."

Tori keeps staring at Melissa, hurt flashing all over her face. "Do you… Do you know a man named Carson Lewis?"

Melissa frowns, and she looks at me. I shrug at her. "Sorry, but no."

"Uh, Tori, hun, what's going on?" Eden asks her.

"She looks so much like him," Tori croaks out.

Eden's body goes stiff, and Lilly's face is now pale. Both girls are looking at Melissa in a whole new way now. Eden finally speaks up. "He's what? Thirty-eight? You sure? Because that puts him at eighteen."

"I-I gotta go," she squeaks out and runs off. I watch her go, with T-bags—oops, I mean Trevor—hot on her heels.

"What was that about?"

"You girls sure you know nothing at all about who your dads could be?"

I shake my head at her, and Melissa says, "No."

"I never saw it before, but Tori is right. You look so much like her husband," Eden announces, still staring at Melissa.

"Come with me," Lilly says. We follow quickly behind her into the clubhouse and to a computer in the sitting area.

I watch her go to a folder and click on it. There are tons of picture displayed in the file, and she clicks on the one at the top.

"This is Carson," Lilly says and slowly turns to look at Melissa.

I lean in close and snap to Melissa instantly. "Oh my God."

Melissa's face is pale. "He's… oh no," she whispers.

The file name, I realize, says this is the Untamed Angels members. Those guys are the worst of the worst. There is no doubt in any way that this Carson guy isn't Melissa's father, or heck, maybe her brother.

"What's going on?" Angel says, sounding concerned.

Lilly points to the picture on the computer and tilts her head at Melissa.

"Shit!" he says after a few moments.

"I just… I need a moment." Melissa takes off toward the boarding room area, and we all leave her alone. When she gets upset, it's best to leave her alone. Otherwise, you will catch hell from her.

"Tori was the one that figured it out. She went pale and got upset," Lilly fills him in.

"I gotta talk to Trevor. After that shit years ago, and now with Tori being here, looks like we'll most likely be seeing the Untamed again. Even if he lets Tori leave him for good, he'll want to know his daughter," Angel states gruffly.

I frown. "He's a bad dude. He probably wouldn't care," I observe, confused.

Angel shakes his head. "He might be a shitty ass person, but he looks after his other kid. Man is a good father, that much I know, but the man himself, as a husband and more… no, not good. As soon as he finds out about her," he says, nodding in the direction Melissa took off in, "he'll want to spend time with her."

I don't like the sound of that. Lilly shuts down the computer, and Angel goes to walk away, but something occurs to me. "Wait, why do you have to talk to Trevor?"

Angel leans in close to me and whispers in my ear, "Trevor is his brother. That would make Melissa his niece."

"Wait, what?!"

"Shh, Tori doesn't know. He doesn't want to tell her yet."

He walks off, and I look to Lilly with wide eyes. "But if Tori knows him, how come she hasn't recognized him?" I ask.

"He changed his last name, and he's had a lot of reconstructive surgery. That's why, but also, it's been twelve years since she last saw him," Lilly tells me.

"What a clusterfuck!" I declare.

BLAKE

The sun starts to set when Angel and the guys start setting up chairs around the fire pit. Some of the women and kids he is helping out are here, but decided to let the guys have family time, so they went into the apartment section of the compound.

Cori and Melissa both look so at peace here, so happy and carefree.

I watch Trevor stare after Tori when she gets up to go to the bathroom. It looks like he's battling something, but I don't know what; just seems to be really protective of her. She goes to the bathroom, he goes too. She walks away for a few seconds, he's right there not long after.

Angel moves and sits next to me on the chair once I lose sight of Trevor. "That's Lilly's cousin. She's married to the president of the Untamed Angels."

I glower and turn to him. "Then what's she doing here?" Untamed Angels are bad news, and if that woman is connected to them, it's only going to bring trouble.

"She ran away and knew we'd help her out, since she helped Eden when she ran off. She's trying to get a divorce. T-bags is apparently Hangman's little brother, the brother Hangman thinks is dead. Turns out, T-bags has known Tori since they were kids, and they were together for a long ass time. But since T-bags was attacked by my father and left for dead, he looks nothing like the man he once was. Tori, it seems, moved on to his older brother, and then later married him. Now, she's here, and she has no clue who T-bags really is." He pauses. "I keep telling him to tell her, but he keeps putting it off, waiting for the right moment to tell her. I just know it's gonna blow up in his face, though."

"Sounds like it will. I just hope it doesn't mean bad shit for your club."

Angel shakes his head. "I'm sure Hangman will find her eventually. Although, Scraper, Hangman's tracker, is with us now, too. So I'm sure it will be a long ass time before that happens. Hopefully."

"Wait, an Untamed member is part of your club now?"

"Yeah, he came with Tori. He helped her leave. Said, after he saw what went down while rescuing the girls years ago, he can't do it anymore. So far, it's been a few months, and he seems fine. Even think he's got an eye for older women," Angel says smirking.

"Oh?" I ask.

"Yeah, Rachel, owner of the diner in town, she's just about forty. Scraper is twenty nine, and he watches her. Man watches her like a hawk and even starts fights with men that sniff around her."

"So he's into cougars. Interesting." I smirk.

Angel throws his head back and laughs, and then leans in close and gets serious. "Gonna need your help with Melissa for a bit."

I raise a brow. "Why? Everything okay?"

He shakes his head. "We just found out some shit, not good shit. Melissa is Hangman's daughter."

103

Stunned, I stare at him before I can speak. "When the fuck did this get revealed?"

"Today. Tori took one look at Melissa, and bam. That was that. Melissa now knows."

"That why she looks like someone died?"

He nods. We hear the girls giggling, and I see Cori with a mischievous look in her eyes. Angel must see it too and sobers. "Fuck, she's up to something, and it looks like Trevor is in her line of fire. I better go warn him." He gets up and swiftly moves toward Trevor.

Before he can get to him, Cori speaks up. "Hey, T-bags!" she shouts. "You tell your new girl here how you got your nickname?" The girls around her start laughing, and the guys look to their boots, trying not to give in.

Trevor narrows his eyes, and his face turns red. Tori, who is sitting beside him, looks at the girl. "No, he hasn't, but I'm curious to know."

"Tori," Trevor growls out at his woman.

Cori rubs her hands together and smirks. "Well, you see, it happened about seven years ago. The boys decided to throw me a huge eighteenth birthday party, just the members, Lilly, and Melly and I. Eden and Moira were on babysitting duty, and T-bags got super drunk and had to take a piss. So, anyways, I walk in by accident to the men's bathroom to see him peeing with his balls resting on Breaks' forehead, who was passed out."

"Wait… what? You didn't tell me that's how he got the name," Zippo yells at Cori.

"That's because, every time I tried to tell you, I couldn't stop laughing," Cori yells across the yard.

The whole group bursts out laughing. Poor Trevor will never live this down.

Another hour passes, and I can see the girls getting tired, so we all say goodbye, with everyone telling the girls not to stay away for so long next time, and then we leave.

CHAPTER 18

Cori

After Blake dropped us off at home, we're both exhausted. It was such a great day. I missed everyone so much, and seeing Lilly, Eden and Moira again was awesome. I can see why Zippo, Reaper and Angel are so taken with them. Moira, even though she is a nurse at the hospital, is now actually a member of the club, as are both Eden and Lilly.

Another piece of info I got was that Eden now owns and runs Momma B's old bakery. She said at first she didn't want it, was going to just sell it off, but after talking with the girls and Angel about it, she decided to just change the name and make it her own instead. Which is crazy to me. I can't believe I've missed so much by not being here. It's not like we haven't talked or visited in years.

If I wasn't terrified of riding my own bike, I'd totally do it. But at the same time, I don't think I could see the situations they go to. I lived a bad situation; I don't want to be part of that mess again. It's why I love my job so much. I just get to read about the cases and tear up, then smile when the case gets resolved.

Blake didn't want to leave tonight. He wanted to talk to me, to stay, but I told him I really needed to chat with Melissa. She seemed totally off all day, and it's bugged me.

Changing into more comfy clothes, I search my sister out. When I find her, she is laying on her bed, just staring at the ceiling.

"Okay, what is going on?" I ask her, flopping down on the bed next to her. "You've been off since this morning, so I know it's not just the news about learning who your dad is."

"It's Dray," she says quietly.

"Okay?" I prompt

"We slept together, last night," she finally says.

I tilt my head to the side, wanting her to continue.

"I wasn't even really that drunk, but after you left, Dray and I got it on. It was amazing, Cori. So damn amazing. When we were done, though, he wouldn't look at me, just told me he had to get back to work. After that, I just got rip roaring drunk. Then I realized that we didn't even use protection."

"Oh shit, Melly. Safe sex. Always safe sex." Well, there goes my hypocritical self. Blake and I haven't used protection either of the two times we've done it.

She cries quietly. "I know, and that's not even the worst part. I saw him leave later that night with some model looking bimbo. Not even three hours after fucking me, he leaves. Looks like I was right all along. He never actually liked me, just wanted me to put out."

I take her hand in mine, both of us laying on our backs on her bed. "His loss, Melly. You're great. He's stupid not to see it."

"I love you, sis," she says, looking at me.

"I love you, too, baby sis." We fall asleep in bed together. I take longer to doze off than she does, since now I'm worried about her being pregnant.

BLAKE

I walk away from Cori and Melissa's condo and go up to mine. I didn't want to leave; I wanted to talk to Cori, spend more time with her, but I knew that she needed to talk with her sister.

It's late, but I don't feel tired. I shrug off my jacket and toss it on the couch when my cell rings. "'Lo?"

"Blake, fuck man, you know that fucking Zambini case I've been racking my brain over?" Adam greets.

"Yeah, what about it?" I would have figured he'd have ended the case a while ago. There is something about it he's not getting, though.

"Wife just fucking showed up dead."

"Shit, man. Her testimony was all we had to go on," I gripe, rubbing my face.

"I know. Fuck. Everyone else collaborated his story, that it wasn't true, even though that boy is in the hospital from abuse and sexual assault. Mrs. Zambini said it was her husband that did it. Now, we have nothing unless that boy wakes up," Adam says with his voice cracking.

"Let me call the Angels. I'll see if they can get surveillance on Mr. Zambini. Hopefully we'll be able to nail that fucker," I offer to him.

"Fuck, man. Sorry. It's late. I'll do that. You probably want to hit the sack."

"I can do it. It's fine," I tell him.

"Don't worry about it. I just needed to vent it out, man. I can do it. You have a good night." Adam clicks off before I can reply.

Shit, that case is brutal. I'm starting to think maybe I shouldn't have passed it off to him.

Lying in bed, I think of Cori. Maybe I should take her on a real date, an actual date. Maybe then she'll be open to being with me. After what Melissa has said to me, I'm starting to think maybe Cori has the same thoughts she does—that I only want her because I now know about the true her. But that is so far from the truth.

I grab my phone, and without realizing how late it is, I call up Angel. Besides Melissa, he knows her better than anyone.

"'Lo?"

"Shit, man. Sorry. I didn't realize the time," I say, looking to my bedside clock. It's one o'clock in the morning.

"Don't worry about it. What's up?"

"Cori. I want to take her on a date, but I have no clue what to do."

He lets out a quiet laugh. "Man, you've dated. Just do that."

I shake my head and sigh. "No, she knows all about those dates. She set most of them up. I need to be different."

"Have you ever taken any of your dates to The Keg?" he asks.

"No, I just took them to cheap yet nice restaurants. All I wanted to do was fuck, so I didn't want to spend a shit load of money on that."

"I should tell you to stay away from Cori, but I'm going to go out on a limb here. You really like her, don't you, and not just in the 'I want to fuck her' way?"

"Yeah," I say gruffly.

"You hurt her, Blake... I swear to God, I will fuckin' hurt you."

"Got it."

"Take her to The Keg. She loves it." With that advice, he hangs up, and I place my phone on my nightstand after powering it off.

Monday night after work, Cori will be coming on an actual date with me. I fall asleep with a huge grin on my face.

Twisted Up In You

CHAPTER 19

Cori

I wake up the next morning with Melissa's heat at my back, and I smile. It's Sunday, my day off, which means it's pig out day. Yesterday was a great day, despite being barfed on. It was so great getting together with my family.

I also remember Melissa's little problem. It's way too soon to find out anything, but until we do, I'm not letting her drink, which I know she'll flip out over. And I remember Blake. I might not understand why he's doing this, wanting me now, but I have to admit I kind of like it.

I roll away from Melissa and get out of bed, thinking it's a good day for bacon and pancakes, when she stirs. "What time is it?" she grumbles.

"Ten. Want breakfast?" I ask her, slipping my feet into my blue fuzzy slippers on the floor.

"Yes please. We have any fizz in our pop machine? Because I could go for an energy boost right about now," she says, slowly sitting up.

I shrug. "I think so. We haven't used it in a while."

We both work around each other in the kitchen, her manning the bacon, me doing the pancakes, when I finally speak up. "Melissa, um, are you on birth control?"

Melissa's hand with the fork in it freezes over the bacon pan. "No," she says quietly.

"You know what this could mean, right?" I ask gently.

She bites her bottom lip and hangs her head. "Shit, Cori. I didn't even think of this last night. What do I do?"

"Well, what do you want to do? If you end up pregnant?"

"I'll keep the baby. You know I want kids," she starts. "But telling Dray... that would be a whole other thing. I don't know what to do about that."

I chew the inside of my cheek. "You'll have to tell him, Melly."

"I know, and if I am, I'll tell him, eventually," she says quietly. "Can we not worry about this right now? It only happened once. What's the chance of me being pregnant after just once? Seriously, let's move on." I want to reply that it only takes one time, but I don't want to upset her.

We finish up breakfast and settle on the couch to pass the time watching movies until Once Upon a Time comes on this evening.

"Oh, Cori, Marcy texted me while you were in the bathroom. She's popping over in a bit just to hang out," Melissa suddenly says.

"Uh, okay?" When the heck did Marcy manage to get Melly's number?

She just grins at me.

"So, what did you," I start to say, but a knock at the door interrupts.

I walk over and open it, expecting to see Marcy. But it's Angel and Reaper instead.

"Uh, hi? What are you guys doing here?" I ask.

Angel holds up a folder and gives me a chin lift. I don't like the look of this.

I let them in, and we walk quietly into the living room.

"Hey, guys," Melissa greets them, smiling.

Angel quietly passes her the folder he was holding.

"What's this?" she asks.

"Everything you would ever need or want to know about your father. You don't have to read it or anything, but I figured, since this has come about, I'd give you that option."

Melissa chews on her top lip and just stares at the file. "I don't know," she says quietly. "I've always wanted to know who my father was, but now that I do, and I know he's a bad man, I don't know."

"There's more, Melissa. Something you can't tell the other women right now. Not until Tori knows, at least."

"What?"

"Trevor is your uncle. Moira is a nurse at the hospital, and she was able to fast track a DNA sample," Reaper tells her.

Her eyes fill up with tears. "Does he know?"

"He does now. And knowing Hangman, Carson, if he finds out about you, he'll want to be in your life," Angel says.

"Trevor is my uncle, Cori," Melly whispers, tears falling down her face.

I give her a small smile. "No, T-bags is your uncle."

She bursts out in laughter over that.

"Thank you for this. I don't know when I'll look at it, but it's nice to know I'll have that choice," she says, looking back to Angel.

Growing up, we never knew who our fathers were, and I was too young to remember who was around when our mother conceived Melly. Somehow, I wonder if we would be better off never knowing. One good thing: at least Trevor is a decent guy for an Uncle.

BLAKE

I decide to head out for a bit. I sent Marcy down to the girls' place to let it slip that I wanted to take Cori on a real date. Pacing my condo is going to wear a whole in the floor, so I call up my buddy Drew, seeing if he wants to go to lunch.

We meet at East Side Mario's and place our orders. "So how's life been?" I ask him.

"Busy, man. This move, the new position… it's rough. But it's getting better," Drew tells me. He recently moved from Devon to here. He was just a cop before, and now he's a detective.

"So, Cori and I are a thing now," I clue him in, picking at some bread on the table.

He chokes on his water. "What? When did you finally do that?"

I shrug. "Not long ago."

"Yeah, but you said you'd never make a move unless she made one first. So how'd she make that move?"

"She didn't. I did. Cori isn't the shy little mouse we all thought. Girl is nuts. You think Melissa is crazy? No, Cori is right there with her."

"Whoa, what? Seriously?" he asks, totally shocked.

"Yep."

"That's great, man."

Our food comes, and we dig in. "So, now that you've decided not to take the transfer after all, how's Keller handling not being able to mooch off you?" I ask him. His friend, Keller, is a Grade-A asshole. He's a hockey player and is worse than any guy I know. When Drew first said he was transferring to a small town, he had Keller move out; he moved to Edmonton, where his girlfriend, Chelsea, has a job.

"He moved with me, if you can believe that shit. Chelsea's gonna have a bitch fit when she finds out, because she's moving here to be with Melissa and Cori, to get away from him. The second I said I wasn't doing the transfer after all, he didn't even ask, just tagged along," he says, shaking his head.

I've never met Chelsea, but I have heard enough about her through Drew. "They break up for good this time, or is it just another phase?" I ask with a chuckle.

"Oh, it's done for good. She found out he not only was fucking around on her on the road, which was a normal thing for them—she knew and was fine with that—but that he was also fucking around on her in town. Chelsea found out when one of the bimbos went into her clinic, pregnant, and was talking about her great love, saying his name was Keller."

"Oh, shit, man. Doesn't he wrap it up?"

"Apparently, not that time. Idiot."

"Not quite sure how you're friends with that moron. Why don't you just boot him out?"

"Hey, he pays half my 'rent'," he says in air quotes. "What he doesn't know is I actually own the house. Figure I'll keep him, pay off my house faster, and then boot him out. I only have about sixty grand left to pay on it."

"Well, that's good I guess then, eh."

"I suppose. Worst part is, he knocked up that society rich bitch and now has her shacked up in some rundown apartment just downtown. Oh, and get this, fucking moron has a new girlfriend," he spits out.

"Anyone we know?" I ask him. I heard about Becky Veldhuizen getting knocked up, but it was always speculated it was her ex-boyfriend, Cameron, who by the way is married, got her with child.

He looks out the window, a muscle in his jaw twitching. "No, but she's a good person. Met her a handful of times. She doesn't deserve to be with that fuck head."

I say nothing. Seems as if everyone I know is having some sort of relationship crisis lately.

We finish up lunch, making plans to go out to the bar this weekend, and I head back to my condo.

CHAPTER 20

Cori

Angel and Reaper finally take off after just hanging out with us for a bit. Marcy arrives about a minute after they leave. The second she comes in the door, she's beet red.

"Holy shit, I think I just found the man that will turn me straight," she breathes out.

I burst out laughing. "Oh, God."

Melly smirks. "Which one? Heavy bearded guy or Mr. Moody?"

"Bearded guy. Holy shit. Wow, just yum."

I shake my head at her.

"No, I'm serious. I would totally be willing to take his cock any day, because um, yum."

"He's married," I say, my lips twitching.

"Well, shit!" she huffs, looking genuinely sad about it.

"Come on. Let's pig out and watch crappy movies."

We finish up watching Mean Girls and go to start searching for another one, when Marcy pulls open her purse and waves a movie.

"What's that?"

She smiles slowly and passes it to me.

"Holy Shit!" I yell. I hold it up to Melly, and she squeals. "We've been wanting to see this, but I felt too creeped out to see it in theaters."

Marcy laughs. "It's not too bad, to be honest."

I open the case and pop in Fifty Shades of Grey. I really hope to see some Jamie Dornan ass. I miss him on Once Upon a Time. He was only in season one, but gah, yum.

Before the movie starts, Marcy speaks up. "I was talking to a certain someone this morning," she sing songs.

"Who?"

"Blake."

"And?"

"I heard he's taking you out on a real date tomorrow."

"Really?"

"Oh, yeah, he sure is. Pretty sure he's taking you right after work tomorrow evening, so make sure you wear something nice," she says, smirking at me.

Holy shit. A date. A date with Blake.

A flash goes off, snapping me out of my daze, and I look to Marcy, who is smiling so huge it's scary. "There, and send."

"What?"

She smiles. "Sent it to Blake. Let him know how happy you are about the thought of a date with him. That stupid dopey look you had going on was super cute."

~

My phone rings, waking me up from a good dream, a dream about Blake. I roll over and check the time. *What the hell? It's so early. Who's calling me?*

"Hello."

"Hey, babe. I'm just outside the building. What number is your condo?" It's Chelsea.

I squeal and jump from the bed. "309. Come right up." I throw the phone on my bed and run to Melly's room, yelling at her to wake up.

We both wait by the door until the knock comes, both of us rushing forward to open it. Chelsea stands there, on the other side of the door, with a huge smile on her face. Oh my shit, she looks so different than the last time I saw her. Gone are her long locks; instead, it's cut short into a pixie style, similar to how Eden wears her hair.

I rush her before Melissa can and squeeze her tight. Stepping back, I let Melissa at her. "I've missed you," we all say at the same time. We laugh, and then Melissa and I finally let her into the condo.

"Thanks so much for letting me crash here for a while. I appreciate it," Chelsea says, pulling her suitcase behind her.

"Yeah, no problem. I'm just happy you finally saw the light with douche monkey," I say, shrugging.

She shoots me a glare and then rolls her eyes at me. "Yeah," she says softly.

"You don't need him. Cori and I know lots of single guys. We can help you move on," Melissa says, sounding gleeful.

Chelsea shakes her head. "Thanks, but no. Last thing I need right now is another man in my life."

"Ugh, men ruin everything lately," Melissa pipes in with her two cents on the subject.

"What about you, Cori? Any men in your life lately?" Chelsea says, raising her brows.

I say nothing and turn my head.

"Oh my God! Look at her. She's turning red!" Chelsea booms out in laughter. "Who is it? Did Blake finally make his move?" she asks

I look to her. "What do you mean, finally make his move?"

She snorts. "Dude, that guy has always had a hard on for you."

"How would you know that? You've never met him."

"He's friends with Drew, remember, who is friends with Keller," she says, winking.

Oh yeah. "Uh, it's really late, or early, however you wanna look at it. We should get to bed. School and work in the morning," Melissa chimes in.

Oh, shit. Yeah, I need sleep.

"We'll catch up more later on," Chelsea says, yawning.

"Uh, you can't. Cori has a date tomorrow night," Melissa says, a huge grin on her face.

Chelsea turns in shock and then grins herself. I pick up the throw pillows on the couch and throw them at the girls.

Heading to my room, over their giggling, I shout, "Night, bitches!" I end up just tossing and turning for the rest of the night. Not sure what time I finally pass out, but it couldn't have been for long, because not long after, my stupid alarm clock goes off.

CHAPTER 21
BLAKE

A text came through on my phone last night from Marcy. She took a picture of Cori, who looks stunningly beautiful, as always. A huge grin is on her face, and she looks dazed.

This is what she looked like the second I said you were taking her on a date. – Marcy

Still being a pussy, I pick the phone back up and look at the picture again. I smile and lay my phone to the side then head to the break room to grab my own coffee.

Cori arrives to work late, which is unusual for her. She looks exhausted. I go to my little mini fridge in my office and pull out her favorite energy drink and bring it out to her, popping it open before placing it on her desk.

She looks up with a smile. "Thank you," she breathes out, grabbing the can and quickly taking a sip.

"Rough night?" I ask.

She shakes her head. "No, my best friend Chelsea showed up at three in the morning. Didn't get to go back to sleep."

I clear my throat. "I wanted to take you out after work, but maybe we can do it tomorrow instead?"

"Actually, Marcy already spilled the beans, and I was actually looking forward to it," she says a bit shyly. That's the Cori I always knew, slightly shy, timid—the Cori I first fell for.

I smile at her. "Great. We'll finish up a bit early and get there before it gets busy, so we don't have to wait around."

She gives me a huge smile. "Okay."

I walk around her desk and place my hand on the back of her neck, staring into her eyes. "Fuck. You are beautiful," I say then slam my lips onto hers.

Our kiss is interrupted by Clara. "Finally!" she shouts.

Cori pulls away, blushing like crazy, and fuck if it doesn't make me want to kiss her some more.

I look to Clara, who has a silly ass smile on her face, staring at Cori.

"What's with the yelling?" Adam says, stepping off the elevator. "I heard it through the doors."

Clara rolls her eyes. "Asshole," she mutters.

Adam hears her—he must have super hearing—and glares at Clara.

"We need to talk," he says to her, not caring that both Cori and I are right here.

She doesn't say anything, just stands there ignoring him, looking at Cori.

"Clara," Adam probes, starting to get frustrated.

"We have nothing to talk about."

"Yeah, we fucking do."

"Sure as hell don't."

"You're my wife!" Adam shouts.

"Won't be for much longer!" she shouts back.

"Oh, shit," Cori whispers.

Clara turns on her heel and walks away, down the hall, probably to her desk.

Adam clenches his jaw, watching her go. I give Cori a quick kiss and grab Adam's arm, taking him into my office.

Shutting the door, I turn to him. "What the hell?" I ask him. "I thought you were married to the sister?"

Adam rubs his face. "I was. Clara finally forgave me for that shit, then once the divorce was finalized, we got back together and got married. Then shit went to hell all over again."

I cross my arms. "Spill it. We're best friends, have been for a long ass time. I didn't know any of this shit."

"She couldn't handle the friendship Sophia and I have. We've always been best friends. There was never, and are not now, any feelings between us. She asked me to choose, Sophia or her, and I couldn't make that choice. She left.

119

Clara's been on about divorce ever since, and hasn't spoken to me since then either, until today," he tells me as he slumps into one of my chairs.

"Maybe we should switch P.A.s?" I suggest. I'd hate to give up Cori, but if I keep her, I highly doubt we'll ever get any work done.

Adam sits straight up. "No, if having Clara as my P.A. is the only way I can have anything to do with her, then so be it. Not giving that up."

"Are you going to sign off on the divorce?" I ask him.

"I don't want to, not at all, but I also don't know how to make her listen to me, to let me explain everything. It will fucking kill me to let her go, to see her move on."

"Hate to tell you this, man, but she already has," I reveal slowly, quietly. I saw her out the other night having supper with Officer Thrane, and the pair seemed cozy. And from what I know of Thrane, since he's lead officer in Airdrie, he's a good guy.

Adam's head snaps to me, and he glares. Standing up, he storms to the door and walks out. I follow him, wanting to make sure he doesn't do something he'll regret. He strides over to Clara's desk and leans on it, glaring at her.

"Who is he?" he demands.

Her eyes narrow, and she glares at him but doesn't answer.

"You are my wife. Does he know you're married?"

Again, she says nothing.

"Fuck this," he says, swiping some of her papers onto the floor before walking away, slamming his office door shut behind him.

I bend down and help Clara tidy it all up. "Sorry about him."

"It's fine. He was bound to find out eventually," she says.

I walk back to my office and see Cori staring up at me from her desk, eyes huge. "This office is never dull," she says, fighting a smile.

Fuck. She's cute. She tilts her head to the side, and I see a few other caseworkers and office staff staring at us, huge open mouthed shock all over their faces.

"I don't pay you to stand around staring. Get to work," I tell them. They quickly do, and I look back to Cori, winking at her, and then head into my office.

CHAPTER 22

Cori

Today has been eventful. Lots of office drama. Word quickly spread throughout the office about Clara and Adam, them being married, and, of course, everyone was shocked as shit about it. Some are team Adam, and others are team Clara. And then there is Marcy, who is team 'Cladam'. Seriously, that's what she's calling it.

Strange girl.

I tidy up my desk and sit in the chair to wait for Blake, when the elevator beeps and out walks Preston Thrane.

"Dude! What are you doing here?" I ask excitedly, coming around my desk and giving him a hug.

"Cori," he says back, returning my hug. For as long as I can remember, he's always had a hard on for Lilly. Even after she got married to Vinny, he still held on to hope that Vinny would fuck it all up. "I'm here for Clara."

"Wait… Shit. What?" I stammer out.

"Preston?" Clara asks shocked.

"Babe, thought I'd surprise you, take you out."

"Um, you do remember the part where I told you that my husband works here, and it wouldn't be a good idea, right?" she says. Ohhh, someone is snappy.

"Yeah, I remember, and I don't give a fuck. He sees you've moved on, maybe he'll wise the fuck up and sign them papers," Thrane tells her with a shrug.

Oh no, this isn't good. Hot alpha male cop up against hot alpha male social worker. I start chanting in my head, *please don't let Adam come out*, over and over again. My chanting doesn't work, because lookie there, Adam is storming over to us.

"Hey, Adam," I say hesitantly.

"Thrane," Adam says, glaring.

Thrane looks shocked and turns to Clara. "You didn't tell me Adam was your husband."

"I told you I had one. His name shouldn't matter," she suggests dismissively.

"Babe, it kind of does," Thrane says back. "Look, talk it out with him. You still feel the same after you actually speak, I'll be here, waiting." He gives her a quick kiss on her forehead and walks away.

"Dude, badass Thrane is a softy!" I say, my eyes bugged out.

Blake walks to me, grabs my hand, and we walk into his office. "Let them have some privacy."

"I want to know what the heck is going on. Clara is so tight-lipped about everything now that we know her and Adam are married."

"It's none of our business unless they make it so. Let's just leave them alone," he says.

I sigh. "Fine."

"Wanna make out?" Blake asks me, grinning.

"I think that can be arranged," I say with a wink.

BLAKE

Cori and I spend half the afternoon making out on my couch in my office, all while we could hear Adam and Clara yelling at each other for a good part of it. When Cori tried to undo my pants, I pushed her hand away. She looked pissed at first, but when I told her I wanted to go slow, back it up a bit and date first, her face got all soft.

"That's actually perfect." She kisses my nose and goes back out to her desk.

I like her a lot, and I respect her. I don't want to fuck this up. We could really have something between us. When I look at Cori, I can see us having a future. When I'm with her, I feel that spark, that piece I've been missing.

Pushing my excitement for our date to the side, I get busy on the work I have been neglecting all morning.

~

I'm finishing up the last bit of paperwork I have when Adam comes in, looking beaten down. "What time do you think you'll be done with your date with Cori tonight?" he asks, slumping into my chair.

"Not sure. We're just doing dinner, and then I'm taking her home."

"Oh, great, so tomorrow."

I chuckle. "No, actually, I told her I wanted to slow down a bit, at least have a couple of dates first."

Adam staggers back in shock. "Dude, what?"

I shake my head and smile. "I like her, man. I don't want her thinking I only want sex from her."

"Uh, okay. Well, think you can be back around ten?"

I frown. "What's up?"

"The case we're working with the Angels? Girl ran away. We have to call them in, find her, give her a safe place, and then get permission to enter their house, hopefully without them knowing this time."

"Yeah, man, I'll be here probably before then. We'll get this done. You call the boys now, though. Get that done, and we'll work on the rest."

"So this shit with Clara?" I raise a brow.

Adam holds his hands up. "I have a phone call to make."

"Right," I quip, shaking my head.

He retreats to his office, and I take out my phone, debating ordering Cori some flowers. I dial the number for my florist but hang up. I don't want to treat Cori like all the other women I have dated. She's different.

CHAPTER 23

Cori

I run my fingers through my hair one last time as I look over my outfit in the mirror of the company bathroom. I don't know why I am nervous. Hell, we have already had sex, and I have known Blake for years.

I'm about to walk out of the bathroom after giving myself a quick pep talk, when Marcy walks in, grinning hugely.

"Look at you! So pretty!" she gushes.

I blush. "Thanks."

"Word has it that you and Blake have been making out in his office all day," she says, winking. "You guys apparently didn't close the blinds."

My eyes widen, and I stare at her. "Oh, shit."

She laughs. "Don't worry. Everyone in the office is loving this." She goes to the mirror and fluffs up her hair. "Oh, what is your sister doing tonight? My date canceled, and I'm bored."

I shrug. "She and Chelsea, I believe, are staying in. Just pop over if you want. I'm sure they'd like that."

"Perfect. I will do just that then," she decides as she walks toward me and loops her arm in mine. We walk out of the bathroom together, and she starts to giggle. "You're nervous. Stop it. By the looks of him, he's just as nervous."

I snap my head up, since I was walking with my head down, and see Blake waiting for me in the lobby of the building. Oh, shit. He's handsome, and he has a small nervous smile on his face. Okay, good. Glad I'm not the only one.

"I wonder how awkward this will be."

DAWN MARTENS

Marcy leans in and whispers in my ear, "You are talking out loud."

"Shit!" I hiss, embarrassed.

"You'll both be great. Trust me."

"Ready?" Blake's deep voice asks me when we get close.

I bite my bottom lip, and his gaze narrows on it, eyes blazing with hunger. "Yeah, I'm ready," I answer, releasing my lip.

"Have fun, you two!" Marcy calls out as she walks away.

We drive in silence until we pull into the parking lot of The Keg. I turn to him, a huge smile on my face. "Really?" I ask excitedly.

He winks at me. "Yeah, I was told this is your favorite place."

~

Our date is coming to an end, a date which I must say was beyond anything I expected. We had great food, then we took a walk downtown and just talked—about nothing really, just talked.

I thought the ending of the date would be better, but when we pull up to our building, he pauses. "Are you coming up?" I ask him with a flirty smile.

He shakes his head. Okay, maybe the date wasn't as perfect as I thought. "I want to take this slow, Cori. I don't want you to ever think I wanted you for just a quick fuck. I like you, a lot. As much as I want to go upstairs with you right now, and lick and suck and kiss every single part of your body as slowly as possible, I'm not doing that."

Oh, shit. That is so sweet. "I'm good with fast," I say breathily as I feel my panties getting wet.

"So am I, but not with you." He leans in, kissing me softly, slowly and then pulls away.

"I'll see you tomorrow at work." He steps back, looking at me. "Go up."

I swallow, nod, and walk in the building, going up to my floor. Tonight was perfect.

BLAKE

Cori just keeps surprising me. I am enjoying getting to know her outside of the shy girl I thought I knew her to be. She is outgoing and funny as hell with a bit of sass. She keeps me on my toes, and I like it. It was so hard to tear away from her kisses and leave her at the front of our building. I knew, if I walked her to her door, I would be tempted to follow her inside. And, besides, why quit while I am ahead? I walk back to my car, whistling, and head back to the office to help Adam on this case.

When I pull in at the office, my phone pings with a text from Cori.

Tonight was really great.

I enjoyed it too. Many more nights like these to come, so get used to it. I text back.

If I would have known before that Cori and I were so compatible, I would have made a move much sooner. Tonight was the best time I have had in a long time with a woman where sex wasn't involved. Great food, easy conversation—it was nice. I shut off my car, tuck my phone in my pocket, and head inside. I wave to Barney, our night security, as I walk past his desk to the elevator.

Adam is sitting in the conference room, papers strewn all over the place, when I get up to our floor. "This everything on the Mercer case?" I ask him, shrugging off my jacket and tossing it over the chair.

"Yeah, I printed everything out instead of leaving it on my computer, so I don't have to go back and forth all the damn time," he says, not looking up from the paper he's reading.

I look over a file he passes me. "Fucking hell. I'm counting over ninety girls in total that lived in that damn house."

"You think that's bad? I have over three hundred boys counted. Look at some of these statements. All the boys just say their time was fine, and they barely remember most of it. But look at the girls. From all the statements the Angels managed to get for us, they all say they were raped, beaten, lived in dirt and filth, and were barely fed," Adam says, growing impatient.

"What about the girl that ran away? What do we have on her?" I ask him.

He digs around on the floor, pulling out a small file, and tosses it to me. "That right there is enough to get them shut down for good. It's also enough to get Mrs. Mercer's brother fired from the police station. The girl that ran? Well, she took photos and recorded shit. The cop brother? Well, whenever a report is made to the station, he intercepts it and gets rid of it. It's why nothing was ever done before."

"That makes no sense. What about Social Services? Teachers? Friends? He can't bury all that shit. No one can."

"This is where it gets a little sketchy. Although, if you look at that last photo, it might all come together," he says, frowning.

I grab the photo on the bottom of the pile and stare. "Untamed Angels? You shittin' me?"

"No, that's the president of that club. Not sure what the hell he's doing out this way, so far from home, but it's another reason we really need to chat with Angel and the boys. If you also run a search on a few of the girls that lived in that home, slightly over half of them are club girls or strippers for the Untamed Angels. It's almost as if the Mercers are fucking recruiters or some shit. I really don't know, but we need to find out."

"All right, let's make some calls, and hopefully we'll get something. The Untamed are nasty fucks, but I don't think they'd hurt kids. That doesn't seem to be their thing,"

I say honestly. From what I know of those bastards, they would do just about anything, but kids are off limits.

An hour later, Adam slumps into his chair. "Let's go get a pizza and watch the hockey game at my place," Adam suggests once we've finished up and have called the Angels and the cops to let them know all we have.

"Sounds good, man. You have beer?"

"No, whiskey. I think, after this mess, we need it."

He's right about that.

CHAPTER 24

Cori

"Babe, you are so much better off without that loser. Famous hockey player or not, dude is shit," I tell Chelsea.

"Yeah, but I was with him for a long time. But enough about me. Tell me all about this Blake and your big date night," she says.

Last night was perfect. The second I walked in the door, Marcy, Melly, and Chelsea all flanked around me, demanding answers, but I could only smile.

We got along so well. We didn't run out of stuff to talk about, even though I was afraid we would because I see him five days a week at work. But it is nice to get to know the man he is outside of all the good stuff he does for the kids he works to protect. He is so selfless. I really had no idea how much time he puts in outside the office, organizing charity drives and doing stuff with foster kids.

Today at work, I thought maybe it would be awkward a bit, but it wasn't. Blake was professional, and at the same time, every break we got, we made out on the couch in his office. Blake wanted to get together tonight, but I told him I was having a girl's night with Chelsea while Melissa was at work.

Blake's smile flashes in my mind, flushing my cheeks. I can't wait to kiss him again.

"Hello… Earth to Cori." Chelsea waves her hand in front of my face.

"Sorry," I apologize, blinking out of my daze.

"Ha! You are blushing! Okay, come on. Spill," she demands as the girl doing her nails jumps, startled when she bounces in her seat.

"It was perfect, Chels. At the end of the night, I thought we'd be in bed, but he left me at the door of the building, saying he wanted to take things slow with me," I tell her.

"That is so sweet! You have to keep him," Chelsea says, sending me a wink.

"I think I might," I say dreamily back. Chelsea grins, and we fall silent, enjoying being pampered.

An hour later, after our nails are done, hair is done, and a massage, we're out of the spa and off to the condo. Chelsea decided we needed to do mud facials, but she doesn't like other people touching her face, so we're going to do it ourselves.

When we get home, I change into a ratty tee shirt and yoga pants and throw my hair up into a messy bun so Chelsea can put her shit-looking mud on my face.

"So, has Keller tried talking to you after everything?" I ask her, and she moves her brush over my face.

"He texts me once a day, at least, saying he's sorry, he didn't realize she lived nearby, all that type of bullshit. Although, it's just that—bullshit. I've seen this bitch in the news, in the paper. She's a fucking heiress of some stupid ass corporation," she says.

"Who?" I ask her.

"The Veldhuizens. Not even joking a little on that shit. Keller got that rich bitch knocked up." She snorts.

I've heard of her. "Wait… Becky? That's her name, right?" Chelsea nods. "Isn't she the bitch that was making Avalynn's life shit for a while?" Avalynn is a girl I heard about from Vinny one day when he was pissed off about Ava painting his bike. I met her briefly at Hilary's funeral. She's four years older than I am, but she and her friend, Kristi, were always into crazy shit that made Eden look sane.

"Wait. Oh, God, yes it is! At least now that crazy bitch is out of her life."

We giggle at the thought of Keller being tied forever to the crazy rich bitch.

"Would you ever take him back, though?" I ask her, hoping her answer is no.

Chelsea sighs. "No, I can't. You know my parents, how crazy their life was for a long time, because of my older brother? Yeah, I don't want that shit. I don't want the baby mama in my life at all. I couldn't do that. And now that Scott is getting married, shit is getting intense again. His mom wants Dad around all the time to help her with wedding shit. The bitch is even trying to say Mom isn't allowed at the wedding. Family only."

"Are you serious? It's been twenty-five years since they married. What is her problem? She can't honestly think that your dad will get back with her one day."

Chelsea shrugs. "Who knows? That woman is the definition of nuts."

Chelsea finishes up putting the mud on her face when a knock comes to the door. "I'll get it," she says in a singsong tone as she skips away.

BLAKE

Knocking on the door to Cori's place, I am taken aback when some chick I don't recognize throws the door open with green shit caked on her face.

"Hey, Blake," Mudgirl says, pulling me in for a hug.

"Oops," she says with a giggle. Her eyes narrow to the green crap she just smeared on the shoulder of my white shirt.

"Chelsea?" I ask.

She rolls her eyes. "You're kind of an idiot."

"Uh, what's on your face?" I ask her.

"Shit," she says, deadpan.

"Ha. Ha. Very funny," I retort.

"Come in, weirdo. Cori is just lying on the couch."

Twisted Up In You

I walk in and down the hallway. Cori is laying on the couch, knees bent, with mud all over her face. "What'd you do to your hair?" I ask her in shock. Gone are her blondes and browns. She's hot pink underneath with a few streaks on top. Her natural blonde with brown streaks in her hair looked way better.

She raises her brows. "What? Don't like it?"

"Uh, well, it's nice," I stammer.

She smirks. "It only looks bad right now because I have it up in a weird knot so mud doesn't get all in it. Trust me. It looks awesome."

"I'll, uh, take your word for it," I relent. I sit down next to her on the couch once she moves her legs off it.

I go to ask her if she wants to do something tonight when Chelsea interrupts. "All righty, chicka, time to wash that off your face."

Cori gets off the couch and smiles at me, the stuff caked on her face cracking slightly with that movement. "Be right back, handsome."

Fifteen minutes later, she comes back out. I was wondering what was taking so long, but not only did she take the stuff off her face, she also fixed her hair. "Holy shit," I say, taking her new look in. She actually pulls pink hair off. It's sexy.

She giggles. "You should see your face. I thought your eyes were gonna pop out."

"You look... Wow."

"Told you so," she says, winking at me.

I clear my throat. "So, yeah, want to go out tonight?" I ask her.

"No can do, handsome. It's my TV night. I record all the shows I love on the other days of the week, and I watch them all in one afternoon and night. However, if you're a good boy and will go out and get me some Chinese food, I will let you stay and cuddle with me."

I hop off the couch quickly and nod. "I can do that." I kiss her and let her go. "Be back soon."

She winks at me, and I feel my cock straining against my jeans. Fuck. I don't want to get Chinese or cuddle. I want to take her to her room and strip her the fuck down, ravage her.

Scrubbing my hands over my face, I try to picture anything other than her naked. I don't think the takeout place would appreciate my hard on. The things men do just to get a little action.

I walk down to my car, giving my head a shake.

Why did I say I wanted to go slow again?

CHAPTER 25

Cori

Blake plants tender kisses along my collarbone. I shove him away. "Dude, I'm trying to watch my show."

He doesn't give up and flicks his tongue over the shell of my ear.

"You're lucky I like you a little," I tease.

He laughs lightly, throwing his head back.

"You guys are too gushy for my liking. I'm off to my room to be normal," Chelsea shouts over her shoulder as she walks away.

Melly stays seated on the couch, giggling. "Melly, move it! I really don't think you want to see your sister getting screwed, because we both know that's what's next!"

"Fine," Melly says, getting up and rolling her eyes.

With the room to ourselves, things get heated quickly. Blake tugs on the hem of my shirt, hinting for me to take it off.

"I recall you telling me we were taking this slowly," I goad him.

"You don't want me?" he questions.

"I didn't say no. I only said slowly."

He grins before claiming my mouth. He plants soft kisses along my jawline. "I can do slow, but can you handle it?"

"Bring it on, big boy."

"I'm plenty big enough, sweetheart."

And, hell, does he take it slow. Waiting for him to decide where he wants to start is excruciating. He keeps teasing me, trailing his fingers down my thigh and back up, going oh so close to my panty line. Feather light kisses tickle along my neck and onto my collarbone.

"Damn, you smell so good." He nuzzles against my hair, working his way along my jaw to my mouth.

Two can play this game. Sealing my mouth shut, I refuse to kiss him back, shoving his hands away playfully. I roll my hips over, straddling his lap, rubbing against him. He immediately goes hard beneath me.

"God, I want you," he whispers against my mouth, eager for a taste of my lips.

"I want you, too," I admit, because taking it slow is for the damn birds.

"Your room?"

"Why don't you take me upstairs to yours," I suggest, biting my lip. I have a feeling we might get loud. Chelsea and Melly could interrupt us at any minute.

"I like the idea of you in my bed."

"Then stop talking and lead the way."

I wrap my hand in his after we untangle from sitting on the couch. Blake is practically dragging me to the elevator.

Inside the elevator, Blake's hands find their way up the back of my shirt. He has my bra unclasped quickly. The ride to his floor is brief and not long enough for things to advance.

He fumbles for his door key, and I find it cute that he can't concentrate on anything but me.

Inside, his apartment is so masculine and so him. The layout is a lot like mine and Melly's place, other than everything being sleek and modern. His appliances are newer than mine.

I walk into his living room, getting a feel for the place. He doesn't have any photos of himself or friends displayed anywhere. It's kind of cold feeling.

"Hey, you." Blake wraps his arms around me, kissing my neck softly.

I turn, melting into him, ready to have my way with him.

My shirt is tossed over my head, and my bra drops to the floor. His mouth is on my breasts, which feels so good.

"Bed. Now," I demand. It has to be hard on him, bending down to touch and taste me. He is so much taller than me.

His bedroom is bare like the rest of his place. Melly and I have shit everywhere at our place. Blake must be a total neat freak. My observation on the lack of personality of his home is interrupted when he kicks his shoes off and drops his pants. My mouth is salivating at the sight of this gorgeous man in front of me.

BLAKE

Cori is lying on my bed with her hands pinned over her head, looking like my living and breathing fantasy come true. Her curves are beautiful. I take my time appreciating every inch of them with my mouth as she twists beneath me. Her hips buck, and her back arches, demanding what she wants most—my cock.

I insert two fingers and go still when she starts to wiggle greedily against my hand.

"Slow down, Cori," I warn, brushing my mouth over her navel.

She stops squirming, so I begin to move my digits in and out, working her pussy slowly.

I look up to see her biting that bottom lip and nearly come undone. My mouth latches on to her pussy, licking and sucking her clit as my fingers continue to please her. She tastes so damn good.

Cori tightens around my fingers, close to her release. Sliding my fingers out, I rock back on my calves and grab a condom from the nightstand.

"Let me." Cori takes the wrapper, tearing it open with her teeth. Fuck. That is hot. She rolls the rubber over the head of my dick swiftly.

With our height difference, sex can get awkward fast. Cori doesn't miss a beat, rolling onto her stomach with her ass in the air, ready for me to give her what we both need.

I slide into her from behind as her ass rolls against my hips. Fucking paradise.

Pumping into her quickly, it doesn't take either of us long to orgasm. All the sexual tension that has been building between us is finally released.

I kiss her shoulder, and she collapses onto the pillows. I go into the bathroom, dispose of my condom, and clean up a bit. When I come back to bed, Cori is snoring softly.

Seeing her in my bed doesn't make me feel panicked. It feels amazing. I want this—her sleeping next to me.

Brushing her hair from her face, I bend down and kiss her cheek, and she sleep smiles. I take a few minutes to straighten up our trail of clothes from the living room to the bedroom. As I crawl into bed, the dipping of the mattress wakes Cori. She smiles and snuggles against me.

"Sorry. I guess I was more tired than I thought."

"Don't worry about it," I murmur, giving her a grin. "We can get some more sleep, or we can go out for a bite?"

"Sleep. Need sleep. Can't move," Cori grumbles.

I chuckle. "Okay, sounds good." I kiss her head, and minutes later, I feel her drift off to sleep. Now that she is sound asleep, I scoot over away from her inviting warmth. Her hot body pressed against mine makes things begin to stir, and right now, we both need the sleep.

Lying on my side, I watch her chest rise and fall until my eyes close. This feels damn good.

Twisted Up In You

CHAPTER 26

Cori

Melissa comes out of the bathroom in tears, holding the stick I sent her in with. She doesn't say anything, just nods and hands me the stick. She's pregnant. Two weeks after she slept with Monster, I wanted her to take the test, but she refused. We waited. After six weeks of her barfing all the time, I finally made her take one.

I sit down on the couch, not sure how long I sit here, when I hear the front door open and Blake call out for me. He comes around the corner, and when his eyes look at what is in my hand, he pales. "Is that?" he starts to ask.

I shake my head no. "It's Melissa."

"She's pregnant? Who?" he demands. He's become protective of her over the last while. If I thought he thought of me as a sister, I was wrong, so wrong, because that's how he treats Melissa.

"Monster," I answer

He frowns. "Monster?"

I nod and sigh. "Dray."

"The fucker that hurt her a few weeks ago? The fucker that slept with her and then left a few hours later with another woman? That Dray?"

I nod again.

"I'll kill him." Blake storms out of the condo and slams the door behind him. Uh oh.

I run to Melissa's room and open the door, seeing her sitting on her bed.

"Have you told Monster yet?" I ask, getting in close to Melissa.

She nods and then snorts. "Said that if the DNA test proves it's his, that we have to get married."

I see red. "That fucker! He demanded a DNA test?"

She nods. "Yeah, whatever. My doctor told me he can get it done in a few weeks while the baby is still in my tummy," she says, rubbing her stomach. "But I'm not marrying that jerk."

"I wouldn't let you, anyways."

She chews her lip. "Uh, he kind of said that, if he is the father, I don't have a choice."

"What the hell?"

"Yeah, my thoughts exactly."

"Um, also, I should tell you, Blake was just here. I told him what was going on, and he left, pissed, saying he's gonna kill Dray."

Melissa looks to me with wide eyes. "Oh, shit!"

BLAKE

I pull up to the club. It's daytime, but I know someone has to be in this place right now. I bang on the door, shouting for someone to open the fuck up. Finally, minutes later, the door swings open and Randy stands there.

He holds up his hands in surrender. "Man, I haven't touched her. I swear on that."

I shake my head. "Not here about you, man. Your bouncer, Drayton. Need him, and need him now."

Randy's eyes narrow and then widen. "What'd he do to Melissa?" he demands.

"Not gonna say it again."

"Okay, fuck, man. He's working tonight. I know that much. But if you want him before tonight, he lives over near Inglewood Drive. I'll run up to the office and grab his address," he offers and then jogs inside the building.

He comes back down with a piece of paper and hands it to me. "That's his address."

"Thanks," I say, looking it over.

"Seriously, though, man, what'd he do?"

"Got Melissa knocked up. Fucker."

Randy's body goes solid, and a muscle in his jaw twitches. "That fucking moron."

I raise my brows.

"I'll deal with him tonight, after you deal with him today. No one hurts my girls," he claims.

"About that," I start.

He holds a hand up. "Don't. I love those girls. Have since I met them. I know Cori's with you now. Don't need to worry about me. There was a time I wanted more from her, but it didn't happen. Just treat her right. I know all about you. When she's drunk, she spills all. You're the love of her life. Treat her well. Otherwise, I'm swooping in, and I don't give a shit what you think."

I lift my chin up at him. "Fair enough."

I walk out and get into my car.

I pull up in front of Dray's house and knife out of my car, slamming my door shut, then stride up to his front door.

I pound on the front door, and barely a minute later, a young blonde wearing a man's shirt opens the door. Her eyes widen in shock. "Um, hi… Can I help you?"

"Yeah, where's Dray?" I demand.

Her brows bunch in confusion. "Who's that?"

"Drayton!" I yell through the front door after I slightly shove the girl aside.

"What the fuck, man?" he says, thumping down the steps. "Oh, fuck," he says when he realizes who's here.

"Yeah, you dumb fuck! Not only did you fuck Melissa, after you've been chasing after her for months, you left with another woman a few hours later… And guess what, you dumb fuckstick? She's fucking pregnant because of your dumbass."

The girl that opened the door gasps in outrage. "You bastard. How could you do that to someone?" She storms past me and Dray and goes upstairs. Seconds later, she is running out of his room, down the steps, and out the front door.

Dray rubs the back of his neck, looking guilty. "May as well come in and have a seat. Want a coffee or anything?" he asks.

"Yeah, sure," I answer.

He brings me a coffee and stays standing.

"You going to sit down or just stand there?"

"Only seat I have to sit on is that couch, and I don't know if I want to be too close with you right now."

I smirk.

"How is she?" he asks me.

"She's fine… pregnant. And she's upset that she ever gave in and let you touch her."

"Fuck," he mutters. "I didn't mean for this to happen. I have shit in my life right now that isn't good. I've been in love with Melissa for years, ever since she turned eighteen and started coming to the club. I've wanted her, always, but was never in a good place to actually pursue her."

"So why did you that night?" I ask him, confused. I look around his place; it is a freaking mess—drug paraphernalia, empty beer bottles, and ashtrays overflowing. He is going to have to get his shit together if he wants to be around for Melly and her child. This is not the environment to raise a child in. I've seen a hell of a lot worse in my line of work, but this shit isn't ideal.

"I was high. Only reason I remembered doing it was because, the next morning, the bitch I took home told me about the girl running out of the club as I left, crying. Then the memories came back." He rubs his face. "I'm such a dick."

I snort. "Yeah, man, you sort of are. You need to fix it. She can't do this alone. Melissa has her sister, friends, even me, but you need to step up, too. You need to clean this place up and get your head straight. Melly is a sweet girl, but this shit…" I motion to the mess surrounding us "is no place to bring a kid around to."

"Yeah, man, I feel ya. Just got a lot of heavy shit. I got down, man, but I won't do her wrong."

"Don't fuck this up, man. Melissa is Cori's sister, and she is important to the Angels Warriors and me. Keep that in mind the next time you start to do something dumb," I threaten.

CHAPTER 27

Cori

Blake comes home, and I'm expecting blood or bruises, something, but he doesn't have any of that. "What happened?" I ask him, worried.

"It's all good. Dray feels like shit. Trust me, he's going to fix it."

"You are amazing," I breathe.

He smiles at me, pulling me into him, kissing me softly. "Want to go out today?"

"Go where?" I ask him.

"Buddy of mine has a shooting range behind his farm. We can go out there, shoot a few rounds, and then maybe go out for supper?"

"Sounds like a plan." I pause. "Does this shooting range have trees hidden out of sight?" I ask, biting my lip.

He narrows his eyes at me. "Yes," he says slowly.

"Perfect. I can have my way with you then."

His gaze turns hungry. "How about we do that now?"

I shake my head. "Nope, we're gonna be adventurous."

~

Blake kicks at my feet. "Your stance is all wrong. Spread your feet. Square your shoulders. Relax your arm slightly. This pistol doesn't have much of a kickback, but you'll still feel it."

"Yes, sir." I grin as he fixes my protective ear muffs for me. I shove my goggles back up my nose because they keep sliding down.

Twisted Up In You

I really love the feel of this gun. I feel powerful and in control. I like it a lot.

Blake teases that maybe I like it a little too much. At first, I thought I would suck badly, but it turns out that I have great aim.

Blake shakes his head, seeing I shot my poster in the head, neck, and heart.

"My girl is a total badass," he boasts, giving me a quick peck before taking his turn.

I watch him as he handles the rifle he's using with ease. He looks so damn sexy holding it in his arms.

"Tell you what. If you can beat your personal best, distance wise, I will reward you handsomely."

Blake fires off round after round but isn't able to beat his record. After turning in our gear, we run through a drive-thru for dinner. Blake brought a blanket for us to picnic on. We settle on burgers and fries with apple pie for desert. All that shooting made me hungry.

"Your arm will be a little sore when you have to type at work, but I have some good muscle rub in my desk if you need it."

"Thanks." I flick his nose with a fry as he kicks his shoes off and gets comfortable on his plaid blanket.

We talk a little about work. I try to pry information out of him about Clara and Adam, but he doesn't know much more than I do. I have just finished my apple pie when Blake leans forward and licks some of the filling from the corner of my mouth.

"Gross!" I shriek, leaning away from him.

"Baby, it isn't gross. I lick your pussy, so licking a little pie from your mouth is nothing," he jokes, testing my temper.

"You have a point." I cock my brow, feeling devious as I think about putting my plan into motion. "You ever mess around in the woods?"

"No, why?" He leans back on his elbows, missing the point of my question.

"Figured we could give the wildlife something to talk about."

He is on me like a bear to honey before I can say more.

Blake's pants are down around his knees in an instant. He strokes his cock, and I lick my lips. I have never been big on giving head, but with Blake, I want to do it for him.

My tongue darts out, swirling his tip, and he groans loudly.

"As much as I want to fuck your mouth, I need in you now."

"That so?" I tease, removing my clothes slowly.

"It's a fact." He goes down on his knees, ready to claim me.

I roll away from him and start bouncing around on my socks. "You have to catch me first."

I barely get around the tree before his arms grab me, hooking around my bare waist. My back goes against the tree, and he commands my body, wrapping my legs around his waist.

"Blake, kind of rough on my back. The bark."

"Sorry." He carries me back to our blanket and orders me to lay down.

"No way. I want on top. I don't want twigs and shit getting all in my hair and having ants crawling in my ass crack."

"Your wish is my command, but if ants get in my crack, I make no apologies if I shoot up from under you."

BLAKE

We made it home in silence, mainly because my backside is itchy as hell since Cori fucked me so hard we moved off the blanket and into the dirt. And Cori bitched about having a mosquito bite on her ass. I go to pull Cori close to me when I hear it. "No!" I hear screamed. I jolt out of bed and look down at Cori, squirming around. "Please don't. Please!" she cries. Her legs jerk as her body shakes in terror.

I lean down, putting my hand on her shoulders. "Cori, baby, wake up. It's only a dream," I tell her, jarring her slightly.

"Please stop! Please! Don't take my baby!" Her words have me frozen to the spot. Her baby? "Please give him back! Please!" Her arms stretch out.

"Corinne!" I shout, lifting her up from the bed, cradling her in my arms. She comes awake in a panic, and her breath comes out raggedly. Her skin is cold and clamored in sweat.

"I haven't had one of those in years," she whispers in a haunted tone.

"It's just a dream, babe. You're safe. You're fine," I placate, trying to soothe her.

She shakes her head. "You're wrong. It might have been a dream just now, but it was real. It was real."

I hold her close. I want to ask more about this dream, but I'm worried it will push her away. I need to call Angel up and ask him to hurry up with her file. I need to find out what the fuck happened to her.

Today was amazing—the way she rode me in the woods, the way she tried desperately to not scream so Mathias wouldn't come out to check on us. And now, I'm holding her in my arms, and she is scared as fuck.

"Cori, talk to me?" I whisper.

"No, Blake. I can't. Not now," she answers, shutting down.

"I'm here, always, if you ever need to talk about those dreams."

Her tense body relaxes some. "I know, Blake," she says sincerely.

I really hope she talks to me about these dreams. I talked to Melissa about them the other day, and she said she hasn't had one in a long ass time. Now they are coming on more and more frequently.

And the shitty part about it? I've been having nightmares about my past, too.

CHAPTER 28

Cori

I wake up to a breeze on my face. I roll over, snuggling in deeper to Blake. As I'm about to fall back to sleep, it's back, only this time, I feel a wet finger going into my ear.

"What the hell!" I shout, sitting up.

Chelsea and Melissa are both grinning down at me. "You wouldn't wake up," Chelsea says with a shrug.

Blake sits up behind me, chuckling. "We tried a few times, babe. You weren't budging."

I glare at him.

"Yeah, we've tried talking to you and poking you. We thought for sure the blowing on your face thing would work, but then Chelsea decided to give you the wet willy," Melissa says.

"By the way, you need to clean your ears. Yuck," Chelsea tells me.

"Well, I'm up now, so what's so important to wake me?"

"I was just sick of your phone going off," Melissa states.

"I just wanted to bug you," Chelsea adds.

Both girls leave the room, shutting the door behind them. I look to Blake and glare at him. "Thanks for ganging up on me. Gee."

He chuckles, pulling me to him, kissing my forehead. "It was worth it. Now you get up, shower, whatever, check your phone. I have to meet up with Adam and the Angels in a few hours. We're arranging a charity thing."

"Oh, Eden and Lilly told me about that. They're really pushing for a bake sale."

Blake's face shuts down. "We're men. We don't do that frou-frou shit."

I burst out laughing. "I know, but the guys are so whipped by their women, if that's what they wanna do, that's what will happen."

"Great," he mumbles.

An hour later, I am ready and out the door.

I get to the entryway of the south doors of the mall and spot Clara standing there, waiting for me. "Hey! Ready for some retail therapy?" I ask her, grinning.

She doesn't grin back, just nods. We make our way through a few stores. I pick up a few things and new underwear, while Clara hangs back each time, just flicking through the racks. Finally, I've had enough, and we find a bench to sit down.

"Okay, enough is enough. You called me for retail therapy, but you are gloomy, and as we continue throughout the mall, you get worse. What on earth is going on?"

"Adam signed the papers," she whispers, gutted.

"Um, okay. Isn't that what you wanted?" I ask her, confused.

"Yes, and no. I don't know," she confides, throwing her hands up.

"Why don't you tell me what happened?"

And she starts. "He and my big sister were best friends, always, never anything more, but the minute I entered high school, I was a grade below him, we were attached. Sophia was over the moon happy for this development. So when the time came that Adam was going away for the summer with friends, before he went off to college, of course my sister went, too. He broke it off with me. God, Cori, it was such a giant blow." She takes a breath before continuing. "Sophia had been acting weird about a month before the summer trip, just off. I never got it until she came home at the end of the summer, with Adam in tow, married, having a baby."

"Oh, Clara," I whisper. Fucking stupid Adam. She must have been devastated. That is horrible. Fucked over by her boyfriend and her sister.

"We worked it out. A year later, they divorced, and once he explained everything to me, both he and Sophia, I forgave them and we got married. The baby wasn't his. Sophia's boyfriend started getting abusive, and since they had been best friends for years, he wanted to help her. They said it was the only way at that time," she explains.

"Okay, but you said you forgave them and got married. What happened to have you want to divorce him?"

"I couldn't handle their friendship. I might have forgiven them for what they did to me, but I didn't like them still being as close as they were—cuddling, Adam babysitting so damn often we never had time together, and then I heard Kayden, Sophie's son, ask Adam to please love his mommy more so he could be his daddy for real. God, my heart broke hearing that. And Adam, he said... Fuck. He said, 'I wish I could, buddy'."

I sit back on the bench and stare at her. "Clara," I start. I want to explain to her what he most likely meant, because his response was actually normal.

"And that's not even the worst of it, because Sophia and Adam didn't want Joel to ever be able to get custody of Kayden. Adam is listed on the birth certificate. They didn't even tell me." She sniffles, getting choked up.

I grasp her hands in mine. "There's more, isn't there?" I ask, dreading the answer.

"Yeah, Sophia was standing behind me when I overheard that, and when I turned around, I lost it. I yelled at her, told her I hated her and wanted nothing to do with her ever again. Adam came running out of the living room, and I told him to choose. Sophia or me. He said he couldn't choose, saying that as he looked to Kayden, so I made it easy on him. I told him I was gone." She takes a deep breath and finishes. "I left, never looked back. I moved away for a bit. Adam always seemed to find my new number or new email address, and was constantly contacting me, all the time, for years. I never replied to him, ever. I was originally Blake's assistant, but when Adam found out I was, he switched me. I didn't even know this was Adam's work place until my first day here. I was gonna quit, never come back, but the pay was too good to pass up. And a small part of me loved being able to see Adam again, even without actually having him."

She cries quietly, and I pull her into a hug. "It will be okay, Clara. I promise you. Either you need to really sit down and talk with Adam, or let him go for good."

"I know. I know."

"Sit on those papers for a while. Really think it over, Clara. If it's what you truly want, go forward with it. If it's not what you really truly deep down want, fight for the man you love."

BLAKE

Melissa and Chelsea left the Clara bonding to just Cori, saying they didn't really know the woman well enough to help her out, so they decided to come to the office with me. I swear, next time, they are taking their own car, because listening to this shit that they have playing is gonna make my ears bleed.

Finally, I park and get out of the car. I see the Angels' bikes all lined in a row and Adam's car in his spot.

I groan as Melissa and Chelsea rush out of the car and skip into the building. I shake my head. They are going to kill me.

I get into the building to see Lilly and Eden standing around, chatting with Melissa and Chelsea.

Angel comes over with a grin. "I know you said guys only, but they begged and we couldn't say no. And it looks like you went through the same thing. But where's Cori?" he explains then asks.

"She's hanging out with Clara today. Those two just randomly put themselves in my car." I point to Melissa and Chelsea. "Moira didn't come?"

"No, she's home with the kids, and Tori is helping her out. They were gonna come, but then we'd have to bring all the kids, so they decided to stay behind."

"We have the best idea!" Eden shouts suddenly.

Angel groans.

"Bake sale!" All four women shout at the same time.

"No!" I yell over them.

"I'll even pitch in on baking," Melissa says, ignoring me.

"Me too. I have tons of recipes to try out," Eden says, also ignoring me.

I throw my hands up in frustration and look at Angel. "Seriously?"

He shrugs. "May as well do it. Otherwise, they'll be after us to do a bake sale every single time we want to do something."

I groan. "Fine. We'll do a damn bake sale."

We talk everything over, and Melissa and Chelsea are in charge of the bake sale downtown while Eden and Lilly are hosting the one in Airdrie. Zippo suggested having the two locations to help bring in more money. They're going to split up the club so they can be in both places for it. We're going to donate all of this money to four new families that the Angels just helped get on their feet, hoping to bring them in more money so they can have a little extra.

A few hours later, we all drive off and head back to the condo. Melissa gets a text and starts getting pissed. "Ugh, I don't want to talk to that dick," she says, shutting her phone off and putting it into her purse.

Chelsea chews on her bottom lip, wanting to say something but backs off. When we arrive home, Melissa stomps out the doors. "Where's she going?" I ask Chelsea.

"Went to get pop."

"She does realize she's pregnant and can't drink all the shit she just bought, right?" On the way home, Melissa made me pull into the liquor store, and she came out of there with a giant box full of rum and some wine.

"Yeah, she does," Chelsea says, looking in the direction Melissa stomped off in.

"I'm going to order a couple pizzas. Anything you don't like?" I ask her as she unlocks the door.

"I like everything. Melissa and Cori only like Pepperoni, though."

I place the order and sit down on the couch, waiting for Cori to get home.

Twisted Up In You

CHAPTER 29

Cori

The second I get home after being with Clara, I feel icky. I like Clara, don't get me wrong, but it has me feeling run down. I do know, when I get my hands on Adam, I'm gonna wring his neck. How could he not be able to choose between his wife and her sister? That's not right.

"Babe, I ordered pizza," Blake calls from the living room as I shut the door.

"Oh, thank God." I walk to him, finding him sitting on the couch, papers all over my coffee table. "Busy day?"

"You could say that. Your damn sister, Chelsea, and the other girls won on the damn bake sale charity," he grumbles.

I smirk. "Told you."

"Told him what?" Chelsea asks, skipping over to me.

"Nothing," I say, winking at her.

"Today was so much fun, and Mason was totally pissed about what Keller did to me. Says he wants to hunt him down and wring him up by the balls. It was awesome," Chelsea says gleefully.

I laugh. "I bet. Where is Melissa?"

"Oh, she ran to the store to get some pop for the mountain of booze she bought today."

I frown. "But she can't drink."

Ten minutes later, the front door opens, followed by the smell of pizza. "Blake, come pay this guy," Melissa shouts.

She comes in the living room, six bags full of pop in her arms, and she sets them down. "Let's get drunk," she declares.

"Uh, Melissa, you're pregnant. You can't drink," I tell her.

"I know that, but I can have a glass of red wine. My doctor said it was okay. The booze is for you guys. I need fun in my life, and watching you all get drunk is the greatest," she says, grinning.

I shake my head at her, and Blake comes in the room with two boxes of pizza. "The works and a pepperoni with extra cheese."

I wrinkle my nose at the works pizza—that's so nasty—and grab the pepperoni box from him. Melissa mixes my drink, and as she's about to start Chelsea's, her phone goes off.

"I'll be home tomorrow," Chelsea says, bolting out the front door, but not before grabbing a slice of Blake's disgusting pizza.

"Where is she going?" I ask.

Melissa looks at me, confused. "Not a clue."

We dig into our food and our drinks, and turn on the TV to re-watch some Game Of Thrones.

I look to Blake after a while, hearing him chew. It's annoying as hell, and I'm about to snap at him when I see him picking a mushroom off his pizza.

"That's disgusting! I can't eat that. Why the hell would you put mushrooms on a pizza?"

"Mushrooms are good," he tells me with a shrug.

"Good for you, but I'm not eating cow shit!"

"It's not cow shit."

"Uh, yeah, it is."

"Almost all food that comes from the ground grows in shit. You still eat that stuff."

"Yeah, but mushrooms grow FROM cow shit. Totally different. That's just wrong," I tell him on a shudder.

He takes a mushroom off his pizza and puts on a show of slowly chewing it as he smirks and gives me a small moan. I gag.

"I'm never kissing you again."

Blake pulls a mushroom from the top of his slice, and then the big jerk flings it at my cheek.

I want to be mad, I really do, but it is kind of funny. I pick a pepperoni from mine and throw it in his direction, missing him completely.

Blake leans over to kiss me, and I take my pizza and smash it against his cheek, catching him completely off guard. He grabs my wrists, pinning me defenseless as we fall from our chairs onto the floor, bringing my slice with us. Freeing one of his own hands, he smears the sauce across my face and down my chest.

"You're dead," I warn.

"I'd go a happy man."

I get a smear of sauce on my finger and wipe it across his brow. He leans down, staring in my eyes, and kisses me hungrily.

"I'm done with pizza. I'm hungry for you," he says, propped on his elbows.

"First, a shower," I suggest, pressing my hand to his chest.

I take off to the bathroom, starting up the shower as Blake strips off behind me. I get in the shower and quickly start washing all the pizza off me. When I go to grab my shampoo bottle, Blake comes up behind me, wrapping his arms around my waist, his cock hard between us. "Blake, no, this is a bad idea."

"No, it's not," he says in my ear as his left hand comes up and cups my breast roughly.

I moan. "Blake, I'm serious. I'm short, and the tub is slippery. Only bad things will come from this."

"Trust me."

He pushes me slightly forward, and in one swift movement, thrusts fully inside of me. "Oh, God," I moan out. He pulls back and slams into me, grabbing my hips, as a possessive growl rips from his throat.

Just as I'm about to come, I start slipping. I swear, it's like slow motion. His hard thrusting causes me to slip, and down we go. We are a tangled naked heap at the bottom of the tub as the water pelts against us.

"Fucking shit!" Blake roars. I'm stunned for a moment, but quickly pull myself off of him and press my back against the wall of the tub. "My dick!" Blake croaks.

I panic, crawling toward him. "I told you this would happen."

Tears well up in his eyes, and he stares at me, cupping his precious jewels. "You broke my dick."

I shake my head. "I told you shower sex was bad. This is your fault for not listening to me."

I try removing his hands to inspect the damage, but he refuses. "No way. You are not touching my dick," he says firmly.

Wow. I've never known a grown man to ever cry before, and Blake is here, sitting in my tub, bawling his eyes out.

"We should get you to the hospital," I tell him, trying to remain calm.

He shakes his head. "No, call your sister. She's a nurse, or training to be. No way am I going to the hospital so I can be laughed at," he says.

My eyes widen. "Uh, what do you think Melly is gonna do? Because I can tell you right now, the whole damn town will know about this within an hour."

"Just get her," he seethes.

I climb out of the tub, wrapping a towel around me, and go in search of my sister.

"Melly!" I shout, running down the hall to her room.

She opens her door and looks at me in question.

"Blake. Broke. Dick," I pant.

She bursts out laughing. "Shower sex?"

I nod.

"Should've known. What did he think would happen? You are only four eleven, he's six two. Good grief," she says, following me to the bathroom.

I step into the bathroom, and Blake is still sitting in the tub, tears in his eyes. I feel bad, but I knew this would happen. I told him it would.

Melissa goes over to inspect the damage. I should feel totally jealous that my sister is doing this, but I'm not. I'm just worried about his dick.

"Well? Is it broken? Will we ever be able to have sex again? Oh my God, please tell me we'll be able to have sex again," I say, starting to panic since this is taking forever.

Melly giggles. "Don't worry, big sis. He's fine, just a little sprain. Gotta say, I'm jealous. He's got a huge monster goin' on."

BLAKE

I slowly get out of the tub I'm lying in, cupping my junk. Fuck. It hurts so damn bad. Melissa told me to take some aspirin if the pain gets too much, and that's what I'm going to be doing as soon as possible. Cori comes back into the bathroom, after following Melissa out, with some loose sweat pants for me to put on.

"I went up to your condo and got you these. Figured they'd be best to wear instead of your jeans," she says meekly, avoiding my stare. "I'm really sorry, Blake," she apologizes in a quick breath. "But I did warn you, so in a way, it's your own fault."

I glare at her. "It's my fault you turn me on and I couldn't wait to have you?"

"Yes, but no sense fighting about it. Here." She hands me some aspirin. "I feel really bad about it. It's going to be so hard avoiding the temptation." She smirks, her eyes going straight to my crotch.

"Don't stare at my dick like that. You are going to make me hard, and I'll end up in the ER and be known as broke dick Blake all over town."

Cori looks as if she's about to cry, so I pull her into me, kissing her softly. "It'll heal. Don't worry. But until it does, I don't think I can sleep in the same bed as you because it will be too tempting."

Her face falls. "You mean, you are going to your condo tonight?" she whispers, sounding almost horrified.

I nod. "Just tonight. I'm going to take some pain meds and get some rest. Fucking thing hurts like a bitch, but I'm still horny. How fucked up is that?" I say with a small laugh.

"Okay, fine. I'll see you tomorrow, though, right?" she asks, worried.

I pull her tight to me. "Of course." I kiss her again and head out.

CHAPTER 30

Cori

Since I sorta, kinda sprained Blake's dick, we've been doing absolutely nothing for the last three months. I've tried getting him to at least go down on me, but he won't budge, saying I broke his dick so my punishment is getting nothing. Jerk. He even hid all of my vibrators.

He stopped icing his junk about a month ago, but still refused to touch me, saying he wanted to give it a little more time, just to make sure. I was worried the night it happened, because he went to his own condo. Ever since we started really doing this thing together, we've never slept apart. I was worried we'd be over.

Thankfully, we weren't.

Tonight, we're lying in his bed, a place I haven't been in months, since we're always at my place.

I roll to my side, trailing my fingers down his chest. "Tell me about you. I know who you are now, but I don't know anything else."

"Not really much to tell. Dad died when I was a month old—Army. Mom couldn't deal with his loss. Gave me to the system. I was in and out of foster homes until I hit eighteen. I wouldn't say I was a bad kid, but I got into enough fights at each home I lived in for them to send me along. One family wanted me, permanently, but foster homes aren't meant to be long term, so I was only with them for a year." That sucks. Poor Blake. "They tried fighting for me, adoption and all that, but they couldn't get approved, which I think is bullshit, because why not? I wouldn't have been in the system anymore, and the government wouldn't have had to fork out cash for my raising." He shakes his head. "I was in a few really bad homes, some so bad I used to have nightmares, but I got talking to a shrink, and they stopped. Haven't had one in years now. But because of how I lived, it's what made me want to get into social work."

"That's amazing, Blake. What you do now is amazing," I tell him.

He gives me a sad smile. "I reached out to the family that tried adopting me years ago, but found out they were murdered. One of the kids they were fostering was bad, ended up murdering everyone in the house in their sleep before slicing his own wrists."

"That's terrible," I gasp.

"Yeah, babe, it is. Shit like that happens. Nothing anyone can do. Fuckin' hurts," he confides. "Tell me about you. I know a little, but I know I don't know all of it."

I still. Do I really want to bring Blake into my ugly? No, I don't, but I can tell him a little bit of it. "Started when I was six. My mom was always shitty. We never were told who our dads were. Hell, mom said she didn't even know. She was a junkie and a hooker. Anyways, I was six when Melissa was just a baby, and Mom said she was going out so I had to watch her. It wasn't anything new, not really. But she didn't come home. The next day, a cop and some woman came to the door. I was always told never to answer the door when Mom wasn't home, but that day, I did since it was a cop. Officer Gilvaja came in, took a look around the house, saw me holding Melissa, who was only 4 years old at the time. It was at that moment the woman started talking to me, telling me that my mom called her and said that Melissa and I needed to get gone and she wouldn't be home until someone got us."

"What happened after that?" Blake asks.

I flop to my back, not really wanting to make eye contact with him. "We jumped around a lot. One time, they tried to separate us, but I wasn't having it. I would run away a lot, fighting, all of it, just to get my sister back with me. They never tried to separate us again. But after about two years, Mom came back for us. Although, that didn't last long. She'd take us back for a few months, then ship us back to foster care. It went on until I was about thirteen. Just before I hit eighteen is when Angel and the guys saved us. They came storming in that house, cussing the place down, and took us away, giving Melissa a better life, an amazing life."

"Have you seen your mother since then?" he asks.

"A few times, but none of them have ever been good. Usually, she wants money, money I don't have, and causes the usual shit storm until Jasper and the guys have to send her off."

I decide to give him a little more. "I used to be a stripper."

He stills, his body coming up and over me. "What?" he growls.

"I didn't want to ask for money. Angel and the rest of the guys found out about it, lost their shit. Came in during my shift, pulled me right off stage, and yelled at me, lectured me, all of it for days. After that, they refused to let me work while I was in college. They paid for everything, and then the second I finished, they got me my job with you."

"So you're telling me that dirty pervy men saw you on a pole?" he questions, abashed.

"Um, yes." I blink.

He growls. "Never again. Mine. Just mine." He kisses me, claiming me as his own. So much passion is seeping from him.

BLAKE

"I am all yours," Cori agrees. Her fingers are tracing the muscles of my stomach, dancing dangerously close to the waist of my shorts.

"Cori," I warn her, moving her fingers back up to my chest.

She gets this devious gleam in her eyes as she leans over and takes my nipple between her teeth, biting gently.

"How about we see how healed you are…" She trails off, kissing her way down my happy trail.

Fuck. It's been too long, and my cock is standing and ready. There is no contest; she will win, hands down. She continues to taste and tease me, her fingers finding their way to my length. Her hair is pulled back in one of those knots, exposing her face as she yanks my shorts down hungrily. My girl is so damn sexy when she takes control.

Her full lips cap over my dick, and she sucks me hard and deep. It's safe to say I am fully recovered. Her tongue wraps around me, sucking and tasting. It's fucking erotic. I glide in and out of her sweet mouth, ready to blow. I try to pull away, wanting to satisfy her, too, but she isn't having it, saying tonight is about taking care of my needs. Can't argue with that. I love that she wants to do this for me, not wanting anything in return but my happiness.

Cori falls asleep before I do, her weight almost completely on me, and I feel at peace. She shared, even though something in her eyes said she wasn't sharing everything, just the fact that she shared at all speaks volumes. I'm glad I was able to give her that piece of me, let her in more. What I didn't share with her, though, was that I also tracked down my mother.

She was living the high life with three kids, all happy while I rotted away. I can't say I completely hate her, since I am who I am now, but she gave me up, just did it so damn easily, then moved on to a new family.

I checked up on her about two years ago, wanted to make sure my half siblings were being treated okay. I found out that their dad is a pretty stand-up guy, but from watching my mother, she seemed to be hiding her pain. You can tell it's there, in her eyes, but when her other children or husband were around, she lit right up.

Twisted Up In You

After that, I stopped checking in to make sure everything was fine. I was going to have her happy little world come crashing down but decided against it. It wouldn't make me feel any better, so there is no need for it.

Cori rolls over, and I follow, drifting off to sleep.

CHAPTER 31

Cori

I wake up and stretch. I groan when I see the clock and realize it's only three in the morning. Why the hell am I awake? Looking over, I watch Blake, who is sound asleep on his stomach. Opening up last night was a bit of a relief, and hearing about his youth was pretty great, too. He grew up, in a way, kind of like Melissa and I did. I trail my finger down his cheek and smile.

"Stop that. It tickles," Blake grumbles.

"Oh, really?" I say teasingly. I move my hand down to his side and tickle slightly.

"That's it," he says, grabbing my hand and rolling over on top of me. "Are you ticklish, Cori?" he taunts me as he squeezes my sides.

"Stop. I'm sorry." I laugh.

"Are you guys playing hide the salami again?" I hear Melly shout through the door. Blake rolls off me, smirking. "No!" I shout back. "We're playing hide the mother fucking jumbo cucumber," I brag, winking at Blake. He shakes his head at me. "Well, hurry up, because I'm sick and tired of hearing 'Oh, Cori' and 'yes, please, fuck'," she says, mocking us. "I need some damn sleep."

I burst out laughing. "Maybe we should take our sex-capades to your place for a while?"

"No, I like your bed better," he sighs, grinning. "Why'd you wake up?"

"I don't know. I woke, stretched, and then realized how early it was," I tell him.

"Something bothering you?" he asks.

"Nope, just woke up." I give him a smile. "Want a blow job?"

"Don't even need to ask that shit," he says, pulling his boxers down to reveal his cock. I lick my lips. "But how about it's my turn." He gives me a wink. "Want me to eat you, baby?"

"Don't even need to ask that shit," I reply, repeating his words.

BLAKE

I am sleeping soundly with Cori spooned against me, when I am awakened by the thrashing of her arms and legs again.

"Please, don't make me do this. Please," Cori whimpers. "I've been good. I've been so good. Please."

I hold on to her tightly. "Cori, babe, please wake up.

"No, please, don't touch her. I'll do it. I will. Just leave Melissa alone," she says, sounding as if she's giving up.

"Cori!" I shout.

She bolts straight up in bed, wiping the sweat off her forehead. "I hate those dreams," she whispers.

"Talk to me. What was that?"

"Nothing, Blake. Please, just let it go. Don't worry about it."

I decide to let it go. We've come far in our relationship. This is something that, if I push, it might end badly.

I'm getting tired of her saying that shit—let it go. I carefully get out of bed once she's asleep and snag my phone.

Need you to call me. Cori's having dreams. They are fucking bad, man. She won't talk about them. I need answers. - B

Tossing my phone on top of my pants on the floor, I climb back into bed, wrapping my arms around Cori.

~

I get to my office and see Angel sitting at my desk. "What are you doing here?" I ask him, confused.

"I got your message last night. Made sure I was here by the time you got in. I have your info," he answers, nodding to the huge file in front of him.

I gulp, starting to sweat. "How bad is it?" I ask him.

His jaw clenches. "Bad, man. While you are looking this over, I'm going to stay right here, because I have a feeling I'll need to keep you calm."

Oh, shit. That doesn't sound good at all. I pull out my chair and take a seat, and he hesitantly hands over the folder.

I scan pictures—Cori bruised, Melissa's eyes dead. The last photo is of a baby. Confused, I look up at Angel. "Who's this?" I ask, pointing to the baby in the photo.

His nostrils flare. "Keep reading."

I flip over to the last page. 'Corinne Treyton claims while she was in this home, she was tied down and raped. An older boy, who was acting weird and sleepy, was forced into relations with her. This photo is the only thing she was allowed to keep of her child, who was quickly taken from her an hour after his birth.'

"What?" Corinne would have been only what—fifteen or sixteen?

Angel shakes his head. "After this happened, they tried to start focusing on Melissa. You were gone by this time, and that's when Cori reached out to a friend at school. That friend knew about us, and we went as soon as we could."

"Do we know anything about the baby?" I ask him.

"We tried getting him out, too, but they had documents claiming that they were that child's biological parents." Angel's face turns dark. "How often do you remember being drugged in that house?"

I rub my temples and lean forward. "Most weekends. They wouldn't drug us during the school week because they didn't want questions asked. But I don't remember anything that happened over the weekends. From the time I ate supper on Friday to Sunday afternoon, it's all a blank during the year I was there."

Angel clears his throat after a few moments of silence. "Reaper is tracking down every boy that lived in that house during that time. That means, man, including you, we're gonna need a DNA sample. Unfortunately, what we don't want Cori to know right now is that the child died."

"Fuck," I whisper out in torture. I wonder how possible it is for me to be the father of that child. "Do we know if they've done this before? Any of the kids housed there ever get pregnant besides Cori?"

Angel nods grimly. "Four more girls that we've managed to dig up have had children. We don't need you for those, because it seems that they only bred one girl at a time. You weren't in the house for those other girls." Angel tugs at his beard. "You are gonna have to talk with Cori, man. If you don't, I will have to, and that is one conversation that could push her to the breaking point."

"You said something about a DNA sample? How? You said yourself the child is dead."

He looks away for a moment before speaking. "We kept the blanket they wrapped that boy in when he was first delivered. It was the only thing they allowed Cori to keep, besides the photo. She had her friend, Chelsea, give her a Ziploc bag, and she put it in there. We have DNA from that."

"When can the tests be done?" I ask him.

"We can't get Moira do to this again, so we need to go to Thrane. He'll pull rank. Because of the club, and who Moira is married to, they are making sure she doesn't abuse the hospital for anything."

"Take it, then. I want to know. The minute you know, I need to know," I tell him.

DAWN MARTENS

CHAPTER 32

Cori

Blake was acting off all day at work, barely spoke to me. We decide to go home together since I let Melissa have my car today. The whole ride home, he's quiet. "Is something wrong?" I finally ask him.

He glances at me and turns back to the road. "No, why?"

"You've just seemed off all day."

"Just a case I'm working. It's stressing me out."

I don't say anything more, and we make it to our condo building in silence. He walks me to my door and gives me a kiss. "I'll talk to you later," he says abruptly, dismissing me.

I stare at his retreating back. "What the hell is going on, Blake?"

He stops and hangs his head down. "It's nothing, okay? We'll talk later."

I stamp my foot. "No, we'll talk about it now. What the hell is wrong?"

"Cori, just go in your condo. Get something to eat, a drink, whatever. I have shit to do right now, okay? I'll talk to you later," he tells me, still not turning around.

"You walk away from me right now, Blake, I won't talk to you later."

He shakes his head. "Cori, I'll talk with you in the morning."

He hits the button on the elevator.

He wants to act like a jackass and not talk to me, fine, but he won't be talking to me later, either. I open my door and slam it shut, locking it. Melissa and Chelsea are in the kitchen and come out.

"What's with the slamming?" Chelsea asks.

"Nothing," I grumble. "Blake is just being a turd today. I'm going to bed early. He comes by, tell him to get lost," I say, walking toward my room.

I close my bedroom door and dig my phone out of my purse.

"Hello?" Lilly's voice sounds on the other end.

"Hey, want some company this weekend?" I ask her.

"Yeah, sure, bring Melissa!" She hangs up quickly, saying that Rose is getting into her make up.

Chelsea comes in. "What's going on? You're in a pissy mood."

"Nothing. Blake was being a turd today."

"Wanna talk about it?" she asks.

"No," I grumble. "What I want to talk about, though, is where the heck you've been lately? What made you take off so fast the other night?"

Her face goes red. "I was just meeting up with someone."

I narrow my eyes at her. "Please tell me it's not Keller," I practically beg.

"Pfft, no. Hell no. Although, bad news is he moved to town. How much bullshit is that?"

"Okay, then, who were you with."

"Promise you won't get mad?" she says, chewing her bottom lip.

"As long as it's not Keller, I won't be."

"Randy." She says the name so fast I almost I almost miss it.

"Wait, Randy? Club owner Randy?"

She nods.

"That's great!" I say happily. "He always wanted more with me, and I always felt bad I couldn't do that with him. You're amazing. He's amazing. Best match ever."

Most people would get all weird about this kind of thing, but Randy has been more of a great friend to me than anything. I just want him to be happy, and Chelsea, well, she is great, so I know they will be awesome together.

Chelsea laughs. Just then, Melissa comes in.

"Melly, get packed. We're going to Airdrie for the weekend," I shout out my bedroom door.

"Woot! Awesome," she says.

I look to Chelsea. "Want to come with us?" I ask her.

"Nah, you guys go. Have a blast. Be nice to be alone for once," she jokes, laughing slightly.

Thirty minutes later, Melissa and I are packed and driving off.

On the drive up, we sing and eat snacks, having a good time naming off random baby names for her peanut.

I thought she was going to spew pop out her nose when I suggested Harriet for a girl. We made a game out of coming up with the worst names.

BLAKE

I should have talked to Cori. But I couldn't. This is something she seems to want to hide from me. I need to be patient with her, and let her come to me on her own. It sucks, because everything in me wants to shake her until she tells me everything.

I almost want to ask Marcy to talk to Cori to see if she'll open up to her and so she can try to convince her to talk to the counselor we have in the building.

A text comes through just when I'm about to call Marcy.

All set up here. How about your end? – Angel
Making the call now. – Blake

Normally, I would get Cori to make the call, but I don't want to talk to her right now. We need a break.

I call up the town office, but remember they close early on Fridays, so instead, I call up the Mayor at home, talking to him about the bake sale, asking for a location, and telling him it will be run by the Angels Warriors. Once I say that, he says I don't even need permission for that sort of thing and gives me the go ahead to get it going.

I lay in bed. Sleep seems to be taking forever for me to find, but finally, I drift off.

"The drugs are wearing off already?" a woman says.

"They are, but we can't give him more right now. We'll just have to get this over quickly," a man tells her.

Where the hell am I? I don't recognize this room, and I'm so fucking tired I can barely stand up.

"Get over here, boy," the man says sternly.

Arms grab at me, moving me forward. I then realize I'm naked, and my dick is hard. What the hell?

I squint around the room and see a small blonde girl tied to the bed. What?

"We need to give him another dose."

"Fuck. Okay, kid. Go get the case over on that table," the man says. Then the man comes at me with a needle.

I bolt up in bed. "What the hell was that?" I say out loud. I wipe the sweat from my face and lay back down. "Fucked up dream," I mutter to myself and get back to sleep.

CHAPTER 33

Cori

Melissa and I head to Airdrie for the weekend to hang out with the club and the women. I didn't bother telling Blake because, honestly, I need away from him since I'm pissed at him for last night. Years I've worked for him, by his side, a friendship, all of it, and now that we're together, it's still so crazy to me, and his aloofness last night, not wanting to be together or talk, has me worried.

We pull into the compound, and Angel comes out, grinning at us. "Hey, girls. Leave your stuff in the car. You can stay at Lilly's place this weekend. We have a full house this month."

We hang out for a bit at the clubhouse. Trevor comes in pissed off as fuck and walks straight to his room, slamming the door.

"What's up with that?" Melissa asks.

"He's just pissed off that Tori spends too much time with Scraper," Angel says.

Shoot, I'd be spending time with that man, too. He is FINE! He's huge, so damn huge. Plus, he makes Reaper and Angel look like choir boys. And he's bald, no hot man is bald, but yeah, he pulls it off. Just looking at Scraper makes my panties wet.

"Why haven't you picked a new name yet?" I ask Reaper.

He shrugs. "It puts fear into the bastards we help take down. May as well keep it."

"What about Scraper, then? You all said he's from the Untamed Angels. I think I can piece together what his name means," I say, wrinkling my nose.

"He's thinking of giving the nickname up all together. Just go by Anthony."

I shrug. Lame name for such a hottie.

"How are you and Blake doing?" Angel asks me.

I feel my face heat up and shake my head, not wanting to talk about it with him.

"It's good, then, I take it. Boy better treat you right. Otherwise, he's gonna see my fist," Reaper grumbles.

"So, uh," I start, wanting to change the subject. "Melissa's pregnant and all, so how come you haven't threatened the baby daddy?" I ask them.

Reaper tenses, and Angel glares at me. "What makes you think I haven't?"

"Oh," is all I say.

We all just talk about random things, and when we finish eating, we drive off to Lilly and Vinny's place.

~

The next morning, Melissa and I are helping Lilly get the girls cleaned up since they decided they wanted to wear their food instead of eat it.

I give Melissa a pointed look. "And you actually want to do this?"

She just smiles at me.

"Looks like my mom is taking the girls tonight, so we can do something fun," Lilly declares, coming into the bathroom.

Rose and Elizabeth run out of the bathroom, giggling. "They are your demon spawn. You can chase their naked asses down," I tell Lilly.

Melissa laughs. "I hope I have a little girl."

"You would," I tease. She snaps my butt with a towel. "Girls are drama and trouble."

"You'll change your mind one of these days," she says dreamily, rubbing her stomach.

I seriously doubt that.

I walk into the living room and flop down on the couch to watch a movie with the kids.

"They love the hell out of this freaking *Frozen* movie," Lilly tells me, rolling her eyes. "Trust me. That song will get stuck in your head, and you will be threatening to burn the DVD before you leave."

Lilly was not wrong. I want to trash this movie.

~

Half way through helping Lilly pack things up to send the girls to her mom's for the night, a knock comes at the door.

"I'll get it," Lilly says, already walking out of the room.

I zip up Elizabeth and Rose's bags and am carrying them out of the room when I hear yelling. I drop them and run.

"You need to leave! You are not welcome here."

"I will be here if I want to be. My son lives here, and so do my bastard grandchildren," some nasty lady says, sneering at Lilly.

"Actually, I haven't put Vinny's name on the deed to the house, so it's still just mine," Lilly points out, standing firm. "It also is a fact that your son has said many times, the last time six years ago when you tried to screw with us, that you were not welcomed in our lives."

I enter the room, wanting to help out Lilly, when the nasty bitch turns to me, fire burning in her eyes when she sees me. "Oh, look, another of Samuel's spawn," she spits out.

"What?" I ask her, confused.

She lets out a bark of laughter and looks to Lilly. "Oh, you didn't see this? She looks just like your father."

My face pales, and I turn to Lilly, who looks so upset I almost think she's going to pass out.

"Mom, what the fuck are you doing here?" Zippo says, coming into the house.

"I wanted to spend time with my son, of course, and those things," she says in disgust, motioning to the girls.

"No, you didn't. Let me guess. You ran out of money? No, wait. I know what it is. Bryce called. He's taking you to court. Seems like you are in a shit load of trouble for taking his trust fund," Zippo says with a nasty grimace on his face.

"Well, okay, I was coming to you for money, but it seems another opportunity has presented itself to me," she says, looking at me with a grin.

"Why do you keep looking at me like that, and will someone tell me who the hell Samuel is?" I demand.

"Oh, this is so great. You didn't know? Really, truly didn't? You and Lilly are sisters. Isn't it obvious?"

"What?" I whisper out. There is no way. If Lilly and I are sisters, there is no way in hell she or Mona would have let me live the way I did, right?

"Oh, God," Lilly chokes out.

"No, she's wrong, right? Lilly, tell me she's wrong!" I plead with her.

Lilly looks at me, tears in her eyes, looking at me in a completely new light. "It can't be," she whispers.

"Get out. Now!" Zippo roars at his mother.

"Fine. Don't come crawling to me when you need something."

"Trust me. I never would," he sneers at her.

The front door slams shut. Lilly and I are still staring at each other—shock, tears, everything. "Please, tell me you didn't know," I beg her.

"We don't know anything for sure, Cori," Zippo says gently. "Should we call him? Have a meeting or something?"

"If you are my sister, oh my God, what you went through... I could have helped sooner," Lilly chokes out.

I back away slowly, and Zippo rushes to me and grips on my waist, pulling me tight to him. "It will be okay, Cori. We'll talk to Sam, find out the truth."

If this is true, how come it took that evil woman to notice it? Why didn't anyone else? I feel as if my heart was just ripped out of my chest. They knew. They had to know. I run from the room, Lilly and Zippo both calling after me, and go into the guest room. Slamming the door shut, I lock it and fall to the floor, tears running down my face. Fuck them all.

No one ever really wanted me.

Not my mother or my father, whoever he is or was…

BLAKE

I haven't heard from Cori since Friday after work, and I'm worried. This is the first time since we've been together that we haven't talked at least once a day. The last four months have been amazing. Fuck. She's the perfect woman in every way. I leave my condo and make my way down to hers, knocking on the door. On the second attempt, Chelsea opens it, looking like she just woke up. I know I need to apologize for what happened Friday night, but I didn't think it would take this long for me to get over the shit going through my head. And I thought she'd at least come to me.

"Uh, hey? What's up?" she asks.

"Where's Cori?"

Her head rears back in shock. "Uh, she didn't tell you?"

I shake my head.

"She's in Airdrie for the weekend, visiting the club."

"Thanks," I say, storming off. Why the hell didn't she tell me?

Just before I get to the elevator to go back up to my place, my phone rings. Zippo's name flashing on the screen. "Yeah?"

"Shit just went down. Need you here. Cori needs all the support she can get." He hangs up. Fucking vague asshole.

I walk back to Cori's condo and knock, again getting Chelsea. "Get packed. Something has happened. You're coming with me to Cori," I tell her and go to my place for my own bag.

We both meet in the lobby, not saying a word as we get into my car. "Do we know what we'll be walking into?" Chelsea finally asks after driving for a half an hour.

"I wasn't told, just to get there as fast as possible. Cori needs me."

"I hope everything is okay. At least I can tell her about the letters. If she's already gotten bad news, may as well get it all out."

"What letters?" I ask her.

She sighs. "For the last three weeks, every day, a letter addressed to Cori arrives. Same as before, when we were in college and she got them, so I knew what they were and just took them before she knew about them."

"Spit it out, woman!" I say, getting impatient.

"Her mother is writing her again," she says after a moment of silence. "The last time, it was bad. The letters only happened for about a week before the woman showed up, trying to cause all kinds of hell for Cori and Melissa. It took Jasper and Mason giving her some money to finally get her to go and stay gone. I'm thinking the bitch ran out."

I grip the steering wheel, knuckles going white. I don't say anything; nothing needs to be said, not right now. I pull into Zippo's drive and shut off the car. "Wait," I call to Chelsea as she starts to get out. "Don't tell her. Not right now."

She says nothing, just nods.

Zippo meets us on his front step, looking like a mix between anger and upset. "What's going on?"

"My mother was here," he spits out. "Caused her usual drama. She took one look at Cori, and shit just hit the fan."

I narrow my eyes at him. "And?"

"She said that Cori is Sam's daughter."

"What the fuck?" I know Sam, not well, but I know him through the guys. He's always seemed like a good man—a flighty man, but good. I also know he recently divorced from Angel's mother.

"Cori locked herself in the guest room. We can't get in, and she won't come out. Lilly's on the phone with her dad right now. He's saying he'll be down this evening. Melissa took the kids out. She's over with Moira and Eden. Angel and Reaper will be here soon."

"I'll go try to get in," Chelsea says, stepping around us.

"If this is true, how did no one know?"

"That's exactly what Cori said. I don't even fuckin' know how we missed this. All those years together, with her and Melissa, and just now, everything is coming out that we knew their fathers. Fathers that would have made sure those girls were taken care of."

"I've been around Lilly many times, though, even Sam, and I never put it together myself." I rub the back of my neck, feeling frustrated.

The sound of bikes coming down the street gives me some relief.

Angel and Reaper get off their bikes, and both look a bit angry. "I'll fuckin' kill her for doing this," Reaper growls out to Zippo.

"Get in line, brother," Angel says.

"Let's move this inside, try to talk to Cori. Right now, she's angry, thinks we knew. She was crying in the room, screaming at us from in there, saying how we let her rot in that house. Fuck," Zippo says.

Fuck is right. After all the shit Cori has been through with her mother, this has to be shredding her.

DAWN MARTENS

CHAPTER 34

Cori

Everyone finally gets me out of the room, but I don't look at any of them. I know they keep saying they didn't know, but how could they not? I don't get it.

Blake is here. I see him the second I hit the living room and go to him instantly, settling on his lap, my face in his neck. I feel so safe and secure in his arms, like nothing bad will ever touch me when I am with him. He is a good guy. I just wish I knew why he was being so weird the other day.

"Babe, it will be okay."

Blake leans away from me to whisper something to Chelsea. She nods and goes to Vinny. He does that stupid chin lift that drives me nuts when men do it, and takes off with her.

"Where are they going?" I ask.

"Just getting something to eat." He shifts me a bit and looks at me, holding my face in his hands. "You wanna tell me why you didn't tell me you were coming here for the weekend?" he asks.

I chew my bottom lip. "I just wanted a little time away," I explain quietly.

"Could have had that, too. I just didn't like that I didn't hear from you. Didn't know where you were. Pissed me off."

"Sorry, Blake."

He kisses my forehead as a response.

"Where's Melly?" I ask Lilly.

"The second she heard Vinny's mom, she took the girls into their room, and once she left and you locked yourself away, she went over to hang with Eden and Moira," she answers.

"I'm sorry for snapping at you, Lilly," I apologize, feeling like a jerk for my reaction. It took me off guard. I wasn't expecting to hear those words. Blake tenses, and he gives me a soft squeeze.

She shakes her head. "Nothing to be sorry for. I'm just so damn sorry I never saw it. God, Cori, if I had known, you never would have went through that shit. Ever. I would have taken you in, even took Melissa, too. I would have done everything I could have."

"I know," I tell her, my eyes welling up with tears. Lilly would have been the best sister ever. She has always been so good with Melly and me. But I don't want to dwell on what might have been. The past can't be changed.

We all talk a bit. Jasper and Mason both still look extremely tense when Chelsea and Vinny come back, arms loaded up with tons of takeout bags from Dairy Queen.

"Oh, what did you get?" I ask excitedly.

Vinny winks at me and pulls out a basket of poutine.

"Oh, God, have I told you I loved you lately?"

"Yeah, Cori, but I still like to hear it," he teases, giving me a smile.

"Can you eat all that?" Blake asks me.

"Uh, no, not even close, but it doesn't mean I don't try." A basket of poutine can easily feed two to three people, but I always get it. He grabs a fork and digs into the basket with me.

Doesn't take long for everyone to finish eating, and then there is a knock on the door. "That's probably Dad," Lilly announces, getting up to open the door. Her face is pale. I think she is uneasy.

I get nervous. I always thought Lilly looked like her mom; maybe that's why no one really put it together that we could be related. Sam walks in the room, looking around hesitantly, until finally, his eyes land on me. He flinches, staggering a bit.

He runs a hand over his face, and I look at him, really look at him. My eyes, my hair color, my chin... Good God.

"What's your name?" he asks me, coming closer.

"Corinne Treyton," I tell him.

"That whore," he curses, looking away.

Blake gets up, leaving me sitting on the couch with Lilly, her arms wrapped around me. Blake walks over to the guys and Chelsea, giving us a slight bit of privacy, but not much.

Sam grabs the chair across the room and drags it over, sitting down directly in front of Lilly and I.

"Your mother, her name?"

"Luanne."

"I was with her twenty-three years ago. I wasn't the greatest man back then. I was only with her twice. Hell, the condom even broke the last time with her, and she promised nothing would come of it. I should have checked in, anyways. I didn't."

"So it's true?" Lilly asks.

"Truth is, I was with her mother twice. We won't know anything for sure without a DNA test, but looking at her, Lil, it's right there. She looks just like Gramma Patty when she was younger," he admits, resolved in the truth of our shared eyes.

Lilly's arms convulse around me.

"I'm sorry, Corinne. If I had known... Fuck. When the boys got you out of that shithole, I was their lawyer on the case. I didn't even think of anything except helping them get you and your sister out."

"You didn't know," I assure him.

"It doesn't matter," he snaps. "I was a shitty ass father to both my girls. What kind of man does that make me? Thirty-three years later, and I'm still a shitty ass father."

"Daddy," Lilly whispers, clutching his hand.

"I throw money at you four times a year, bought you this house. Anything you wanted, I gave it. I just didn't give you me. Done that shit for years. I wasn't a father, Lilly, and you know it. Then I find out, after twenty-three years, that I have another one. The hell she grew up in, I let that shit happen. This shit is on me."

BLAKE

Taking in the scene on the couch, I watch Cori and Lilly cry together, Sam losing it. I want to go over, but right now, they need this.

Angel, Reaper, Chelsea, and Zippo are all just standing around with me, watching them and taking it all in.

"You remember Phil?" Sam asks Lilly.

"Yeah, the Lawyer Hilary was working with here in town." She scrunches her brows, appearing confused for a moment.

"He wants to retire. I'm taking over. I'm moving back to town," he clarifies. "I know, Corinne, that you don't live here, but you aren't much further away. I want to prove I can be a better father, a good father, learn about you girls, really actually do this father thing right. I know it's thirty-three and twenty-three years too late, but I need to do this."

"But, Dad, what about your practise?" Lilly asks.

"When Jasper's mom left me, saying I was too devoted to my work and that I was ruthless, I took a look at my life, and the other partners bought me out. I fucked shit up with Vincent's mom." Zippo gets tense at the mention of his mother. "I fucked everything up with Ann. Should have put a ring on her finger, but I didn't want that life back then."

I watch Lilly react to what he's saying. "Wait a minute," she says, gleaming, her eyes lighting up. "Are you saying you love Mom? And you want her?"

"It's doubtful that will happen, Lilly. It's been too long."

"Yeah, but maybe she'd stop hooking up with losers," Lilly mutters. Sam goes stiff at the mention of Ann with other men.

Twisted Up In You

"The point is, I need to be here. This is where my family is, my kids and my grandkids, so this is where I need to be," he states.

"Okay, Dad."

"Everyone calls me Cori. Corinne is such an old fashioned name," my girl declares. I smile, knowing he just got the green light to go ahead and get to know her.

Maybe this is something that Cori needs to help her to open up. Maybe she can finally break free from her past and her mother.

187

CHAPTER 35

Cori

A week passes, and everything is back to normal. Finding out about my father was hard. Learning Lilly is my sister, though, that was the best part of it all. Although, it was rough. Blake and Chelsea, along with Melissa, ended up going home, and I spent the rest of the night and all day Sunday with Lilly. And we just talked. She shared with me about growing up with a father like Sam. Told me I didn't really miss much. But she was upset because she felt that she could have saved me from my hell.

I texted Blake last night, letting him know I would be late today, since I'm going with Melissa to her ultrasound appointment. Melissa keeps getting calls and texts from Monster but refuses to talk with him. She's still pissed about him dismissing her after she finally screwed him, and then him being a dick when she told him she was pregnant.

But now, I think she's taking it too far, so behind her back, I texted him and told him about the appointment today. He said he'll be there, so we'll see how Melissa handles it.

Sitting in the waiting room, Melissa starts complaining. "I have to pee so badly."

"Just wait. You'll be in soon."

I spot Monster walking into the office, and I quickly look to Melissa, who is reading her magazine. "Um, Melissa," I say hesitantly. I am not sure how she is going to react. She needs to see if he can be the man she needs. She owes it to her baby to give him a chance. People make mistakes all the time, but it doesn't mean they will always be that way. I would have never dreamt Blake and I would have actually gotten together like we have.

"Yeah," she answers, not looking up.

"Um, Dray is here."

"What?" she says, looking up, and her eyes find him. "Shit. How did he know?"

"I'm sorry, Melissa, but I told him. He's the father. He should be here," I tell her gently.

"It's fine. It will be fine. Whatever," she concedes, still staring at Dray.

"Cori. Melissa," Dray cautions, finally coming to us.

I give him a small smile, and he takes the seat next to Melissa. "I'm sorry for being a dick, Melissa," he apologizes honestly. "I want to be here for you, the baby. For us," he claims, sounding hopeful.

I can't see Melissa's face, but I think she's crying because Dray's big hand moves to her face, wiping at it.

"I want us to be together. I want to try. Please, let me make it up to you?"

"Okay," Melissa whispers tearfully.

Dray is holding her hand tight, like he never wants to let go. So sweet. I hope I don't have to kill him someday. I do like him, even if he is an ass. He comes off all tough and big, but deep down, the guy is a soft teddy bear. I saw him once downtown, holding an old lady's hand as he helped her cross the street. No badass would ever do that.

Seems like drama is over. Minutes later, Melissa is called back into the room. Hopefully, we'll be able to find out what she's having.

BLAKE

Adam barges into my office with a huge grin. "What's up?"

"Bad news first. Untamed Angels and Cop Mercer's dealings have nothing to do with our case. Something different. We don't need to know that shit. So the bad news is, we have no idea how these idiots keep getting away with shit. Good news is, we were able to shut them down!"

"Are you serious? Finally!" I say happily.

"More good news is, all of the old foster children are speaking out against them. Angels Warriors, along with a few officers, arrested the couple this morning. Judge set bail, and an hour later, the brother bonded them out. So the bad news is, they are back on the street until the New Year, which is when this shit goes to trial. But still good news, they can't hurt any more kids."

"Fuck, man, this is awesome."

Sort of. The guys still need to finish up searching for stuff concerning Cori. That part of the case won't be closed until something comes up.

I hear the ding of the elevator, and Cori steps out with a huge grin on her face. "Why are you so happy?" she asks.

"Closed a hard case today is all. What about you?" I ask, seeing her eyes shining bright.

"Melissa is having a girl! Oh, and Dray got his head out of his ass, and they are working at being together! Best day ever, it seems," she declares.

She doesn't even know how her words ring true. It's better than she could probably dream of.

I smile at her. I want to tell her the news about today, but I'm reminded about how much her life was shit when she lived in that home, so I put it aside.

I pull her to me and kiss her, hard.

"That's amazing. Congrats to Melissa." I smile at her.

"Yeah, it's great. I can't wait to buy her all the most annoying toys in the world. Although, it's gonna be weird having a baby around the house. I already told Melissa I'll never change a diaper." I smirk at her.

I go to tell her she'll be an amazing mother one day when Adam comes into the office.

"Hey, need you in the conference room. Marcy just had a kid come in for his shots, and suspicious bruising was on his arms. She wants you to take a look and talk to the kid while I talk to the parents."

Cori stills in my arms.

I sigh and kiss Cori on the forehead. "Can you grab the recorder? I'll need you to record everything while I talk to the kid."

She nods and follows me out.

CHAPTER 36

Cori

Listening to the little boy the other day, while he talked about what life was like at home, was hard. Blake's face was angry, but he had to wash it away for the kid. He whispered to me and told me to call the police. Work was not boring that day. Adam was even punched in the face by the kid's father. Both parents were arrested, and Johnny, the boy, was placed with a good family, a family that Blake and Adam approved of. I hope those two never get out of prison.

I'm in the kitchen, getting some baking done for the bake sale coming up next week, when someone starts pounding on my door. I'm not the greatest baker, but I can do the few things Melissa asked me to make. I put the mixing bowl down and wipe my hands.

Peeking through the peephole, I'm stunned. I don't want to answer it. On the other side of this door is my mother. I grab my phone quickly, texting Jasper.

She's here. - C

Do not open that door, Cori. - J

I have to. She's still banging. - C

Let her do it. I just called Blake. He'll be there soon. – J

I'm opening the door now. – C

Do.Not.Open.That.Door. – J

I toss my phone to the couch and open it, facing her.

"Mom," I say.

She sneers at me, looking me over. "'Bout time you answered."

"I was busy. Sorry."

She walks in and looks around my place. "Fancy. Looks like you have money now."

"Not really, I work as an assistant."

"Yeah, word is you help out on cases concerning little brats like you were."

My phone pings nonstop with incoming texts. Mom just stares at me. She looks and smells as if she hasn't showered in days. She's fat. How is she fat? All she does is drugs and drink. I don't get it. Maybe the drugs make her get the munchies? Her light blonde hair is still natural, but I notice she has bald spots on her scalp.

"What are you doing here?"

"I came to see my kids. Why else would I be here?"

"You don't even like us," I state the obvious.

"Got that right, but you're my kids," she says with a shrug.

"Why didn't you ever tell us about who our dads were?" I ask her, really needing to know this.

"They aren't worth shit. That's why."

"Did you know Melissa's dad is the president of the Untamed Angels?"

Her face pales, shock written all over her. "No, that's not true. His name was Carson."

"So you knew. And, yeah, Carson, that's him. Goes by Hangman now."

"Does he know?" she asks urgently.

"No, but everyone else does, so I bet he'll find out soon. I also found out who my father is, and that I have another sister."

"Let's go back to Melissa's father," she says, panicking. "If he finds out, he'll kill me."

I brush her off, because from what I've heard, there is a big chance that will happen. "No, let's get to mine. I'm sure Hangman, or Carson, will deal with you eventually." Her face pales, and she quickly washes it away with a scowl.

"Your father was scum. He was nothing."

"He's actually the best damn lawyer in the country, so I beg to differ," I tell her. She looks at me in shock again.

I'm not sure if it's because I'm somewhat standing up to her, or because she realizes that Melissa and I both know who our fathers are.

Then her face goes back to her sneer. "Doesn't matter about any of that now, anyways. You're my girls, my daughters. You're nothing. Scum. Like mother, like daughters."

Melissa walks in, followed by Chelsea, both girls laughing over something. Melissa's face pales when she see's Mom.

"Mom, what are you doing here?" she demands.

"See, what'd I say?" Mom says, throwing her hands out at Melissa. "Scum, nothing, forever and ever, nothing. I bet you don't even know who the father is."

Melly bursts into tears, and I want to slap our bitch of a mother. But I can't. My feet freeze. I am back to being that little girl again who wants nothing more than her mother's love and approval. I just wanted to be good enough for her.

BLAKE

I get calls and texts from Angel, telling me to get to Cori's condo immediately because her mother is there. I rush over as fast as I can, calling Drew to come over as well. Figure I may need him. I pull up to the building and see his car already here.

"What are we walking into exactly?" he asks.

I give him the run down, and he follows me up, telling me he actually has an arrest warrant for her so this is his lucky day.

We step off the elevator and hear screaming. Chelsea.

"You mother fucking cock sucking bitch! How can you treat them this way, huh? You're their mother! And you make them feel like scum! You, woman, you are scum! That's all on you. Fucking crack head junkie whore!" Chelsea screams, but she isn't done. "You made them suffer

194

for years, you stupid cow. I hope like fuck Hangman finds out he had a kid by you, because I would love to see your insides strewn around town."

"Shit," Drew says, moving fast to the door.

I swing the door open, and it bangs off the wall. Cori and Melissa are just staring down at the floor, arms wrapped around themselves, tears streaming down their faces.

I look to the woman Chelsea is facing off with. I'm thankful neither one of her daughters looks like her—worn down, hair falling out, too damn fat.

"You Luanne Treyton?" Drew asks from behind me.

She puts her hands on her hips and throws attitude. "Who's asking?" she snaps out.

"RCMP," Drew growls.

Luanne's face pales, and she looks away.

"Yeah, she is," Chelsea speaks up.

I go to Cori, wrapping her in my arms. "It's okay, baby. She can't do shit to hurt you. Not ever again. I promise."

I hear the cuffs being placed and Drew reading her rights, when she finally speaks up. "My slutty bitch of a daughter got herself a hot shot? Well, you should know she ain't nothing special. Get out before she ruins your life like she did mine."

"Shut the fuck up, woman," Drew growls. He marches her out of the condo as I'm holding on to Cori.

Chelsea wraps up Melissa.

"I don't get it. I'm good with everyone else. She shows up, and I'm so fucking stupid I can barely speak with her. Why can't I stand up to her? I started to, and then I couldn't," Cori says, her voice sounding dead. "I just wanted her to love me. Melly too. She never accepted us or showed us anything but hate, and still, here I am, hoping she would be proud of the women we've become."

"This is my fault," Chelsea speaks up.

"What? How's it your fault?" Cori asks her.

195

"You were getting letters again. I took them, hid them. If I had just told you, you could have been better prepared or something."

Cori shakes her head. "No, you did the right thing. Thank you."

"What did they say?" Melissa says, finally speaking.

"The usual. Give me money or I'll show up. Shit like that. It's always shit like that," Chelsea explains.

"I told her about our fathers," Cori says. "She was terrified when I said Melissa's father is the president of the Untamed Angels. She didn't seem to know that."

"I'd be scared, too, if I found that shit out. Have you heard of those guys?" Chelsea says. "It's all over the news, all the damn time, about how they keep finding bodies and shit. Cops say it's the Untamed, but there is never evidence so nothing ever happens."

"Well, shit," Cori breathes.

"How about we finish up the baking, and I take you out?" I say, stepping into their downer conversation.

"That sounds perfect," Cori says, sounding relieved.

CHAPTER 37

Cori

A week after that terrible face down with my mom, things are finally getting back to normal. I'm now wondering about Blake's mom. He said she gave him up after his dad died, but he didn't say anything else after that about her, just about the family he tried to find that wanted to adopt him.

I'm bored today, so I'm swiveling around in my chair at my desk when Blake comes out of his office, looking amused.

I stop spinning and grin at him. "What? I was bored."

He shakes his head. "Well, now you can get un-bored." He hands me a few files. "Close those and file them. Then come in my office."

I give him the look, the look I always give him when I want it, and he shakes his head at me and just tells me to hurry.

I do what he asks quickly. I make sure no one is staring as I scurry into his office, and then make sure the blinds are closed this time. Blake loosens his tie, his hungry eyes devouring me as I begin taking my dress off after locking the door.

"We keep this up, you are going to need a new couch in here before long," I tease.

"You complaining?" He cocks his brow at me, undoing his cuffs.

"Never." I smirk, stepping out of my dress. We meet at the couch, crashing together full of want and need.

His lips are latched to mine as he explores my clit with his thick fingers.

The phone on his desk rings.

"Ignore it," I demand.

"I want to, but I can't." He licks my bottom lip and picks the phone up from the receiver. "Blake here."

Saddling up next to him, I go down on my knees. His eyes go wide as I take him in my mouth. "Sounds good." He groans, hanging up quickly.

"You don't play fair."

BLAKE

I'm watching Cori getting dressed when she asks the question I didn't want to answer before. The question I've been waiting for that has never come.

"What happened to your mom?"

Sighing, I sit in my chair, and she comes close.

"You don't have to tell me. I just wanted to know."

"She's living in Chilliwack with her family. Husband is a doctor, and she has three kids. Two girls, one boy."

"What? You can't be serious."

"I am. Once I learned that, I stopped wanting to know anything else. Seems she got remarried three years after she got rid of me."

"What a fucking bitch!" Cori explodes. "You need to confront her. Her new stupid ass family needs to learn about the bitch she really is."

"No, Cori, just leave it alone."

"What's her name?!"

"Cori."

"What. Is. Her. Name?!" she shouts at me.

I rub the back of my neck and relent. "Fuck, Cori, don't do anything, okay? It's Linda. Happy now?"

"Yes, yes, I am. Thank you," she says curtly.

She leans over to me, hands on my shoulders, and gives me a kiss.

"Thank you for telling me. She doesn't know what she's missing out on, how amazing you are."

"Have you talked to your dad recently?" I ask her, changing the subject.

She perks up. "A bit. Mostly, we do three-way calling—me, him, and Lilly. Plus, you should see my bank account. He's going crazy. I talked to Lilly about the money, and she said it's the same amount she's received from him so far, too."

I raise my eyebrows. "How much money are we talking about here?" I ask her with a grin.

"Nope, I'm not telling you. I won't become your sugar baby," she says sarcastically.

I kiss her forehead, and she pulls away, looking at me oddly. "What?" I ask her.

"Well, Dad emailed me last night, and um, the weird thing is that he sent me house listings. I called Lilly about it, and she said it's his thing. Apparently, he even bought Lilly a house when she turned eighteen, and he seems to want to do the same for me," she says, looking a bit put off by it.

I don't want him buying her a house, because when I can manage it, I want us to buy a house together. For now, she needs to stay in her condo.

"Don't worry about it. He's just trying to make up for lost time and all that," I tell her.

"You're probably right." She sighs and goes to the door. "I should get back to work. I wouldn't want my boss to catch me away from my desk." She throws me a wink and saunters out.

Great. Now I want her again.

CHAPTER 38

Cori

When I leave Blake's office, I'm still feeling angry about his bitch of a mother. I know he was trying to change the subject, so I let him, but still not letting go of the shit he told me about her. I get that she lost her husband, but giving up a child, and then a few years later remarrying and having more kids without even bothering to find the child she gave up? I want to wring her damn neck.

I walk to Adam's office and don't bother knocking. He looks up, shocked at seeing me, probably because it's rare I ever actually come to see him.

"What can I do for you?" he asks.

"Linda Lexington. She's married now. Don't know that name. But you are to find me everything you can. Mailing address preferred," I request.

He gives a slow blink and stares at me. "Blake know about this?"

"Nope, and you're not going to tell him either."

"And why wouldn't I?"

"Because I'll stop trying to tell Clara to hold off on filing the divorce papers, and I'll root for her doing it," I threaten.

He sits up straight in his chair, looking at me. "She didn't file yet?"

I shake my head. "I told her to hold off a bit, make sure it's what she really truly wants first. But you tell Blake that shit, I'll make sure she knows my opinions on it has changed."

He swallows visibly and nods. "I'll find what I can."

Twisted Up In You

I smile sweetly at him. "You're so awesome, and here I was pissed at you because you're a moron... Thanks, Adam."

"Wait. You were pissed at me?" he asks, looking put off.

"Well, of course. What you did to Clara? Not cool, dude. Not even a little bit," I say.

He looks at me in shock. "She told you?"

I nod. "Yep, about everything, including how you wouldn't choose between her and her sister. Shit move, buddy, but the choice was obvious. Your wife. Always first. Forever and always."

"Fuck," Adam mutters. "It's not what she thinks. I couldn't make that choice in front of the kid. Plus, shit started happening again, bad shit, and I couldn't abandon Sophie."

"Too bad so sad. You made your bed. I think it was dicky of you, but whatever. If I didn't like you so much, I would be shouting at her to move on to Preston and make beautiful babies with him. But hopefully, you'll fix your shit soon. Now, back to my thing," I say, changing the subject.

"Yeah, I'll do it. Don't worry. But, just so you know, if Blake finds out, he'll be pissed," he warns.

I wave him off. "Let me worry about that."

He shakes his head at me, and I watch him walk down the hall, staring longingly at Clara.

I hope the two of them can work their shit out or move on. They need to give in to each other or get closure. It isn't healthy walking around with all that stuff hanging over a person.

BLAKE

I watch Cori talk with Adam, and at first, I think she might be going behind my back, but when I open the door

201

quietly, I hear her talking about him and Clara. Happy to know she isn't disrespecting my wishes, I shut the door and go back to work.

I see Adam is no longer talking to Cori, so I buzz her phone. "What's up, handsome?" she asks, answering.

I smile. "Need you to run down to all the floors. Need all of their statements for everything," I tell her.

"Righty-o, boss man." She clicks off, and I watch her leave. Tax season isn't for four months, but I always make every floor send me up all their numbers and shit once a month so I can make sure everything is running properly. Adam is in charge of getting their rent, and I look over numbers they bring in to see what can be a write-off and what can't.

Cori brings everything up about forty minutes later. I don't bother looking at her because I know, if I do, I'll take her again.

Two hours later, my phone lights up, and I hit the speaker button. "Yeah?"

"I'm heading out now, babe. I'm starved. Want me to pick you up something?" Cori asks.

I look at the clock and realize it's an hour past closing. "Wait for me. We'll go out."

"Okie dokie," Cori says, sounding perky.

~

We end up a Chinese buffet, and Cori loads her plate with the basic stuff—chicken balls and fried rice. "That's it? We're in a Chinese place. You don't want anything else?" I ask her.

She wrinkles her nose. "Eww to everything else. This shit right here," she says, showing me her plate, "is the only good Chinese food."

I shake my head, and we eat, talking randomly about shit. She tells me what she learned about Adam and Clara. To say I'm shocked is an understatement. Hell, Adam threw me when it came out that he and Clara were married. We've been friends for years, and I never knew.

Cori gets a call, and she rolls her eyes. "What?" she answers. "I'm out. Eating supper with Blake." Pauses. "Dragon City." Pause. "Fine." She hangs up.

"Who was that?" I ask.

"Melissa. She has a craving," Cori says, smirking. "It's starting to drive me nuts. The other night, she made me get out of bed at two am to get her pickles," she says with a shake of her head.

"No, you didn't," I state. She was with me all night.

She smirks. "You were asleep. I left and came back, and you were still passed out."

"That's weird. Normally, I wake up easily."

"Well, as you said, my bed is the best ever."

She gives me a wink, and we finish up. After ordering take out for Melissa, we head home.

CHAPTER 39

Cori

Adam came through for me. The following week after I asked him for Blake's bitch mom's information, he handed it over. Told me to really think about it first, though, because if Blake finds out, he'll be livid. I just shrugged at him because, after it happens, I don't know.

Blake can find out all he wants. I just need to do this first before he knows.

Linda,

You don't know me, but I'm writing this in hopes you open your damn eyes and get with the program. You lost your husband, gave up your newborn baby, and didn't even think twice about him once you had your new family. What kind of mother does that make you? I bet your kids and husband don't even know about Blake, do they?

I'll have you know, Blake is the best man in the world. He's a social worker, saves children from all over, and even works very closely with the Angels Warriors.

You have no idea what you gave up when you left your son to rot in the system. Thank God he's a better person then you ever were.

> *Cori, the woman so totally in love with your son*

I never said that to Blake yet, but I know it; I feel the love I have for him, and it kind of scares me a bit. I write down Blake's numbers and his address, hoping something comes from this.

I finish typing it out and print it off, sealing it in the envelope in my drawer, stamping it, and writing her address on the front. I see Marcy coming off the elevator, and I rush to her before Blake knows she's here.

"I need you to run that down to the mail box right away."

Marcy looks at me then the envelope and back to me, her eyes guarded. "Be back," she mutters.

"Was that Marcy?" Blake startles me.

"Yeah, she came up but then forgot something. She'll be back," I lie.

He stares at me, and the way he's looking at me, it's as if he knows. I kiss him quickly, because his stare is going to make me blurt out the stupid thing I just did.

I pull away and stare at him. "How about a quickie?"

He groans, shoving his face into my neck. "As much as I'd love that right now, I'm swamped with work. We just got another case we need to work on, and Marcy just came back up."

I smile, pulling away from. "Rain check then." I sigh.

He nods and walks away.

"What was that about?" Marcy asks.

"He was looking at me weird, so instead of blabbing about what I did, I tried to see if he'd go for a quickie."

Marcy bursts out laughing. "You're a nut. I just hope what you just did doesn't get found out. Blake will have a shit fit."

Nine days later, Blake had a shit fit.

BLAKE

Cori has been acting weird the last few days. Every time I've asked what's up, she panics and just starts rambling. Even Adam has been avoiding me lately.

I shake it off when my cell rings. It's a number I don't recognize. "Blake."

"Is this Blake Lexington?" a gruff voice asks me.

"Yes, can I ask who's calling?"

"Jaris Morena." I still when he answers; that's the name of the man my mother married.

"What can I do for you?" I ask, my voice gone cold.

"I didn't know. She never told me," he says, his voice cracking. "When we met, I knew she was a widow but she said she never had kids. It's what I always believed. I got this letter in the mail two days ago, addressed to Linda, and I opened it. I shouldn't have, but I did. Your girlfriend, Cori, wrote to her, telling her off, and I couldn't believe it, so I had you looked into. And it's true."

I clench my jaw shut, glaring out my office window at Cori. I told her to leave it the fuck alone. She sees my look through the window and looks away quickly.

"If I had known, I would have gotten you... or something. I didn't think she was that type of person," he continues to speak, not giving me room to say anything. "I've spoken with her. Right after I found the proof, I spoke with her. The kids overheard us as they were over for supper. They want to meet you, away from Linda. Linda, even faced with the truth, won't admit to knowing you or having you."

Fuck. That hurts. I go to talk, but he keeps on going.

"You have a brother. He just turned eighteen, name is Kevin. Your sisters are twenty-three, twins. Both are married. Lorraine is expecting her first child, and Layla has a four month old." He's telling me the names of my siblings. Shit.

Finally, I get my chance to speak. "Thank you for calling me. I have to be honest, I didn't know my girl was going to do this, and I'm pissed as hell at her for it, too. I told her to leave it alone. But if my brother and sisters want to meet up at some point, I'm all for it."

"Good, son. Good. I hope to meet you at some point, as well. Even if Linda doesn't, I would like to," he tells me.

"That would be nice."

We talk for a few more minutes, my anger at Cori still simmering at the top when I let him go. I sit for a few moments after clicking my phone off, wanting to make sure I don't completely lose it.

Twisted Up In You

CHAPTER 40

Cori

Uh oh. Going by the look Blake just gave me, I think he knows. What else could it be? I brace when he walks out of his office and stands on the other side of my desk. "In my office. Now," he growls at me.

I rub my lips together and quietly follow him. The second I make it past the door, he slams it shut.

"Why? Why would you go and write my mother a damn letter? I told you to leave it the fuck alone!" he shouts at me.

"I know! Okay, I know, and I get it—it was wrong. I get that. Promise I do, but Blake, she needed to know what she gave up! I wanted to make her hurt!" I shout back at him.

He stares at me in silence. "What you did, though, Cori, has just ruined her marriage. And her other children are pissed at her."

"That's not my problem. That's hers!" I snap at him.

"What don't you get? You say you get it, but you really don't. I am happy with my life now. She was happy in her life. You just ruined it all. Now, I have a step-dad that wants to meet me, siblings and kids that want to meet me. And still… a mother who is still denying she ever had a son before my twin sisters were born." I gulp at his words.

"I'm sorry, Blake," I whisper, tears forming. "I just wanted to make her hurt, sorry, something. I care about you so much, and she just abandoned you and moved on with her life, and that pissed me off."

We stare at each other for a few moments before he moves, pulling me in for a hug. "Fuck, Cori, I'm still pissed you did that, but I understand why you did. Hell, I got after your mother for pulling shit on you," he says, his face in my hair. I let out a sob. "Stop crying," he demands.

I jerk back and glare at him. "You can't tell someone to just stop crying. Crying stops when it's ready to stop."

He looks at me, amused. "I just did, and you stopped."

"Yeah, except now I'm annoyed."

"Then stop doing that, too." I only stop because he kisses me.

His arms are around me, and it feels so right. I don't know how I got so lucky with him, but I am so glad I did. After all the dates I have planned for him and the flowers I sent on his behalf to other women, I never thought I would be his. We just fit together. He's mine, and I am his. I sometimes feel scared by how strongly I feel for him. He has become such a part of me, and I don't ever want to let him go. I don't want to lose the feeling of home I get when I am with him, but things never stay good in my life.

I have this nagging feeling in the back of my mind that something will come between us and bring everything crashing down.

BLAKE

I love how much fire Cori has in her. I am still pissed she went behind my back, but it's really sweet that she went through the trouble. Guess I know why Adam is avoiding me. That fucker had to have aided her.

"Let me make it up to you," she stresses, undoing my zipper and stroking my length.

"You drive me wild."

I grip the back of her neck, clamping my lips to hers. Her sweet tongue caresses mine as she continues to test my limits.

My pants fall around my ankles, along with my boxers. Turning Cori around and shoving her skirt up, I shove her face down across my desk and slide in from behind.

"Gotta be quick. I have a meeting in a twenty minutes."

"Sure thing. The girls are coming to take me to lunch." She wiggles her ass, and I thrust deep and hard.

I let go inside of her when my office door flings open, and Melissa and Chelsea are there, now suddenly closing their eyes. "Oh my God. I so did not want to see that."

"Get out," I bark at them. Melissa practically runs out of the room.

"Can I look? Because I just saw your ass, and damn, boy," Chelsea says through a smirk.

"Get out, Chelsea!" Cori shrieks at her.

Once the door is shut, I start laughing, which causes Cori to slap at me. "It's not funny, Blake! They just saw us, post awesome, and your ass."

"Babe, it was funny. Next time, we need to remember to lock the door."

Cori growls at me as she gets dressed. I just smile.

"You go hang out with your girls. I need to chat with Adam and Marcy."

Her eyes go wide. "Don't. Please don't. They told me shit would backfire on me, tried talking me out of it. Please don't be mad at them," she begs.

"They still should have told me so I wasn't blindsided. What's done is done, but once you sent that letter, they should have said something." She goes to argue, but I cut her off. "Nothing you say will change my mind, Cori."

"Fine."

I grab her, pulling her in for a kiss. "I'll see you at home tonight."

"Okay," she whispers.

She walks out but quickly comes back not even a second later. "Oh, be home by seven. We're going out on a double date tonight with Melissa and Monster," she says and takes off.

Twisted Up In You

CHAPTER 41

Cori

Melissa and I finish getting ready for our double date. Things seemed to change for her after Blake's confrontation with Dray, and he's around a lot now, trying hard to get on Melissa's good side. They seem to be doing okay, and tonight, they invited Blake and me out with them.

Melissa is wearing a simple red flowy dress that hugs her just right and shows off the baby bump she's sporting. When I look at her, it hurts. Sometimes, I think about telling Blake about the baby I wasn't allowed to keep, but I don't want him to look at me in disgust. I've often thought about asking Jasper to look into it, but decided against it, because honestly, what kind of mother would I make?

I'm sure, wherever my child is right now, he or she is having a much better life than I could ever give.

I pull on my new dress I picked up from Suzy Shier. It's simple but a bit long, obviously, since I'm so short. I swear, that store only has tall people in mind for their clothes, but it hugs me perfectly.

We end up going to one of those kiddie places with games where you earn tickets to buy shitty plastic prizes, but we have the best time. Dray and Blake are competing at shooting hoops, while Melly and I play something simpler—Skeeball. I don't win many tickets, but Blake doesn't let me down, earning enough to get me a giant panda bear. Melly is pouting because Dray only earned enough for a smaller snake. He keeps teasing her, saying she can't handle his anaconda.

He is being super sweet and attentive with her, keeps rubbing her belly, pulling out her chair and opening doors for her. After we have had our fill of games, we share a large pizza and a pitcher of Sprite. Normally, we would have ordered beer or something, but with Melly and her baby, we didn't want to make her sulk more.

I pull Blake into the photo booth, and we make out like teens as the camera snaps our photograph. I love that I can be as silly and goofy as I want with Blake, and he matches me being just as goofy. I've never felt this comfortable just being me with any of the guys I have messed around with. I like this feeling a lot. I hope I can keep it… and him. We just feel right.

BLAKE

Our double date goes well. Melissa ended up going home with Dray afterwards. I spoke with Adam and Marcy after Cori left the office. Marcy was first, and all she did was give me lip, saying her loyalties were with Cori. Betraying bitch.

I let it go and went to Adam. He told me about the blackmail, saying Cori would be cheering Clara on with the divorce if he didn't help her. At first, I was pissed off all over again, but then I got over it once I saw what Cori was wearing tonight.

"Can we go out?" Cori says, sitting next to me in my car.

"Where? We were just out."

"I know, but we are always either at home or work together. I want to go out—dance, drink. Something."

"Sure, that sounds fine. Where do you want to go?" I ask her. I'm hoping she'll pick Randy's club, especially since I know that Stacy is banned from that place. I haven't heard from her since the mess at the office months ago, and I want to keep it that way.

"Randy's club. I get free drinks there, good stuff, plus—VIP section."

I nod. "Should we invite anyone out with us?" I ask her.

She gives me a hungry look. "Nope."

I adjust my pants and debate if we should just go home instead.

~

Randy comes over to us after I drag a highly drunk Cori off the dance floor, and he smiles at us. "You okay to drive?" he asks me.

"Yeah, man, I only had two beers when we first got here. Time to take her home before she barfs on your floor," I tell him.

He gives his head a shake and chuckles. "Nice to see you two together," he says and stalks off.

"Come on, drunky. Let's get you home," I say to Cori, holding her tight against me.

"You're so handsome, Blakey poo," she slurs.

"You're pretty adorable when you're drunk. Hopefully you won't be miserable at the bake sale tomorrow," I say to her.

She yawns and wrinkles her nose. "I almost forgot about that."

I get her into my car, and she instantly passes out. Arriving to her place, I call up to Griggs, the night doorman, to help me out so I can carry her upstairs.

I lay her on the bed and tuck her in.

CHAPTER 42

Cori

I wake up with a hangover from hell and groan. I check the time and panic. "Shit!" I yell and then clutch my head. Holy fuck! That hurt.

"What?" Blake asks, bolting straight up beside me.

"It's ten. We're late," I say, throwing the blankets off me and running to my dresser to put clothes on.

Both Blake and I make it out the door twenty minutes later, neither one of us taking a shower, just loading up on deodorant.

We make it to the event and run past everyone. I spot Zippo and Trevor standing ahead of the crowd. Melissa and Chelsea are both passing out baked goods while taking money. Shit, they look swamped; taking money is supposed to be my job.

"I'm so sorry. We over slept," I say, out of breath.

Melissa smirks. "All good, sis."

I stand behind the cash box and start doing my job. Blake is at Chelsea's table, helping her with cash.

A little boy, who looks about three, and his mom come up to the table, and he smiles at me. "You're pwetty," he tells me.

I smile. "Thank you."

"Will you be my giwlfwiend?" He can't say Rs, and it's adorable.

"I would, little guy, but I'm already taken," I tell him softly.

He frowns. "Can I at wease hab a kiss?"

I laugh, and his mother looks embarrassed. Before she tells him no or takes him away, I come around the table and bend down to his level. I tap my cheek.

He leans in, kissing me sloppily, and backs away, face beaming brightly.

"Hey, you stealing my girl, kid?" Blake asks teasingly to the little boy.

"She's pwetty," he declares.

"Yeah, I suppose she is," Blake says, winking at me.

"Okay, Ryder, time to go. Say goodbye."

They walk off, and Blake pulls me in for a kiss. "Gee, even hungover, you've got people swooning over you," he tells me with a chuckle.

I laugh. "Get back to work," I say, pushing him playfully off me.

"Yes boss." He mock salutes me.

~

Today was such a good day. The club made over ten grand just at the Red Deer bake sale alone for the families they are helping. Of course, not all of that was baked goods, but also because some of the club members offered rides to the public. People loved that idea.

I curl into Blake. I'm so happy, so damn happy. Everything over the last seven months has been absolutely amazing. I love him, and I need to tell him that. So I do.

"Blake?"

"Yeah, babe?"

He looks at me, and for a moment, I want to chicken out and say something else, like 'go get me food' or something, but I don't. I face this fear. "I love you. I'm so in love with you," I say quietly as tears well up in my eyes.

"Fuck, Cori, I love you so fucking much, too."

BLAKE

I push Cori on her back when I see the tears in her eyes after telling me she loves me. Fuck, I love those words.

Twisted Up In You

Her gaze holds mine; she has me hooked. I can't imagine my life without her in it. She is so perfect for me. I want to frame this moment forever in my heart. Her hair spills over the pillow, framing her face, and she looks heaven sent. Leaning forward on my elbows, I plant kisses along her jaw, wanting to show her just how much she means to me. She is so damn sexy in nothing but her panties.

My hands roam over her curves, touching and teasing her. She is soft and warm, everything a woman should be and more. Her fingers stroke my hair gently as I kiss my way down her stomach and slide her panties down her toned legs.

She squirms, ready for some lovin'.

"Gonna lick you from head to toe," I warn and promise. I want to taste her sweet essence on my tongue.

Not wasting any time, I fulfill my promise. I suck on her clit and finger her tight channel. She is so damn juicy and excited. I love it. Her hips buck, and her back arches up off the bed as she surrenders to her passion.

"I want you to come riding my face," I tell her.

I trade her places as she gets into position, grinding her slick heat on my tongue. Perfection.

I snake my arms around her front and rub on her clit, knowing she is on the verge of ecstasy.

She surprises me, leaning forward and taking my erection in her mouth and sucking me hard.

"Let's finish this together," she whispers.

Fuck yes, let's.

She cups my balls, massaging them, as her tongue glides up and down my shaft in a circular motion.

The pressure begins to build, and I can't stop when I shoot down her throat. Cori caps her mouth over my cock and takes it all. I press harder on her clit, and she tightens over my mouth, shattering into a million pieces.

"Damn, woman, that was..."

"Wonderful," she finishes for me breathlessly.

I hold her in my arms, enjoying our closeness.

"I love you, but I gotta go brush my teeth," she teases, getting up from the warmth of our embrace.

I can only shake my head at her. She is so funny about sex sometimes.

CHAPTER 43

Cori

Blake and I have been together for eight months. Tonight, we decided to go out to celebrate us. It's not a year or anything, but eight months together is a pretty damn good thing to celebrate. He took me out to The Keg, the place we had our first date, and then we walked around downtown, again redoing our very first date.

It's been the best evening ever. Blake breaks from kissing my neck as we walk into my room, when he says something that causes me to have a mini panic attack.

"God, Cori, I love you so damn much. I can't wait until my ring is on your finger, my children in your belly."

His words cause me to stiffen. "What?" I whisper.

He pulls back. "What do you think this is?" he asks, staring into my eyes.

I shake my head. "I don't want kids, Blake," I tell him, feeling as if my throat is closing on me.

He steps away from me, his face pale. "You don't want kids?"

I shake my head.

"Never?" he asks me.

"Never, Blake," I confirm stonily.

He turns around, placing his hands on my dresser. "You're positive? Nothing will ever change your mind?"

"I'm positive." I could never bring children into this world, not with how I was raised. I would never bring a child into my messed up life. I would be a horrible mother. How can I ever have any more children after my own child was torn away from me when I was just a child myself? I can't do that.

"This changes everything," he concedes, brokenly. "I want kids, Corinne," he says when he turns around to face me. "I've always wanted a few of them."

"I'm sorry, Blake," I whisper, knowing this is the end of us.

"Adoption?" he asks, sounding somewhat hopeful.

I shake my head no. "None."

"What does this mean for us, then?" Blake asks me.

I gulp. I'm gonna be sick. I don't want to lose Blake, ever. But I can't do this. "I'm sorry," I say on a sob. He wants children, but I can't give him children. I can't go through that again.

He comes around my counter, pulling me into his arms, his face going into my neck. "I love you, Corinne. I'll always love you. But I can't sacrifice this." He kisses me softly.

This is it, the end of us. Forever and always. Finished.

BLAKE

I leave Cori's condo upset. It takes everything in me to keep from going back, shaking the fuck out of her, and telling her too bad so sad. I want forever with Corinne. I want children with her. I know she never did tell me about the child that was taken from her, the one Angel told me about, and since it's such a hard thing to bring up, I decided against it. But it's been years. I know that Angel and the guys are still working hard to look into the Mercers and the little boy that Cori had, but so far, just dead ends.

I get back to my condo, and I feel like punching the fucking wall. But I can't because the buyers might back out if they see the damage. Everything is fucked now. I had plans to move in with Cori. We were basically already living together, and now it's all screwed.

I just lost my girl. I'm losing the condo. What's next? Fuck!

I call up Adam and ask him if he'd like some company, and he tells me to come on over. I make it there quickly and walk in.

"Hey, man, what's up?" Adam asks, seeing my solemn face when I walk in.

"Cori and I just broke up," I tell him brokenly.

His face turns to shock. "What? Why?"

"I need a drink," I say, moving to his living room and throwing myself onto his couch.

He brings in a bottle of Whiskey and a glass, setting them on the coffee table in front of me. "Okay, now tell me what the hell happened."

"She doesn't want kids," I tell him.

He frowns. "But, she's already had one."

"Doesn't matter. She said she doesn't want any, ever. I told her I did, and it was something I couldn't compromise with her on."

"Shit, man. Why don't you just talk to her about what you know, about her kid?"

"I'm not pushing shit on her. You know her, Adam. If she's not ready to talk about something, she won't budge on it."

"Yeah, but with this, you should just do it. Fuck, Blake. Something like this, you have to fucking talk."

That pisses me off. "Look who's talking. You're the dick that's losing his wife because you wouldn't fucking talk to her." I sneer at him.

His face goes blank. "I've tried, though. At least it's better than giving up like you are doing."

"Fuck you, Adam. You've given up. I also heard the entire story of how much of a cunt you were to your own wife. I hope Clara files those papers." I shouldn't have said it. Fuck. Why am I being a dick right now?

"Whatever, Blake. Finish the bottle. Puke your guts out. Crash on my couch. Hopefully tomorrow you won't be such a tool." He stalks off, and I hear him slam his bedroom door shut.

CHAPTER 44

Cori

Work has been awkward. Blake barely speaks to me, but sometimes, I catch him staring at me out his window. I want to talk to him, something, but I can't, because I am not changing my stance right now about what he wants. I will get married, we can do that and be happy, but I don't want more children. I can't do that.

When Blake does talk to me, it's reserved, and he only talks to me about filing this or getting coffee. Now, on day four, I've had enough, and I've started looking to find another job. Melissa is finishing up her nursing degree, and since she's about two days away from her due date, she's thankful that she doesn't have to delay getting her degree.

I print out my resume, hoping like hell Blake will give me a good reference. Then I think differently of it, so I put Marcy's name on references, followed by Jasper, Mason, and Vinny's. If anyone is a good reference, it will be the Angels Warriors.

I hear the elevator ding and look up, seeing Marcy walk toward me, scowling.

I go to say hi, but she puts her hand up to stop me. "Don't talk to me. I can't believe how stupid you are being about this. Blake loves you. He stopped fucking everything skanky for you. He wanted a life with you, and I know you want that, too. So what's the problem? You don't want kids? Bullshit. I think it was just your way of pushing Blake away. Well, congrats. You've done it. I never thought you were a selfish bitch before, but I know now I was wrong."

Her words cut through me. She casts me one last glare and walks away, back to the elevator.

My phone rings at my desk, and I pick it up. "Hello? Lexington, Blake Lexington's office, Cori speaking. How may I help you," I answer.

"Hey, it's me," I hear Clara say.

"Hey, where are you?" I ask her.

"Listen, um, I'm not coming in. Think you could do me a favor, and after Adam leaves work tonight, can you pack my things up for me?" she asks.

"Um, yeah, sure. What's going on?"

"I'm done. I filed the papers. It's over. I'll call you next week, let you know when I can grab my things from you. Thanks, Cori." She clicks off, and I put the phone back down.

I work quietly at my desk for a few hours, and as I'm about to pack in for the night, the elevator dings open and my dad walks in. "Hey, Cori," he says to me.

"Hey, Dad. What's up?" I ask him.

He holds up an envelope and looks grim. "Need to see Adam."

"Oh dear," I breathe out.

"Yeah," he mutters.

He walks off down the hall to Adam's office and knocks. "Sorry to do this, kid." He hands Adam the brown envelope and waits while Adam opens it up.

"She did it?" he whispers, upset.

He moves into the office, slamming his door shut. I hear him smash a few things, and lots of banging.

"What's going on?" Blake asks, coming out of his office.

My dad speaks up. "His divorce is finalized," he says, sounding upset for him.

"Shit," Blake mutters.

"Cori? You done for the day?" Dad asks me.

"Yeah, was just about to head out," I tell him.

"Good," he says with a smile. "Come have supper with me."

I smile. "Okay."

We walk out of the office to the sounds of Adam tearing his office apart.

BLAKE

I leave work with Adam and Marcy. Both are having life issues like I am. Clara didn't show up for work today; instead, Sam did, giving him papers declaring the divorce was finalized. Adam had a shit fit in his office and broke down crying. I found Marcy in the break room earlier crying; I guess her girlfriend was cheating on her, so they broke up.

We're a bunch of sad idiots tonight, so we're going out to a bar I used to frequent before I started dating Cori. We grab a seat in a booth along the back wall and pile in. A server comes over, and we order a pitcher of beer and some wings.

"Have you talked to Cori at all?" Marcy asks, breaking our silence.

I shake my head no.

"She needs the stick out of her ass," she complains.

"It's not what you think, Marcy," I defend.

She raises a brow. "How isn't it? She only said no to kids because she just wanted a reason to push you away, and look at you—you're letting her do it."

"That's not it. Cori already had a kid," I blurt out. Shit, everyone is finding this shit out now, and Cori doesn't know we all know.

"What?" she mouths.

I fill her in, telling her about the foster care and her mother, but she waves me off as I start those topics as she already knows. Cori already told her. So I get right to the part about her baby. Marcy starts crying.

"I was such a bitch to her today. I'm going to have to apologize."

Silence engulfs us again as we drink, and as I'm about to order another pitcher, I see her. Shit.

"Blake!" Stacy squeals when she sees me.

Marcy glares at her, and Adam looks annoyed.

"I haven't seen you in forever. I heard that you were dating that skanky whore Cori, and I couldn't believe it. But here you are, not with her anymore. I knew you couldn't be that stupid," she says in her whiny ass voice.

"Listen here, bitch. Cori is my best friend. They are fine, happy. We're just having a guy's night out. Now leave before I punch you in your fake ass tit," Marcy growls at her.

Her mouth drops in shock. For the first time, she is speechless. She huffs and puffs, trying to find her words, failing miserably. Adam shakes his head with laughter. Marcy is still scowling at her.

"Why are you still standing here? Shoo! Go away." Marcy swats at her like a fly.

"Blake?" Stacy whines, still not moving away.

"Did you not hear what she said? Go away," I say without even glancing her way.

"Fine!" she says, stomping her foot and walking away.

CHAPTER 45

Cori

Another week passes, and work just keeps getting more and more awkward. The worst part is that he left me a note on my desk this morning, asking me to send a flower shipment to some woman. Fucking dick is moving on, and it's only been two weeks. How could he do this?

My cell phone rings as I finish the online flower order, and I grab it. "Hello?"

"Is this Corinne Treyton?" a man asks.

"Yes, it is. How can I help you?"

"I'm calling from Ashley's House, and I wanted to call you personally to offer you a position here." Ashley's House is basically a shelter for women and children. I applied there last week.

"Are you serious? Yes. I would love that," I tell him excitedly. The sooner I get away from Blake, the better. I'll be able to move on without having to see his handsome face every single day.

"Can you start in two weeks?"

"Yes, and I'm sorry, but I didn't catch your name."

"Sorry about that," he chuckles. "Name's Ashley."

"Wait. What? That's a girl's name." I hear him burst out laughing. "Oh, I'm so sorry. That was mean."

"Don't worry about it," he says, a smile in his voice. "Looking forward to meeting you in person." He clicks off, and I smile.

I slip a note under Blake's door, letting him know I'm off for lunch, and meet Marcy down in the lobby. She called me the other night, apologizing for what she said. I told her it was fine, so we're moving on from it.

I smile when I see her. "What's got you so happy? Blake and you finally talk?" she asks, sounding hopeful.

"No, I got the position I applied for at Ashley's House in Devon."

"What?" she whispers.

"They didn't call you? I thought they would. I listed you as a reference."

"No, they did, but I didn't think you'd really go through with this."

"I need to leave, Marcy. You have to understand that.
"

"I do, but this is shit. First, Clara leaves, and now you. I need to kick Adam and Blake's asses."

Clara left us a week ago. I have talked to her since, and apparently, she was going to work it out with Adam, went to his house to chat, but her sister opened the door. She was hurt, and that same day, she took the signed papers to the courthouse and had them filed. Now, they are officially divorced. She said she can't be pining away after a man that can't choose her.

I feel for her. It sucks, but last night, she called saying she got a job working in Airdrie as a receptionist for my dad. I think it's kind of cool, not totally losing her.

It sucks, but we are all moving on with our lives. I will miss working for Blake, but I can't be around him and not be with him. It hurts too damn much. And my sister is so freaking happy all the time now that her and Dray are solid and starting their family.

Chelsea spends most of her time with Randy. It's kind of cool how fast those two are moving with their relationship, but I'm happy because they both deserve it. Chelsea does after being with stupid ass Keller for so long, and Randy for having me string him along.

"If you leave, Cori, I'm going, too," Marcy declares.

"Don't," I say, shaking my head. "You love this job. Don't leave because of me."

She shakes her head at me. "Come on. Let's go eat," she grumbles.

BLAKE

Cori comes back from lunch looking different. The flowers I got her to order were for my sisters, but she doesn't know that. I was hoping for a reaction out of her, letting me know she still cares at least, but she gave nothing away.

The phone on my desk rings, and I answer. "Blake here."

"It's Angel. We need to talk."

"What time? I'm open all today."

"I'll be there in about twenty. I'm in town already." He clicks off, and I put the phone back on the desk.

I walk out to where Cori is and smile sadly. Ever since we broke up last week, it's been weird between us. I'm scared to lose her completely, especially since I know she's been looking into getting a new job. I might have lost her in my bed and my life, but I refuse to be without her altogether, even when we both finally move on.

I miss her—the softness of her curves, her snarky comments, all of it. But I want a family, and she doesn't. I understand why she doesn't, but that shouldn't stop her from moving on with her life and starting over, forgetting about her past.

"Cori, Angel will be here soon. Please let him come right in my office," I say. Without waiting for her to reply, I walk back in my office. I want to say more. I want to shake her and tell her I love her.

Fifteen minutes later, Angel walks into my office, frowning at me. "What'd you do to her?" he demands.

Sighing, I rub the back of my neck. "We broke up."

Angel clenches his jaw. "Why?" he barks at me.

Twisted Up In You

I tell him about what happened, how and why we broke up, and his face softens. "Maybe, after today, you'll get her back."

I sit forward in my chair with hopeful eyes. "What do you have for me?"

"Bad news, man. We found the body of the baby Cori had," Angel says gruffly. "They fuckin'... Fuck! They buried that child in their family plot east of town. Even threw in a picture of the kids' father and Cori."

"You're shitting me," I whisper.

"Fuck, man, no. Of course, Reaper loves a little grave digging every now and then, dug the body up." Angel holds a file up.

"What's this?"

"The results of the DNA test, also a picture. Fuck, man. I'm sorry to tell you this, but the baby that Cori had was yours." He tosses a file on my desk, but I don't reach for it. I sit back in my chair, stunned.

"What the fuck? How is this possible?" I know the possibility was there when we first talked about this, considering the drugging and the reports from others that once lived there. But for this to happen to me, and to Cori, I just can't believe it.

"I'm gonna have to bring Cori in on this, man. Sorry, but she needs to know everything. Zippo has surveillance on the place, and we have more than enough to raid it and get every single kid out and to lock those fuckers up." He opens the file he tossed on my desk and flips a few pages. "We also have statements from all past foster children that lived in that house. They are all willing to come forward and testify against them."

"Fuck," I mutter. I press the button on my phone. "Cori, get in here."

"I'll call in some others, even Melissa. You go over the case with her, but wait until I'm back to talk about the baby." Angel gets up and walks out of the room with his phone.

Cori comes in, looking confused. "What's up?"

"That case I've been working on? The one I closed?" She nods. She doesn't know what family, though. I never told her. "We found more intel on them."

She smiles brightly. "That's great."

"There's something you need to know, though."

"Uh oh, that doesn't sound good," she states, frowning.

"It's not. This house is the one you were saved from." Her body stills, and tears form in her eyes.

"Finally," she breathes. "I need to tell Melissa."

"Wait. Angel will be back in a few, and there is more, but I can't tell you yet."

CHAPTER 46

Cori

I'm not liking this. Blake's face doesn't look right. I've never seen him look like this before. Something is seriously wrong. I take a seat in one of the chairs by his desk and fidget. I'm worried about what more is going on.

Not long after I sit, the door opens, and Angel, followed by Lilly, Zippo, Reaper, T-bags, and Melissa come in. Melissa looks confused as to why she's here.

"Melissa, go sit with your sister. We have something to share with you both," Angel says to us gently.

She comes to me instantly and stands by me, arm on my shoulder. Lilly comes over, too. The rest of the guys have grim looks on their faces.

"First, the family you stayed with, your old foster family, are being brought down. Tonight. We're going in hard," Angel starts. "Second," Angel looks to me, eyes boring into mine, "we found your child."

The room feels as if it's closing in on me, and I can't breathe. This is something I didn't tell Blake. I put my head down, not wanting this to get out, not after we broke up because I told him I didn't want kids.

"Breathe, Corinne. It will be okay," Melissa says, tears clogging her throat.

"More news… Now, this is going to be hard because we only recently learned of this, but it needs to get out before we tell you the worst part. The child you had, we know who the father of the baby is."

My head snaps up. "What?"

Angel hands me an old picture, so I look at it, confused at first, but then I remember. I knew him. I remember him. I also knew how completely high he was, too. The entire time, he was apologizing for doing this, for hurting me in this way. I look more closely at the picture... The eyes, they are familiar. I've seen these before, after the time in that hell house.

I look up, staring at Blake. Oh, shit. The same eyes.

"Blake here was in that home while you were there. However, he never knew girls even lived there. And, as you know, you thought the same thing about the boys until we raided and got you out."

I nod my head. I was shocked to learn there were boys in that house the day we got taken out of the basement and put into the main house. But, then again, I wasn't at the same time, considering they found boys to rape us girls all the time.

"Blake was the father of your child, Cori," Angel says gently.

"No, that can't be. How? What?" I stutter.

"He was drugged. He had no clue what was happening. Now, he does." At least he doesn't have the God awful memories like I do.

I don't... I can't. Oh my God. I will be getting my child back. "Wait, you said was. What does that mean?" My heart sinks.

Angel's face falls for just a moment. "Did you know what you had?"

I shake my head no. "They wouldn't tell me. They wouldn't let me know. They just kept the baby wrapped up in that blanket I kept." Tears fall from my face, and I finally look Blake's way. His face is pale, and he looks just as shocked as I do. "He was my first," I blurt out.

That shocks Blake out of his stillness. It probably wasn't the time for that admission, but it just came out. I forcefully lost my virginity to Blake. And now, here we were, together—well, sort of.

"Cori, there were other boys in that house at that time. You can't know for sure that Blake was the one," Reaper says from his spot in the office.

"No, I do. I wasn't drugged. It was always the same boy they put me with. I knew he was out of it, but at the same time, he kept telling me he was sorry. He couldn't help what he was doing. That much I do know."

The room tenses at this revelation. It's something I didn't tell them when they saved me.

"You had a son, Corinne," Angel says quietly. He comes close, kneels at my feet, and takes my hands in his. "There's more."

I frown. "What? What more could there be? I want to get my son back."

Angel looks at our hands, and I notice the room is deathly quiet, except for a few sobs I hear coming from Melissa. "Your son, Cori sweetie, is dead," he says so quietly I almost miss it.

BLAKE

I watch her fall apart in front of me, Melissa hanging on to her. I want to reach out and hold her myself. Hearing that I was her first… Fuck. It killed me. She remembers me. Hearing about everything has me remembering the nightmares I've been having lately. But I thought they were just that, nightmares. Now, I know they were, but they were also real life nightmares, too.

I had a kid, a kid with Cori. That kills, hugely. We could have so much together. Maybe now that this is all out in the open finally, maybe I can win her back, be what she needs. Maybe I can finally get her in with the counselor downstairs.

I hear Melissa groan. "You okay?" I ask her. I know she's due anytime now.

"Yeah, just been getting twinges of pain all day. It's fine." She waves me off.

"You sure you're not in labor?" Angel asks her.

"Nope, I'm fine," Melissa says.

Angel backs off. I turn to him. "What are we going to do about this?"

"We were able to get the trial moved up. This will be presented as evidence, too. Sam is going to help us out with things. He's got a few friends that are judges around the area, so this trial will most likely be fast-tracked."

I nod.

"Melissa, why don't you and Cori go on home," Angel suggests to her gently.

"Yeah, that's a good idea."

CHAPTER 47

Cori

I walk out of the building in a daze. My son is dead. Hearing Angel say that my son died of SIDS made me not believe him, but they had an autopsy report done, so at least I know those terrible people didn't hurt my child.

And on top of that, Blake. It's like our whole lives were twisted up in each other's.

"Uh, Cori," Melissa says urgently from beside me.

"What?" I mutter.

"My water broke," she states.

"Oh, shit." I grab her arm, rushing her to the car. "Please, do not have the baby in this car. Keep it in," I tell her.

"Yeah, sure, I'll try," she says, clenching her teeth. "Oh, God," she moans in pain.

I grab my phone and hit speaker once it starts calling. "Yeah."

"Get to the hospital. I'm on my way now. Melissa's in labor," I tell him.

"Shit! Okay, be there soon!" He hangs up, and I race off, hoping to get to the hospital before she ruins the car.

~

"She's so beautiful." Melissa says, tears running down her face as she holds her daughter. She looks up at me and smiles. "Want to hold her?"

I shake my head no.

Melissa frowns. "She's your niece."

Dray stares at me when I look away from my sister, and frowns.

"I'll hold her," Chelsea pipes up.

I can't be here. Without a word, I grab my purse from the chair and take off. Dray shouts for me as I run down the hall, but I don't stop. I can't be here. I can't see that.

BLAKE

I go to follow Cori out of the building, but Angel stops me. "We need a chat," he stresses, looking pissed at me with his jaw clenching. Angel is a tough fucker, and I have never wanted to be on the receiving end of his anger. I once watched him beat the shit out of a man who danced with Eden at a club. It was a beating I doubt the man will ever forget.

"What I need to do is go talk to Cori."

Angel hangs his head down. "I should have gotten her help when she lived with us. The reason she doesn't want kids is because of her son being taken from her," he confides in me.

"I think I got that," I mutter.

"Well, it's all out now. Only thing left to do is finally move on." Reaper comes forward with a file. "What's this?" Angel asks.

"Just found out how the Mercers were able to get away with this shit for so damn long."

"Their cousin is a social worker. Shit. She's the one that kept getting the cases. How'd she do this, though? She's family. She wouldn't have been allowed," Angel says.

"Different last name, and she never told anyone she was related to them. But Zippo was able to figure it out. Had a check done on the woman," Reaper says. "Also, before Wayne Mercer's father died, he was a highly respected Judge in these parts. That family has a lot of friends. The one and only time a warrant was ever issued to search their house was when we pulled rank on it. Everything otherwise was thrown out before anything was ever brought to light because of all of this."

"Well, shit. What happens now? We have a brother and a cousin helping to cover this shit up, and judges," I say.

Zippo speaks up. "We gave that shit to Drew, and he's getting warrants now. Lyle Mercer was fired this morning, and Candy Smith was as well. Both can't be found. They ended up taking off, but they won't be able to hide long. Anthony is searching for them, while Trevor is searching for their buddies."

"I'm gonna go see if I can talk to Cori," I tell them. I want to help them more with this case, but Cori needs me right now.

Angel nods. "Make her listen to you. Don't let her go, Blake," he tells me sternly.

"I'll do my best," I say and stalk off.

I get home and change before going down to Cori's condo. As I'm about to leave, a soft knock comes to the door. Thinking it's Cori coming to me, I open it, feeling relieved. What I see instead has my anger bursting at the seams.

"What do you want?" I sneer at her.

"Can we talk?"

"Oh, about what? The fact that you gave me up and had other children, and didn't give a shit about me?"

"Blake, please. I never meant for any of this to happen. I wanted you to have a better life than the one I would have given you. I wanted to heal," my mother says.

"No, what you wanted was to forget I existed," I tell her. "Because of you, I grew up in some of the worst foster homes, abused, starved, raped. It's why I do what I do now. Your husband called me, by the way. Told me I have siblings, the children you actually did care about."

"Blake, honey, I do care about you. I always have," she pleads with me.

I shake my head. "Nope, not true. Even when presented with evidence, you still denied it all. Get away from me. Stay away from me. My step-dad and my siblings want to get to know me, and you know what? I'll gladly have them be a part of my life. But not you. Never you." With that, I slam the door in her face and listen as her footsteps walk away from my door.

I rub my face. "What a fucking day," I mutter to myself.

CHAPTER 48

Cori

I'm on shot six when Randy comes over and sits next to me. "Hey there, big guy. Wanna go into your office?" I slur.

"No, and you don't either," he says.

I snort. "Yeah, I do, actually. Need to drink and fuck away my problems right now."

"Chelsea told me everything, Cori. You need to talk to someone," he chides, leaning close to me.

"Nope. I really don't." He leans in closer, and I grab the back of his head, pulling him in for a kiss. He pulls away almost instantly.

He shakes his head at me and holds my hands in front of me. "Stop this, Cori. You know I've been seeing Chelsea. Don't do this to your friend. I also know how madly in love with Blake you are."

"Oh, fuck you." I sneer at him. "You don't know shit. You don't know what it was like being tied down and raped by someone who couldn't stop it even if he tried. You don't know what it's like having your child taken away from you, and then years later, finding out the child died. You don't know shit!" I scream at him.

His face softens. "No, Cori, I don't, but self-destructing like this? Don't do it. You'll only hurt yourself more in the end."

"Whatever."

"Not whatever. Why are you even here? Didn't Melissa just have her baby?"

I nod. "Yeah, saw her born then I left. Couldn't be there."

Seeing her have what was taken from me, and what I will never get back, was too fucking hard. Melissa understands that I can't be there right now. As much as I want to, it isn't a good idea. I can't be around her and Dray, all happy and smiling over their daughter. I'll never get to hold my son and know what that feels like. Neither will Blake, unless he meets someone who will give him everything that I can't. Part of me hopes he does, but another part of me dies at the thought.

Randy looks at me with sympathy. "Cori, why don't you go home and sleep this off," he suggests.

I shake my head. "No, I need a little more courage, and then I'm going to do something I should have done a long time ago," I tell him cryptically.

"Don't do anything stupid," he warns.

"Oh, fuck you."

"You want to get shit faced, great, but not here. I hate seeing you like this."

"What is your problem, man? Huh? Chelsea turned you into a pussy, but don't worry, she'll break you soon enough. If Keller comes sniffing around again, she'll be back with him faster than you can say her name." I sneer. Shit, I'm a shitty friend right now.

"I'm going to let that go, considering how drunk and upset you are, but I'm not letting you stay here. Let me get you a cab." He tries pulling at my arm, and I shove him over, watching as he falls back into the chair.

"Don't touch me. I fucking hate you!" I shout at him and storm out of his club.

No one gets what I'm going through. I can't do this. It hurts so fucking bad. My anger continues to boil.

BLAKE

I'm pacing my office. I went to Cori's place after I was sure my mother left the building, but no one was there, so I figured I can help out in some way by being here, hoping to accomplish something. Anything.

"You need to fix whatever mess is going on," Marcy declares, walking into my office.

"I'm trying, okay. We just got hit hard with bad news shit. Give it some time."

"We don't have time, you idiot! She's leaving, Blake. She got a position in Devon at Ashley's House. She starts in just over a week, and if you don't stop it from happening, I will leave, too," she snarls at me. She leaves my office, slamming the door shut behind her.

"Fuck!" I yell, throwing the phone on my desk across the room.

I grab my cell and try calling Cori, but only get her voice mail. "Cori, fuck! You get this, you call me!" I shout into the phone. I try calling Melissa, and her phone is turned off. I try Chelsea, and she finally answers.

"Hey, where is Cori?" I ask her.

"She went out," she says in a hushed voice. "I'm not supposed to be on the phone right now. The nurses are giving me the stink eye."

"Nurses? Where are you?" I ask her, worried.

"Hospital. Melissa just had the baby."

"Does Cori know?" I ask.

"Yeah, she brought her here, stayed until the baby was born, and then took off. She's not answering anyone's calls. Randy was just here with me. I guess she showed up at his club, was getting drunk as hell, tried kissing him, and she got all pissed that he wouldn't take her. She left, and no one knows where she's at," Chelsea tells me in a rush.

I'm frozen. She tried to sleep with someone else? I am livid and hurt. I know she is lashing out, but that fucking cuts deep.

I run out of my office and see Angel and Trevor talking in the parking lot. "Good. You're still here."

Angel looks alert and worried. "Everything okay?"

"First, Melissa had her baby." Angel smiles. "Second, Cori's missing. She was at Randy's club, tried to fuck him. He turned her down, and then she took off. No one knows where she is."

"Shit. Okay, I'll get Reaper and Zippo to help. Anything else?" he asks.

"Cori is planning on moving to Devon. Can't let that happen."

Angel puts a hand on my shoulder. "Don't worry. It won't. You go to her apartment. She might turn up there eventually. Trevor, I'm pulling you off of searching for the judge friend. You go up to the hospital. Go meet your new niece. I'll get calls put out looking for Cori."

We break off, and I head to her condo to wait.

CHAPTER 49

Cori

I know I'm drunk, but you know what? Fuck it! At least I'm in a cab, not driving. I tell him to take me downtown to any place at all that sells guns. Since the main stores are all closed right now, he takes me to a small little shop next to a tattoo parlour. The place looks run down, with bars all over the windows, and I see a few guys in the alley next to the shop smoking a joint. I don't want to be here, but I have to. The Mercer family has to pay. "Want me to wait?"

"Would you?" I slur out slightly.

He nods, and I smile at him.

I walk into the shop and head straight to the front counter. The man behind it gives me a look and does something at the wall.

"Turned the cameras off," he tells me, seeing the look on my face. "You here for something not quite legal?"

I nod. "The family that had me raped and took my child from me, the son I just found out about that is dead. They need to pay," I tell him steely.

He pulls out a glock. "Just got this in. Was gonna hand it over to the police, since it looks like one of theirs, and normally, I never just hand over a gun to just anyone. There's a process, but you need this." He hands it over, and I grasp it in my hands, somewhat shocked at how easy this is. "You get caught, leave where you got that gun from out of your statement. Good luck," he tells me.

"Thank you," I whisper out to him as I hand him over the giant wad of cash I pulled from an ATM on the way over.

I run back to the cab and give him the address to the Mercers'.

~

The cab driver pulls up to the rundown house and watches me. I go to give him money, but he waves me off, not wanting the money. "You need me to stay?"

"No, I'll be here a while. But thank you."

"Stay safe, girl. You need a getaway, call me," he says, passing me his personal card then peels away from the street when I close the door. I walk up to the house and knock.

"Who is it?" I hear called through the house.

"Got a delivery for Wayne Mercer."

The door unlocks and opens, and I rush in, waving my gun, the gun I bought from the local gun shop, at my old foster mother. "How could you do that to me? To anyone!" I scream.

Mr. Mercer looks older, uglier, and even fatter than before. Disgusting old man. Mrs. Mercer is on her knees, pleading with me to put the gun down.

"No, I'm not putting it down. You deserve to die. You deserve to have everything taken away from you!" I scream.

"You're right. We do. Please, just, we'll call 911 right now and turn ourselves in."

I shake my head no. "I'm not letting you do that. That's getting you off too easily."

"We'll take you to his grave if you put the gun down."

"Why should I believe you?"

I cock my head to the side, staring at them with as much hate as I can muster.

"What was the purpose of it all, huh?" I shout at them. "Tell me!" I screech. They take too long to answer me, and I shoot Wayne in the foot. He screams out in pain, and I laugh.

"We'll tell you," Jill Mercer shouts. "We couldn't have children. We wanted a boy so badly. Every girl we had all ended up with girls. You were our favorite. When we found out you were having a boy, we were over the moon happy. So damn happy. But then we lost him a few months later," she proclaims, brokenly crying.

"He was MY son!" I scream. I put the gun to her forehead. I want to pull this trigger right now, end her miserable life.

BLAKE

I pace the length of Cori's condo, getting more pissed by the second. The door swings open, and Angel walks in with a look I can't quite figure out. "Well, did you find her?"

Angel's jaw clenches and nods. "Reaper and Zippo are watching her right now. Man, we need to leave before she does something she's going to regret for the rest of her life."

"What does that mean?" I ask, running out behind him.

"She's at their home, with a gun," is all Angel says before hoping into his SUV. I barely get time to get my door shut before he takes off speeding.

Angel's phone starts ringing, and he hits the speaker button. "Speak."

"Shots fired. Wayne Mercer screamed. Zippo looked in the window, and looks like Cori shot him in the leg," Reaper says.

"Fuck!" Angel roars, punching his steering wheel. "Don't let her do something really fuckin' stupid! Get in there before she does something she won't be able to live with," he orders them and shuts the phone off.

"Should we call the cops?"

"We'll assess when I get there and then bring them in," he tells me.

"This is my fault. Fuck! I should have talked to her sooner about all of this."

"Don't blame yourself, man. I had her in my home, living with us, and I didn't tell her. We'll all help get her through this, and we'll get our Cori back."

I nod, agreeing. I just need her back.

Half an hour later, we pull up outside the house and notice the front door open, with both Reaper and Zippo trying to restrain Cori.

"Let me the fuck go!" Cori shrieks. The sound of her voice is so ugly it throws me for a minute.

Angel runs ahead of me, wanting to calm her down. "Cori, honey, please. Look at me. You don't want to do this. You'll go to jail."

"I don't care," she sobs into his chest.

I walk up to Reaper and Zippo and notice both the Mercers on the ground, blood oozing out of Mr. Mercer's leg and blood pouring out of Mrs. Mercer's shoulder. "She went to shoot her in the head when we stormed in. It startled her, and her shot went wide, nicked the shoulder," Reaper says.

"Would she really have done that?" I ask him, worried.

He shrugs. "Can't say for sure, but in this moment, I wouldn't put it past her. Cori is a wreck, man."

CHAPTER 50

Cori

The police arrive after Angel calms me down. "Hate to do this to your kid, Angel, but I have to place her under arrest."

"What?" I squeak out.

"You broke into their home and shot them," the officer tells me.

I look to Angel then Blake, pleading with them. Blake looks upset; Angel looks angry. Angel comes to me and cups my face. "Don't say a word until Sam meets you at the station," he tells me. I nod, and he kisses me on the forehead as the officer puts cuffs on me.

I'm read my rights and put into the back of the police car. I sigh and lay my head against the window. At least this guy was nice enough to put the cuffs on in front instead of behind my back.

We pull up to the station, and he leads me out. "We're told we can't talk to you until your lawyer is present, so we're just going to leave you in this room until he's here. Someone will be in to ask if you are hungry or thirsty soon," he says as he takes my cuffs off and gestures for me to sit down.

He goes to walk out the door but turns around. "Only reason you aren't in a holding cell until that happens is because I respect the hell out of those Angels, and I know you're one of theirs," he says then leaves.

I lay my head on the table and have myself a little nap. I'm so damn tired. An hour later, I'm woken up when Sam comes into the room with a briefcase.

"Hey, Dad," I say quietly.

"Corinne," he says, not sounding happy with me. "You're not to say a word when those officers come in here to question you. Let me handle it."

I nod but say nothing. He seems really ticked off at me.

He pulls out all his papers and about a hundred files, and places them about the table. He opens the door and tells the officers we're ready.

Dad doesn't say much. He mainly just pushes files across the table at the cops, and they read them. Their faces go slack, looking at me with pity.

The officer that brought me in closes the last file and gives it back and sighs. "We're letting you off with a warning. This isn't going into the file. Do something like this again, you'll be in jail."

"Thank you," I whisper.

"If you need a good therapist, talk to that boyfriend of yours. He has a few good ones working in his building." I go to say I don't need to see anyone, and he cuts me off. "Don't even say it. You've held this shit in for years. Tonight, you exploded. It's natural, it's normal, but it's over now. You need to talk to someone, so do it." With that, he leaves, and Sam and I walk out the door.

Outside, my dad shakes me and then pulls me into a hug. "I'm so sorry you went through so much." He starts to cry, and I let everything go, crying right with him.

BLAKE

I see her coming out of the station with Sam, and I move forward, taking her hand in mine when they finish hugging. "You're coming home with me," I tell her. She doesn't put up a fight, just looks down and moves with me.

The guys all left the minute Sam showed up, but I stuck around, wanting to talk to Cori. I close her door, and Sam calls my name.

"I wasn't there for her. Hell, I didn't even know she existed, so it might not be my place to say this right now, but don't let her go," he tells me.

I nod. "Don't worry. She isn't going anywhere." He grins smugly at me and walks to his car.

I get in the car and start it up. Cori turns the radio on but I shut it off. "What was in your head tonight, Cori? You leave your sister at the hospital right after she has her daughter, then you take off to get drunk and try to fuck another man, and then you are stupid enough to get a fucking gun and try to get revenge?"

"I…" she stammers.

"Don't want to hear it right now. I'm pissed as hell, but that's not the reason why," I say. "Why didn't I know about this new job you were taking?"

"I didn't want to tell you," she whispers, looking away from me. I can feel her guilt and shame.

"What were you going to do, just leave without telling me?" She nods as a tear rolls down her cheek. "Well, just so you know, first thing Monday morning, you're calling them up and declining the position. You're not leaving me, Cori."

"I'm sorry, Blake," she whispers to me. "I just wanted to feel something. Anything. Melissa's baby… Shit. I couldn't do that. I couldn't be there, not when I just learned about my own child," she tells me.

I grab her hand as I pull over to the side of the road. "Look at me, Cori." She looks up from her lap. "I love you, and I'm telling you right now that I will never let you go. You can run, you can push, but I'm not going anywhere. And deep down, you know it. I'll never stop fighting for us."

"I love you, Blake," she whispers at me, tears streaming down her face.

I grab the back of her neck, bringing her in for a kiss.

"Let's go home," I tell her when I let her go.

"Okay."

DAWN MARTENS

CHAPTER 51

Cori

Four months. That's how long it's been since the police finally locked away the Mercers for good. I ended up getting a warning. It wasn't fun, being cuffed. Angel pulled strings, though, as did Blake, and, of course, my dad showed up with all the files of what the Mercers have been doing over the years. And I was let off. The same wasn't said for the Mercers, though. Their family and friends were all charged with a slew of things.

All the previous foster kids came forward. Two of the girls that had children were working on finding out where the kids were, and of course, the Angels were helping them out with that. The other two that had children from living in that house of horrors said they didn't want to know.

I ended up calling the office in Devon to let them know I wouldn't be taking the job they gave me. Instead, I'm back working for Blake.

Sam visits me often, and I make sure to visit him as well. Now, he's really trying to push a home on me, and no matter how much I say no, he still emails me once a day with a listing for me to check out.

Lilly is thrilled. She's finally spending time with her dad. She never really had him around much growing up, she said. Now, he's pulling double duty, being a father to me and her.

It took me a while to get used to having a baby around all the time. Mikayla is now four months old and as cute as a button. But I'm still not all that comfortable around her, especially when she shits all over me and pukes everywhere.

Blake is amazing with her, though. He's constantly offering to babysit so Melissa and Dray can go have a date night, or so Melissa can go to school. He says he doesn't want to see her struggling to pay for child care. I think it's sweet, but it also hurts at the same time, knowing all the things I have missed out on with my own child—the child I will never know.

Blake also made me speak to one of the counselors that work in the building. At first, things were hard, but talking about everything, finally every single thing being out in the open, has me feeling like a brand new person. I'm not weighted down by the pain and anger and hurt I once stored inside me. I haven't heard from my mom since the day she showed up at my condo. According to Blake's friend, Drew, she'll be in prison for a long while. Part of me hopes she dies in there, but the other part hopes she'll learn and become a new person.

It's almost closing time when Marcy comes to my desk and smiles. "I have an errand to run, and you are coming with me," she declares.

"Oh, really?" I say, fighting a grin.

"Yup," she says, popping the 'p'.

"Fine. Let me just talk to Blake first," I tell her.

She rolls her eyes and sits on my desk. I get up and knock on Blake's door.

"Come in," he says, so I do. His face lights up when he sees me.

I go to him, sit in his lap, and kiss him deeply. "Marcy is dragging me out."

He grins. "I know. She told me earlier today, said I can't keep you to myself all the time."

I wrinkle my nose at him. "But having you all to myself lately has been the best." I purr.

His hands tighten around me. "You should leave before I take you on my desk again."

I chew on my bottom lip.

He stands up, taking me with him. "We'll finish later. That's a promise," he says, gently pushing me out the door, closing it swiftly behind me.

Marcy looks up and sees my face, probably shock or something all over it, and bursts out laughing.

I glare at her and walk to my purse and snap, "Let's go."

BLAKE

I meet Melissa and Chelsea at the mall, and we start looking. "It has to be special," Melissa says, moving the stroller around to keep Mikayla happy.

"It will be. Why do you think I brought you all with me? There are six jewelry stores in the mall, so we'll find something," I say. I was able to get Marcy to take off early and get Cori out looking at houses. Marcy is saying she's looking for something to buy instead of rent. Hopefully Cori loves the final house they are going to see, since I already bought it and am just waiting to close on it.

The first two stores were a bust; nothing jumped out at me. One ring that Melissa found and loved, I snapped a picture and sent it to Dray. He asked Angel for permission to marry her, and just said he needed to find the right ring. I get a text back, but before I can check it, Chelsea and Melissa squeal.

I go to them, putting my phone back in my pocket. "That one!" they both say loudly, waking Mikayla.

I peer into the glass. It's perfect. Pear shaped diamond, not too fancy but classic. Cori isn't into being flashy. I know she will love something more traditional and simple. The sales woman comes over, and before she says a word, I point to the ring. "I want that one."

Her brows go up, and then she smiles. "And the size?"

Chelsea takes the ring from the woman and tries it on herself; I brought her because they are the same size. The ring fits perfectly. "That one, exactly that one. I want it now."

"Caveman," Melissa says, chuckling.

I ignore her and watch the woman package the ring, and I hand over my credit card.

I walk out of the mall, the girls trailing slightly behind me, both grinning hugely, the ring bag gripped tightly in my hand.

I get to the car and stop them from getting in. Pulling out my wallet, I pull out every bill in it and hand it over to the girls. "Get a cab, go shopping, whatever. Just don't come home for a while."

"Err, why can't you just take her to your condo?"

"Because I sold it."

Both girls' eyes bug out. "You aren't living with us," Melissa tells me.

"Don't plan on it. In a month, I'm closing on a house. Cori will be moving in with me."

"Dude, that's wicked awesome!" she says excitedly.

"Until then, I'm staying with you guys, so stay gone. Go to Dray's house or something."

She mock salutes me. "Sir, yes, sir."

Chelsea snorts. "Have fun."

~

My hands roam over Cori's bare hips as she snuggles against me. Her skin is so soft, silky even. I will never get over how good she makes me feel. Cori completes me in ways I never knew possible. All of my life, I thought I'd never find the one. But here she is–my one, my crazy, sexy girl. She joins her hands in mine as I plant kisses down her arm. She is Heaven on Earth.

Her legs are tangled with mine as we make sweet passionate love. This is what it's like to love someone and belong to someone else. I'd give or do anything to make her happy. I just hope she finally sees that she deserves everything and more with me.

 Our bodies move together as one as I fill her with all I have to give, both physically and emotionally.

I pin her under me. "Open your eyes," I tell her.

She does slowly and smiles up at me. "I love you."

"I love you too, Blake," she says, tears welling up in her eyes.

I reach over the side of the bed, bringing her to sit up with me, as I grab the ring I hid before she got home from an errand I sent Marcy on.

I grab her left hand and hold up the ring. "Marry me."

Cori starts sobbing, nodding, and grabs the ring from me, putting it on herself. Finally, after she looks it over and tackles me, she screams, "Yes, yes, yes, yes, yes!"

I smile and kiss her again. "How do you feel about us living together?" I ask her.

She smiles and rolls her eyes. "That's basically what we're doing now anyways."

"I mean, actually living together. In a house. The two of us?"

She smirks. "That's what today was, wasn't it? We weren't looking at houses Marcy was looking to buy. We were looking at homes for you and me."

I give her a sheepish look. "Yeah. What did you think about the last one?"

"I love it. It was my favorite."

"Good, because I bought it. We move in next month."

She doesn't get a chance to say anything as I move over her, kissing her softly. This is it, forever and always.

EPILOGUE

Melissa

I stand just outside of the church doors, waiting for my chance to walk down the aisle with Jasper at my side. I was shocked that he readily agreed to walk me down. He said it was only right; he basically acted as mine and Cori's dad, even though he's not old enough to be our dad.

My dress is perfect, even though I am still packing some extra weight from my pregnancy. It's been fourteen months, but I've been so busy trying to finish up with school, planning my wedding, and taking care of my daughter.

"You sure you want to do this?" he asks me.

I smile and look to my fourteen month old daughter sitting on my hip. "Yes. I am."

I have always wanted Drayton; I just never gave in to that urge until I stupidly slept with him without protection. And once we found out we were having a baby, he went full force to make me his, after of course being a total jackass. His promises of me being his one and only were met with reluctance and even a visit from some kick ass bikers and Blake, Cori's husband. But over the last few months, he's kept his word.

I still think it's too soon for marriage, but I'm willing to give this a go.

Blake and Corinne got married about six months after the mess Cori got into at our old foster home. They wasted no time at all in starting their family, because now, four months later, Cori is pregnant. I rolled my eyes at her when she first told me, and then, of course, rubbed it in her face and mimicked her whole 'never having kids' rant. But she just smiled. She's so over the moon happy now.

Twisted Up In You

The only family drama we've had lately is the fact that Tori went back to her husband, and it's killing Trevor. She finally found out who he was, and that was the end of them apparently. No one has heard from her in three months. Then there was the drama of meeting Blake's half siblings and step-father. His mother tried to tag along to the meeting, but her husband, or should I say now, her ex-husband, told her to get lost. Cori is loving all of this extra family she now has, and I as well, since Blake's family is pretty damn amazing.

The wedding march sounds, and I loop my arm in Jasper's while holding tight to baby Mikayla, and we start down the aisle. I smile up at my soon to be husband, and he smiles right back at me. I hope I'm making the right choice by doing this.

I'm still scared, mainly because he still works at the club as a bouncer. I know women throw themselves at him, but I need to put some trust and faith in him that he won't step out on me.

Just as we're about to say 'I do', the church doors burst open and about four very large men storm in. One looks scary as hell. Looking closer, I realize he's the man that is said to be my father. Oh my God. His hair is pulled back into a man bun, and for an old dude, he doesn't look too bad like that. His hands and neck are covered in tattoos, and his beard is even longer than Angel's is.

Jasper, Mason, Trevor, and Vinny instantly stand up, as if guarding me.

"You didn't think to tell me I had a daughter?" the man says, glaring at Jasper. He looks to me quickly, eyes settling on my daughter. "A granddaughter?"

"How'd you find out?" Jasper answers back.

The man looks to me, and his face softens slightly. "Who do you think? I finally get my wife back, and not only am I just finding out that I have had a daughter who is twenty-two years old, but my brother, who not only is alive,

257

but got *my wife* pregnant and is living with your pussy club!" he roars.

"Hangman, watch yourself," Mason growls, stepping ahead.

I look to Trevor, and his face pales slightly.

"She doesn't want me. She begs me every day, every fucking day, to send her back to you, to sign the divorce papers. Well, she got her wish. I'm giving her the fuck up, but not before I go a few rounds with my *dead fucking brother!"* he roars again.

"This isn't the time or place for this," Jasper declares, throwing his hands out.

"No, it's the perfect fucking time." Just then, a woman steps forward from behind Hangman's men, and she glares at Dray. She is stunning, tall, and looks like the perfect black woman, all ass and tits.

Dray's entire body stills, and his face pales—which is kind of weird, because I didn't realize black men could pale.

"You son of a bitch, what do you think you are doing, huh?" she shouts at Dray.

The crowd murmurs. I'm confused. I look to the man that is my father, and he's glaring at Dray as well.

"Shayla…" Dray starts.

I interrupt, wanting to figure out what the hell is going on. "Um, I'm sorry, but who are you?" I ask her.

For a moment, I feel as if she's going to go all exorcist on my ass.

"Who am I? Well, this is great. Now, I actually feel bad for you," she says, her eyes softening slightly before turning hard and angry when she looks back to Dray. "I'm his wife."

With that, the whole world feels as if it stops. "Wife?" I whisper out in shock.

"I never signed his stupid ass papers, so he probably didn't realize we're still married. I told him before what my conditions were. He visits his children, talks to them, then and only then would I let him be free," she says, tears forming in her eyes. You can obviously tell she still very much loves Dray.

I feel as if I've been punched in the gut. He's married and has children.

"This isn't how I wanted to meet my daughter for the first time, but when I found out about the fuck head she was marrying, I had him looked into," Hangman says.

I look to my sister, who is rushing to me, taking Mikayla out of my arms quickly who is babbling on about mama and dada.

Dray's *wife*, Shayla, looks back to me, her eyes again softening, and then her eyes finally rest on my daughter. "You had his child?" she whispers, a hand going to her throat.

I nod as tears that were forming in my eyes leak out, and with that, I run down the aisle and out of the church, all while Dray is calling out for me to stop. I never should have trusted him, ever. How could he do this?

I hear Hangman yelling at Dray, "You hurt my kid, you mother fucker. Why shouldn't I hurt you?"

"Melissa!" I hear Cori's voice.

I stop and look back at her, tears streaming down my face. "It's okay, sweetie. We'll get you through this. I promise."

"We need to leave. It's going to be a blood bath in there," Blake says, jogging to us, taking Mikayla from Cori. "Angel's men are flanked around Trevor, and Hangman is totally losing his shit right now. Seems he's not sure who to go after first, Dray or Trevor, and that Shayla woman is screeching like a crazy lady at Dray, who is trying to get to you."

"Let's go. I never want to see him again," I croak out.

My mother was always right. I'm nothing. I'll always be nothing. This is my life—what a fucked up mess. The only good in my life is my daughter. I'll make damn sure I'm the best mother I can possibly be. For her.

DAWN MARTENS

THE END

This is not the end, not really. Melissa will have a story. Find out how she manages after the truth about Dray is revealed. Will they find their happily ever after together? Or will someone new come into the picture. And how does her life change, now that it's come out she is Hangman's daughter?

Trever, aka T-bags, AND Hangman will have stories as well. Who will get Tori in the end? How will Hangman react when he and his baby brother finally face off after years of thinking he was dead?

Of course, Chelsea, Adam, Clara, Thrane, Blake's friend Drew, Bryce, and loads more characters will eventually get their own stories. First up next, though, for this year, I have tons of super cheesy cliché romances. And I will eventually get to work on Kellie and Jaxon's story from Just Love.

Lots of things are going on. I wish I had super powers to knock them all out at once, but I just can't do that. Just know, I have stories, tons of stories coming for the next few years. Hopefully, my brain doesn't explode from all the books I've started. Ha.

ABOUT THE AUTHOR

Dawn Martens is a young, spunky Canadian Author.

Being a wife to Colin, and a mother to three beautiful little girls (Sarah (2007), Grace (2010), and Ava (2014)) hasn't stopped this Canadian Firecracker from pursuing her dreams of becoming a writer! Dawn's number one passion in life is the written word, and she's extremely thankful that she has to ability to share the ramblings from the characters inside of her head with the rest of the world! She also may or may not have the hugest girl crush on Author Kristen Ashley, who is her personal idol and helped inspire Dawn in the beginning of her Indie career.

Other books by this Author:
It's Just Love Not a Time Bomb
UnKiss Me – Angels Warriors MC
UnTouch Me – Angels Warriors MC
UnBreak This Heart – Angels Warriors MC
New Love – Angels Warriors MC Novelette
Coming soon – Never Let You Go – The Cliché
novella series Book 1

68616723R10145

Made in the USA
Charleston, SC
15 March 2017